"Matt, Why Did You Leave Me?"

she asked. "Why did you run out like that just when I needed you?"

His body tensed and his knuckles showed white on tight fists. "I think it would be a good idea if you'd pack now, Alexandra."

Infinite regret clutched at her with a sharpness that caught at her throat. "Matt, I'm so sorry. I didn't mean to pry."

"It's all right," he said sharply. "It's just that it's pointless to wallow in what's past. It would make much more sense if you would just leave as soon as possible. We'll both be better off."

JENNIFER JUSTIN

is a veteran romance writer. She lives in California and writes about her major interests and hobbies. *Passion's Victory* is her first Silhouette Special Edition.

Dear Reader:

Silhouette has always tried to give you exactly what you want. When you asked for increased realism, deeper characterization and greater length, we brought you Silhouette Special Editions. When you asked for increased sensuality, we brought you Silhouette Desire. Now you ask for books with the length and depth of Special Editions, the sensuality of Desire, but with something else besides, something that no one else offers. Now we bring you SILHOUETTE INTIMATE MOMENTS, true romance novels, longer than the usual, with all the depth that length requires. More sensuous than the usual, with characters whose maturity matches that sensuality. Books with the ingredient no one else has tapped: excitement.

There is an electricity between two people in love that makes everything they do magic, larger than life—and this is what we bring you in SILHOUETTE INTIMATE MOMENTS. Look for them this May, wherever you buy books.

These books are for the woman who wants more than she has ever had before. These books are for you. As always, we look forward to your comments and suggestions. You can write to me at the address below:

Karen Solem
Editor-in-Chief
Silhouette Books
P.O. Box 769
New York, N.Y. 10019

JENNIFER JUSTIN
Passion's Victory

Silhouette Special Edition

Published by Silhouette Books New York

America's Publisher of Contemporary Romance

SILHOUETTE BOOKS, a Simon & Schuster Division of
GULF & WESTERN CORPORATION
1230 Avenue of the Americas, New York, N.Y. 10020

Copyright © 1983 by Jennifer Justin

Distributed by Pocket Books

ISBN: 0-671-53590-0

First Silhouette Books printing April, 1983

10 9 8 7 6 5 4 3 2 1

Map by Ray Lundgren

SILHOUETTE, SILHOUETTE SPECIAL EDITION and
colophon are registered trademarks of Simon & Schuster.

America's Publisher of Contemporary Romance

Printed in the U.S.A.

Passion's Victory

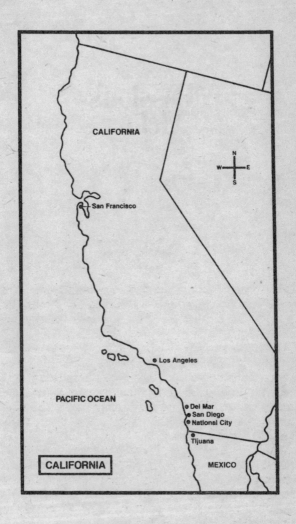

CALIFORNIA

San Francisco

Los Angeles

PACIFIC OCEAN

Del Mar
San Diego
National City

Tijuana

CALIFORNIA

MEXICO

Chapter One

The chestnut colt raced down the backstretch, dirt flying up from its hooves. Turning for home, he leaned into the curve with a classic motion of contained speed.

Alexandra's hands tightened on the rail as she watched. She was standing by the white fence between the practice track and the paddock area, just past the finish line. A familiar surge of adrenaline made her pulse leap as the horse neared, straining toward the finish with the young jockey pressed low and flat against its back.

Standing beside her, Jason Randolph opened his palm. In it was the large gold stopwatch that had clocked two Derby winners in training, both of them Randolph horses. With split-second precision, his thumb came down on the stop button. He noted the time on his clipboard with a lack of enthusiasm.

"Four furlongs in forty-five," he said, more to himself than to her.

Alexandra searched his face. It was excellent time for the half mile. Anything under forty-seven seconds was cause for celebration, but Jason looked unimpressed, almost impatient.

"That's good, Jason. Very good." Something was bothering him. She had sensed it all morning; now she was sure of it.

"Bullet's a morning glory," he said. "He does all right in morning workouts, then fades in the afternoon trials."

It was almost a rebuke. It wasn't the words, just his tone—as if she had said something crassly stupid. She turned away from him abruptly.

The hot-walker, a boy in his early teens, was leading the colt around the paddock in leisurely circles. She watched the thoroughbred cooling off after the practice run, muscles rippling beneath glistening flanks as he moved.

"He's a magnificent animal, Jason. You've worked with others like him. With a little patience—"

"It so happens that I'm out of patience," he snapped.

She turned to face him. "Yes, I can see that. I can certainly see that." She glared at him, her moss green eyes dark with anger. She hated that edge to his voice. She'd heard it before, but he'd never addressed her that way. A strand of auburn hair whipped across her face and she pushed it away as she confronted her fiancé.

He had light gray eyes, usually pensive, sometimes cold, as they were now. His hair was fine, silky, the color of lightly toasted bread. A tall willowy man of thirty, he moved with a languid air of superiority. It was understandable. Jason Morris Randolph III was, after all, the result of generations of selective breeding between the very best horse and tobacco families. A Kentucky aristocrat. Still, he had no right to use that arrogance on her. She wasn't one of his hired hands.

"I want to win the Derby, Alexandra. No, I must win." He spoke urgently, as if the statement explained away his rudeness.

"You will, Jason." She realized the tension in him had nothing to do with her at all. "You always win."

Her resentment subsided, and she was left with that hollow, off-centered feeling which plagued her intermittently. Watching Jason now, as he took her hand with a quick, apologetic squeeze and led her away from the track, she couldn't seriously doubt that he loved her. He had asked her to be his wife, to bear his children. It was just that sometimes it seemed his only real passion was for his horses, his obsession with repeating the greatest triumph of the Randolph family, the Triple Crown sweep. It felt as if she were pitting herself against his three great loves: the Kentucky Derby, the Preakness and the Belmont.

But she was trying to adjust to her place in his life, and to remember that she could only judge Jason in context. He was at the end of a long line of Randolphs, quintessential Southern gentlemen whose regard for womanhood had changed little since the Civil War. It was natural for him to assume their physical relationship would not begin before their wedding night.

The truth of it was, she was relieved by the old-fashioned decorum that kept his behavior so chaste; she needed more time. It was absurd when she thought about it, but she had never been able to erase another man's imprint on her mind and body. It might as well have been a cattle brand. She had tried to argue, to ridicule, to laugh herself out of it for five years. Nothing worked. Sooner or later, she'd have to let it go. In three months, Jason would be her husband. But the thought of sexual intimacy with him still seemed spurious somehow, just something she wasn't prepared to cope with yet.

She turned to watch Jason giving instructions to the hot-walker. No, it really wasn't horses that came between them, it was her memories, held too long and too vividly. She had to face it. Those memories had put her entire life on hold.

This summer, she had let the chance of a lifetime slip through her fingers for the same stupid reason. After two years of apprenticeship with Fratelli Conti, two years of running menial errands and fielding leers and Italian pinches with a sunny smile, she'd had her chance. Fabio Conti, the senior brother, had finally acknowledged her talent and offered her carte blanche in designing the winter sports line. It was to be all hers and she was ready for it. She'd earned it, slaving at the Roman fashion house every day, sketching, cutting and sewing like crazy every night, just to show what she could do. She'd even turned down profitable modeling jobs just to prove she was a designer.

The offer, of course, had the inevitable strings attached. It wasn't surprising. The fashion industry was as competitive as show business, and you couldn't go two steps in Rome without tripping over the proverbial casting couch. But any other young designer would have jumped into Fabio's bed for the chance of a showcase line like that. Instead, she had told him to go to hell and boarded the next plane home.

Fabio wasn't old, unattractive or effeminate. The models adored him. Alexandra would have given her eye teeth for that job. But those ridiculous, worn-out memories blocked her path. Only they weren't worn out. Not yet. She was an anachronism.

Blast you, Matt Farraday, she thought, as Jason returned to her and they crossed the paddock to his car. *You're not going to blow it for me again. Jason and I are right together. He'll have his stables and I'll have my fashions. I'll be a good wife, a good mother and a good designer. I'll have it all.*

She turned to kiss him as he opened the car door for her. "Don't get so uptight about it, darling. You've done it before, you'll do it again."

"Yes, you're right. I will win." His eyes took on that over-the-rainbow look. "Only the horse won't be Bullet."

He raised his head and inhaled deeply as if he could smell success emanating from the bluish rain clouds that lowered in the October sky. "Fortune's Lad." He intoned the name like a mantra. "Fortune's Lad. That's my next winner. No doubt about it."

"Fortune's Lad." It was a new name to Alexandra. But they were all new names now. She'd been away from the world of Kentucky thoroughbreds for a long time. "Is he that spectacular?"

After she was seated, Jason slipped behind the wheel of the station wagon and threw his clipboard over his shoulder onto the back seat. "I haven't seen him yet, but I've heard. He's a maiden. I'm going to California on Wednesday to take a look at him. If everything the grapevine says is true, I'll make my offer. I may want to see him run in the Oak Tree Meet at Santa Anita first, but if I do wait, it's going to cost me plenty."

"California?" Alexandra asked. "What's a thoroughbred doing in California?" She was as bluegrass as Jason, born and raised in Fayette County and steeped in horse lore. The rules were well established: when you wanted decent thoroughbreds, you looked east or to Europe. The West had dude ranches, not bloodstock.

And sportswear, she thought suddenly.

Jason grinned at her. "You've been away a long time. The field's opened up in the States."

"All the way to the Pacific?"

He nodded. "Santa Anita's running $250,000 purses now. It's a class track and they've got class studs out there these days." The grin faded. "Right now, they've got Fortune's Lad."

Alexandra let the words sink in as Jason tooled along the gravel driveway. It would be a good idea to get away somewhere with Jason. It could bring them closer. Besides, she'd devoted two years of her life to sportswear design and had never even seen California, the mecca of year-round sports. It was high time.

"Terrific," she said, tucking her feet up on the bench seat and turning to face his profile. "I'm coming with you."

Jason glowered through the windshield and she saw a cord tighten under his jaw. "Absolutely not."

She couldn't believe it. He always wanted her around. He was "training" her, he had joked more than once, eager to have her begin sharing his lifestyle. Even before he'd placed the diamond on her finger, he'd become very possessive of her time. In fact, ever since he'd learned she was back in

Kentucky, and unattached, he had more or less appropriated her. She didn't react, just sat silently beside him as he drove, trying to figure it out.

Presently they turned into a narrow dirt track that formed a shortcut to the Randolph house.

"You'd be bored out of your mind," he said at last. "It's just going to be a business trip. You wouldn't have time to go sight-seeing. It's just another stud farm. Nothing new."

They were skirting a grove of tulip poplars, lambent with scarlet and gold. She'd forgotten how beautiful Kentucky could be in the fall.

"Bored? Of course I won't be bored." She laughed. "God knows, I'm used to horse trading. If it drags out too long, I'll rent a car and go off on some side trips."

He pulled up in the driveway and cut the engine.

"There's a lot I want to see. I could just leave you to your haggling sessions and—" She noticed something grim about his expression.

"Jason, what is it?"

He was staring straight through the windshield at the colonial facade of the house with an elaborate concentration. "Alex," he began, then stopped to take a deep breath, "the man who owns Fortune's Lad is Matt Farraday."

It was like missing a step in the dark and falling a full flight. "What?" she whispered.

"He owns one of the most successful thoroughbred farms on the West Coast, Vista del Lago."

"That's impossible, Jason. He was dirt poor. Just a farmhand." She had the sensation that her tongue had become unhinged and was babbling on while her mind floated free. "That was only five years ago. Rags to riches doesn't happen that fast anymore. Not in real life."

Jason shrugged, watching her carefully. She wasn't ready for this. Her mind rejected the idea, skittering around it, probing it tentatively, then drawing back. She was hearing Matt's voice again.

"I'm so poor, I don't even own a name," he had cracked once. The Farradays were only Matt's foster parents, tenants on Randolph land who didn't have two cents to rub together. He didn't know his real parentage.

It wasn't until she actually saw the Farraday place that she knew what he meant. That was after he had disappeared, just dropped out of her life. She had waited for days, then when she hadn't been able to stand it any longer, she had ridden across the common land to the Windermere property until she found his home. The roof was rusty corrugated iron. She ran up worn gray steps to the tiny porch.

"I don't know where he's gone," Mrs. Farraday had told her through the patched screen door. "But he's a good boy. Whatever Matt's doing, it must be the right thing."

Weeks later, when she was packing to leave for Livorno, Alexandra learned that Mr. Farraday had been stricken with a crippling stroke—the night before Matt took off.

Now, they were both long gone, the old couple who had raised Matt. She wondered if Mrs. Farraday had gone to her grave still believing in Matt's innate virtue. Such a beautifully timed exit, leaving a seventeen-year-old head over heels in love with him and the only father he had ever known helplessly paralyzed.

Her father had summed it up neatly. "For a girl with your advantages and your looks, you sure picked one helluva loser."

She sat wrestling with the idea that Matt Farraday had surfaced with lots of brand-new money. From what? she wondered. A rich wife? A rich mistress? How on earth could that penniless, irresponsible nobody own a horse that was shaking the grapevine all across America? And why should she care anyway?

Jason seemed to be pondering the same question. He was sitting dejectedly beside her, making no movement to get out of the car. He pulled the key from the ignition and tapped it idly on the dashboard.

"I don't know how he got his money, not for certain, that is. With a type like that, all kinds of possibilities come to mind." He gave her an oblique glance, then turned back to examine his key ring. "There's plenty of talk, of course. About gambling in Las Vegas. There was a long winning streak at the tracks evidently. But that's quite recent. And land speculation. A little of this, a little of that. I don't suppose someone like Matt Farraday is too fussy about how he gets what he wants."

There was venom in his voice, something she'd never heard before.

"One thing's for sure, though; it's definitely the same man. I've seen his picture in newspaper clippings." He looked at her pointedly. "A guy like Matt Farraday always finds a way to get what he wants."

Once more she wondered if Jason knew the whole story of her affair with Matt. He'd always known that she had cared for Matt five years ago. But that it was a body-and-soul commitment on her part was something she had never been able to tell him, for the simple reason that he didn't want to hear it. She would have much preferred a clean slate with Jason, but he refused to listen.

"I don't want to hear a word about you and Farraday," he'd yelled in an uncharacteristic fury. "Whatever it was, it's over. Finished business."

Perhaps she really didn't have to tell him after all. It was possible he already knew they'd been lovers; it would certainly explain his intense dislike for a man who was only a minor employee at Windermere.

There was only one living soul with whom she had shared her crushing humiliation—her father. But if Jason had known all along, or guessed . . . Well, it was touching that he was still willing to treat her like some antebellum virgin bride. Suddenly her heart went out to Jason. She would have preferred one less ambiguity between them; she really wanted to make a success of this marriage. But why dredge up the past when it would only make him miserable?

"So you see," Jason was saying crisply, "the trip is out of the question for you."

Her hand went up to his cheek. "It's over, darling. It's been over for a long time. Finished business— remember?"

Jason reached up to his face and took her hand, tightening his grip until it hurt. "Is it?"

"Please don't do this to yourself," she pleaded. "I was seventeen. It was only puppy love. For heaven's sake, I haven't even seen him in five years."

Jason stiffened and his mouth became a thin straight line. "I don't like the idea in the least."

"Why? I really don't see why you can't let go of something that happened years ago . . . a whole lifetime ago." Who was she asking, she wondered, Jason or herself?

"Because it's not necessary," he snapped.

"Do you mean 'proper'?"

"Proper, then. Yes."

But proper or not, it was crucial, she knew suddenly. She needed to face Matt once more, to show him—and herself—that she had survived. She had to face Matt Farraday one more time and finally lay to rest this awful, ridiculous heartache.

"Please listen to me, darling," she said with quiet urgency. "There was a time when Matt Farraday was the most important thing in my life; there's no use denying it. But only because I was young and naive and vulnerable. It's over, and I want to prove it. I need to prove it for both our sakes."

Jason closed his eyes. "Why do you have to prove anything?"

She took a deep gulp of air. "Because I just can't live with your doubts. I couldn't be happy or make you happy. And don't tell me you don't have any doubts. Look at you. You've been tight as a drum all morning. And why, for instance, are you grinding my knuckles to a powder right now?"

He released her hand. "It's not my feelings that are in question, it's yours. When we're married, is he going to be lying between us in bed for the rest of our lives?"

She gave a convulsive shudder and wished Jason could just put his arms tightly around her and squeeze out all the doubts she was denying. At least it was out in the open now.

"I'll admit I've thought about him sometimes over the years, but . . ."

"But?" Jason held her chin and brought her face to his.

"It's the best way of letting go of the past. Why not face up to it instead of spending the rest of our lives always wondering?" Tenderly she ran a fingertip across the deep frown lines on his forehead. "Please. Let's go together and be done with Matt Farraday in our lives, once and for all."

Jason waited a beat, then wrenched open the car door. Before he got out, he looked across the front seat at her. "Pack for two weeks," he said. His voice was flat. "The flight's at 8:15 A.M. from Lexington."

Thomas O'Neill sat at the battered cherrywood desk that dominated his study. As she walked in, he looked up from a letter, and Alexandra thought she saw something close to desperation in his face. But the look dissolved into a delighted grin as soon as she was through the double doors.

He tossed aside the letter as if it were junk mail and rose from his chair, holding out his arms. She moved into them and gave him a hug.

"Ah. At last I get my kiss. You were off early this morning. I didn't hear you go."

"Jason came over to get me, father. You were still asleep. He wanted me to see Windermere's finest working out this morning. He has this beautiful two-year-old called Bullet." She flicked some shreds of pipe tobacco from his tweed lapel and noticed a drawn look about his mouth. "I heard you pacing down here very late last night. You're still having trouble sleeping, aren't you?"

"No, no." He brushed aside the suggestion with a flourish of his head. "You need less sleep as you get older." Still beaming at her, he subsided into his chair.

She sat down across the desk from him, unconvinced.

"I thought you might be over at Windermere," he

said. "And how's my future son-in-law this fine morning? How's my boy?"

Alexandra winced at the near-obsequious eagerness in his voice. It was always there when he spoke of Jason, and it grated on her, much as she understood it. To her father, her marriage would be a godsend. It would mean financial rescue for Thomas O'Neill and for Laurelwood.

Coming home after five years abroad, Alexandra had been shocked to see what had become of Laurelwood. But she was beginning to understand that it wasn't sudden at all; it had been happening gradually, all through her childhood.

Thomas had always shielded her from the realities —and how easily she had been deceived, how willingly. She had taken her upbringing for granted—the elite girls' academy in Louisville, the finishing school outside Berne in Switzerland, the expensive Institute of Applied Arts in Italy. It had all seemed no more than the appropriate follow-through for a child who, at four years old, had been placed into the arms of an English nanny, nothing out of the ordinary for the only child of a bluegrass horse breeder.

She had never guessed that for Thomas O'Neill it was extraordinary, reckless spending, sheer self-destructive stubbornness in the face of steadily dwindling funds. He was a true O'Neill. It occurred to her that the family should have a coat of arms with the motto "Spend Every Last Penny" beneath a stallion rampant.

Her mother had died in Alexandra's infancy, leaving no memories except those she imagined, conjured up from a yellowing photo album. The silver-framed portrait that stood on the desk was just a young woman with a bouffant hairdo from the fifties and a dreamy expression, the face familiar only because it had smiled out from her father's desk for as long as she could remember.

Thomas O'Neill had compensated in grand style for her lack of mothering, showering her with love and attention and everything money could buy. She had soaked it all up like a sponge, never questioning her privileges. Then she had taken off for Rome and a career in fashion design.

Not once, in all the time she was in Europe, had he mentioned any difficulties in his letters. When she arrived home in June, she knew immediately. How could she have been so blind?

Now, with the adjusted eyes of a stranger, she could clearly see the differences between Laurelwood and the beautifully kept, well-staffed estates of their friends. Those differences may have been subtle once, but now they were glaring.

The stables were reduced to two mediocre brood mares and an aging stallion who brought in paltry stud fees. It had reached the point now where she hesitated to answer the phone; the caller was often one of many creditors.

But he wouldn't discuss the extent of his troubles with her even now. The most he would admit to was a "temporary setback" due to some poor investments on the commodities exchange.

Alexandra knew it wasn't temporary, and it wasn't the commodities exchange that was to blame. Bad racing bets and her own overlavish education had carried off the O'Neill legacy.

Her father was a rash, impossible man, but he was all the family she had and she loved him more than she had ever been able to show. She groaned inwardly, remembering her homecoming four months ago. She had arrived in a Conti original that sold for three thousand dollars, with her savings tucked away in a Gucci purse—less than four hundred dollars after the exchange from lira, the plane ticket and the cab from the airport.

"Hello, father. I'm home. I just quit my job," she'd announced blithely, not a care in the world, when his world was crumbling around him. What a shock it must have been to him.

Jason had seemed like providence trying to tell her something. There had been such undisguised pleasure at seeing her again, such sweetness in his courtship. When they married, she would be living just a mile from her father, able to give something of herself in return for all the years when she'd never given a thought to his utter loneliness. It was such a comfort to know that Jason would help him out of his debts after all those desperate years. That was understood. Not only would it be a drop in the bucket for Jason, considering his resources, but a Randolph would never permit a foreclosure in his wife's family. At Windermere, that would amount to a public scandal.

Alexandra took in the litter of papers on the scarred desk top: bills, demand notes, third and fourth notices, veiled threats—some not so veiled.

"Jason's just fine, father. He's going out to California on Wednesday. I'm going with him."

He fidgeted in his chair and flushed slightly. "But how's that to look? I mean, a trip like that. So far, and you not married to him yet."

"Surely, father, you don't have any doubts about your boy being every inch a Randolph gentleman, do you?"

"No, but—" He stopped and fussed nervously with some papers, rearranging the chaos before him.

"But what?"

"I just don't want anything to go sour in your plans. God knows, Alexandra, I'm happy for you. I've prayed for this. I want you to get married and be content. I want you to lead a whole life, and to—"

"Pay off the liens on Laurelwood?" she broke in, then hated herself for saying it, but it was too late.

His flush deepened painfully, and for a few moments he busied himself looking for his pipe. He located it finally under an open manila folder. "I only want you to have the best. You've had it so far. I think I've seen to that," he said a little defensively. "If Jason can afford it, and he wants to help me over this little problem, can you blame me for accepting? Would you rather see Laurelwood in the hands of some developer? You know what they'd do, don't you?" His mouth tightened. "They'd turn it into one of those subdivisions with a lot of little frame houses and bowling alleys."

"Oh, father, I'd hate that as much as you. You know I would." She hadn't realized how much until now. The very thought made her ache with loss. "But I'm not marrying Jason just to pay off our debts."

"Of course not, of course not. And they're my debts, lovey, not yours." Suddenly, under the halo of crinkly gray hair, the grin appeared, twinkling like the first evening star.

"I just thank the luck of the Irish that you fell in love with the right fella this time. You don't blame me for being glad about that?" He reached across the desk and squeezed her arm. "I can't tell you how happy I am that you're back and planning to make your life here, instead of *there*." The last word sounded as if he were referring to a leper colony in darkest Africa.

She smiled back at him. "I'm glad too."

It hurt to see how much he had aged during the past few years. He looked much older than fifty-eight as he tilted back in the chair and the light from the window hit his lined face.

"We'll be taking an early flight Wednesday morning, and I'll call you when we arrive. We're going to a stud farm called Vista del Lago."

The pipe seemed to jump out of his hand, and the panicked look she had glimpsed when she entered the study reappeared in full bloom. He shook his head fiercely. "No, I won't have it. Farraday's out of your life. I won't have him messing you up again."

Alexandra sat rigid as the blood drained from her face. He knew. He'd known where Matt was all along and never bothered to mention a word to her. How could he do that, knowing how much Matt meant to her? Knowing what she'd gone through?

He registered her shock, and his tone softened. "Alexandra, listen to me, love. That rotter almost ruined my little girl's life. Don't give him a second chance. Leave it alone. You're going to be Jason's wife."

"How long have you known where Matt was, father?" Her hand was shaking and she tightened her grip on the arm of the chair.

"I've known a little while."

"How long?"

He shrugged. "A couple of years, maybe. I read about him in *Racing Digest*. You were in Rome then. What does it matter?"

"Two years? What does it matter?" She struggled with a wave of nausea.

"You think I should have told you? Is that it?" His face was wracked with outrage. "Over my dead body! I'd see him in hell before I'd let him lay eyes on my girl again."

"You had no right to do that," she said tightly. "How could you? I'm not a child, I'm a grown woman."

"Then act like one," he thundered, pounding the desk. "Face up to the fact that Matt Farraday never cared about anyone but himself in his entire life, girl. It's obvious he never really cared about you."

"How would you know what Matt Farraday felt for me?" she shouted.

He sagged in his chair and seemed to shrink before her eyes. "Do you think he would have left you like that if you'd meant anything to him? *Anything at all?* Without a word of explanation—and you believing it was forever and ever, near dying of love for that good-for-nothing . . . that . . . that—" he sputtered, then stopped short for a moment, grinding his teeth. "Could you see Jason ever doing a thing like that?"

"Matt never had Jason's resources. There could be a million reasons—"

"He's rich enough now," Thomas cut in. "He could well afford such luxuries as a long-distance phone call. A postcard." His voice was sour with hate.

Alexandra stared at him defiantly, ignoring the tears that streamed down her face. She couldn't refute a word he said. It was all true, and it hurt so very much. It had no right to hurt. Not after all this time, all the effort to forget. She struggled with the sense of victimization, summoning all the bitterness she could for strength.

"I'm catching that plane on Wednesday morning,

father—like it or not." She stood up and went to the door, stiffening her spine. "I'm going with Jason, the man I'll be marrying in three months—just as you want me to. But I'm going. And as far as Matt Farraday's concerned, he can be in California or on the moon, for all I care."

Chapter Two

$\mathcal{M}$R. JASON RANDOLPH.

The hand-lettered sign caught Alexandra's eye as she and Jason emerged from the jetway into the arrivals lounge at Los Angeles International Airport. The huge area was not crowded, but a cluster of eager greeters stood jostling for space on either side of the cordoned exit as they walked through it.

She tugged on Jason's arm, drawing his attention to the small, dark-clad man who held up the placard. The man stood alone, apart from the path of the emerging passengers. As they approached, he lowered the card, and she saw precise Japanese features beneath a peaked chauffeur's cap.

"I'm Randolph," Jason said, setting down his briefcase in front of the man and rearranging the two flight bags whose double weight was beginning to destroy the elegant fall of his suede sports jacket.

"Aoki, sir. I am Mr. Farraday's driver." The small

man dipped his head in a greeting that blended pure California speech with Asian deference.

Jason handed over the bags and the luggage claim checks. Within minutes, they were seated in a long Rolls-Royce parked outside the terminal, while Aoki returned through the swinging doors to claim their baggage.

Alexandra suppressed a feeling of anticlimax. She had expected Matt to meet them and was braced for it.

Outside the car window she watched a man extricating himself from a band of Hare Krishnas, smiling as they solicited money. She was familiar with the vagaries of airports, but this one was special, with a unique breed of people attracted to the razzle-dazzle of show business, the year-round balmy weather and the free lifestyle.

Two long-haired young men in Day-Glo shirts and tight jeans walked hurriedly to a waiting limousine, each carrying a guitar case. They were gone by the time she realized she had just seen a famous rock star and his lead musician.

Soon Aoki returned, stowed their bags in the trunk and threaded through the airport traffic into wide, urban Century Boulevard. Their route was festooned with enormous billboards and a motley procession of buildings ranging from the streamlined to the ramshackle.

She slipped off her shoes and curled her stockinged toes around the sheepskin footrest Aoki had pulled out from beneath the front seat. Leaning back against the tan upholstery, she breathed in the pervasive smell of hand-processed leather overlaid with the trace of an elusive perfume, subtle, costly. It brought back the scent of the customers' dressing rooms at Fratelli Conti.

Jason was silent beside her. He had slept through the last hour of the flight and was stretched out with his eyes closed, the late edition of the *Herald Examiner* lying on the seat between them. Alexandra wished she were so relaxed, but the thought of seeing Matt again in less than two hours banished all hopes of a nap. She distracted herself, looking around the car's luxurious interior—Matt's car.

Between driver and passengers was a sliding glass partition which moved at the touch of a button set into the armrest. It reeked of casual wealth, power, and expensive women, she thought with a twinge of bitterness. What did she expect? That he would remain celibate? Hardly. Even when she was an innocent seventeen, she had known instinctively that he was already a practiced lover. There must have been many women before her and many since. Had any of them loved him the way she had? she wondered.

Anyway, there was no reason to panic; not only was he very wealthy now, but from all she'd heard about the "new Matt Farraday," he was an altogether different man from the one she had known. Probably she would see him as a complete stranger and act accordingly. At least she could hope.

Jason woke and turned to her, his eyes still drowsy. He reached for her hand and lightly kissed her fingers. "It won't be long now," he said.

"Is the hotel near the water?" She had packed a swimsuit.

"We're not staying at a hotel." He looked away, as if her question bothered him.

"Well, where are we—" She broke off, suddenly appalled. "Jason, we're not actually going to stay there!"

"There's nowhere really convenient to the ranch.

28

Vista del Lago's miles from the nearest decent hotel.
I won't have you staying in some crummy place."

"What about San Diego?" she protested. "You
said it was close."

"Impossible. The traffic would kill half the day for
me. I want to be at Farraday's to catch the morning
workouts."

"I can't believe we're actually going to stay with
him." She shook her head incredulously.

"Hey, you wanted to come, Alex," he said crisply.
"Well, here's your chance to get rid of all your
doubts. All of them." He turned his head away
sharply.

Jason's pride was fragile on the subject. But what
about hers? He'd tricked her into accepting Matt's
hospitality. Now she would face the intolerable
humiliation of having to sleep under his roof and
accept food from his table. The sudden anger that
surged through her stiffened her resolve. She'd be
poised and distant during her stay. She would never
let Matt hurt her again. This time he'd be meeting an
ice queen, not a trembling young virgin.

Jason withdrew into silence again as they glided
down the interminable freeway, car dealerships and
oil refineries giving way to orange groves and straw-
berry fields. "Orange County," Aoki informed them
over the intercom.

Soon, the fields gave way to rolling golden hills.
The six-lane superhighway curved gently around a
bend and suddenly the Pacific gleamed through the
right window. She watched, dazzled by the sight:
wall-high waves curling and breaking in bursts of
white foam at the shoreline, tall palms at the steep
cliff edge, and below, surfers riding the great swells.

It was breathtaking. For a moment she felt more
excited than she'd felt in years. It was all she could

do to stop herself from asking Aoki to pull over so that she could fly down the steep steps and wade into the silver-blue water. She felt like a little girl.

"Little girl," he had called her, stressing the ten years of experience that separated them.

"Are you okay, little girl?"

She was seventeen, and just two weeks out of the graduating class of Kennington, a refined private academy for refined private girls. Even though he was a local farmhand, Matt had been a stranger to her in every sense of the word, his harsh clothes, his laconic bluntness, his crudities. But the morning his truck backfired and made her gelding throw her, he was suddenly the most seductive, the most gentle of strangers. She knew vaguely that he worked for the Randolphs, but he had none of the subservience of Randolph hands; he didn't have a subservient bone in his body.

As she lay in the hard dirt, her eyes had traveled up the long faded blue jeans in silent fascination. He was bending over her, and her gaze came to rest when it reached his eyes, incredibly dark blue. The fall had winded her, and for a moment she could not speak. Before her breath came back, he had swept her up and carried her into the truck.

When she was able to tell him that she was perfectly all right, he caught her by the shoulders and frowned at her.

"Are you sure, now? I thought I damn near killed you, you got tossed so high. You're too pretty to leave this world."

Somehow she knew that the throbbing sensation at the base of her throat had nothing to do with the fall.

It was the beginning of summer. It was the beginning of life, womanhood, a world that began and ended with Matt, totally suspended in time and space. When he left without warning three months later, she was faced with the formidable task of picking up the pieces of her life.

She was no longer a little girl. She lived more cautiously now. Her feelings for Jason were complex; she might have wished them simpler, but she was happy to settle for this. She would be living the kind of life she understood, the kind she had always led except for that brief interlude. But she had come to California to bury that for good, she remembered.

With a jolt, she noticed they had left the freeway and were riding down a private road. The massive sprawl of a Spanish house loomed ahead, its white stucco blinding under an unclouded sky. There was no mellow fall here. On either side of the drive were huge trees aflame with scarlet blooms, and on the ground, clusters of purple and white flowers on long, slender stalks.

A young man hurried down broad steps from the house as the car slid to a halt. "I'm Scott Maddox, Mr. Randolph," he said as they got out of the car. "Miss O'Neill, welcome to Vista del Lago." As they shook hands he said, "Matt's expecting you in his office."

Alexandra felt a hot gust of wind brush her cheek, and she reached up to anchor her broad-brimmed hat.

"The Santa Ana's blowing up," Scott Maddox said. "From the desert. The Indians used to call them Devil Winds. They make the horses act up—

sometimes people, too." He grinned. "Anyway, they clean the air. By tomorrow, you'll be able to see the mountain range behind us."

Maddox wore blue jeans and a clean-cut smile. Sun-streaked hair topped a dark tan. As she and Jason followed him up the flagstone steps, Alexandra smiled to herself. The young man was a walking billboard touting the golden lifestyle of California.

Massive oak doors that suggested an old monastery led into a dim cool interior punctuated by curved archways. Arches beckoned in all directions, and gave an impression of endless spaciousness.

From his friendly monolog, Alexandra gathered that Scott Maddox was Matt's right-hand man. General manager was the term he used, not foreman or overseer. In spite of his almost beachboy appearance, she noticed an educated Eastern inflection in his voice. His manner was welcoming, but not excessively respectful.

At the end of their trek lay an imposing study, functional, almost austere in furnishings, but comfortable. Dark rosewood and leather furniture would have made it gloomy but for the picture window, which looked out on manicured lawns and a glittering lake beyond them. The view was framed by the rhythmic sweep of arches curving up to meet the eaves and forming a shaded terrace walk outside.

Scott seemed taken aback at finding the room empty and went straight to the desk telephone.

"Mr. Randolph is here with Miss O'Neill," he said quietly into the mouthpiece. "We're in your study."

"Matt extends his apologies," Scott said after he hung up. "He's just returned from Europe and he's struggling with jet lag."

Alexandra knew from Jason's expression exactly what he was thinking. To Jason, a trip to Europe meant only one thing. Matt was buying bloodstock. To Alexandra, the trip-to-Europe bit sounded like a pat excuse to keep them waiting, a deliberate snub. She was willing to bet Matt hadn't extended any apology. Scott was just sensitive enough to compensate for his employer's bad manners.

Scott poured them drinks, and Alexandra accepted a tall Scotch and soda, drinking it seriously and suddenly realizing why people drank to escape. If she could have found a way to leave the room, leave the state without seeing Matt Farraday again, she would have done it thankfully at this point, particularly when she heard footsteps approaching the study door.

Carefully, she set down her glass on the side table and gripped the arms of her easy chair, forcing herself to appear cool. But when the doors swung open, her attention was riveted to the man across the room.

Yes, it was Matt Farraday, she thought, trying to suppress a gasp. After five years, the tough frame, the midnight blue eyes, the stubborn chin were quite unmistakable. There was the same striking combination of face and form, and yet the Matt she'd known was gone. In his place stood a self-assured, very detached captain of industry.

He was evidently fresh from the shower, his black hair still slick with moisture. He wore an expensive knit shirt and slacks. He appeared to be casual and yet, as he stood at the door, he might have been any chairman of the board about to sanction a stock merger.

He paused to nod curtly toward them. "Randolph," he acknowledged, and then flatly, "Alexandra."

He was so cool and unflustered at seeing her, that

she could only be grateful that she had dressed with care to give a very businesslike impression. She wore an understated pale coffee linen suit. Her hair was tightly drawn back into a chignon and hardly visible under the wide black straw hat. It was her cool no-nonsense look, but from the eyes she'd drawn from the passengers while walking down the aisle of the plane she knew it was also stunning. She reassured herself that outwardly she looked just as unmoved as he did.

Matt carried a small document case. After the minimal greeting, he went to his desk, threw down the leather pouch and seated himself in the swivel chair. Immediately, he reached for a stack of mail and messages.

"I see Scott's taken care of your thirst," he said, riffling quickly through the papers. "Would you like to freshen up? Or would you prefer to drive straight down to the stables?"

"Let's go now," Jason said quickly. "I want to get a good look at Fortune's Lad before it gets dark."

"I thought you might." Matt's smile was bordering on malicious. "And you, Alexandra? As I recall, you're interested in horses. I think that's how we met."

"I'd prefer to stay here," she said, sounding chilly.

Matt pressed a buzzer on his desk, and in moments Aoki appeared at the door.

"Show Miss O'Neill to the guest suite in the east wing, Aoki. Then take Mr. Randolph's bags into the guest house by the pool." Matt turned to Jason. "I think you'll find the accommodations ample."

"Ample perhaps, Farraday, but not acceptable," Jason said firmly.

Alexandra felt her stomach muscles tighten, sensing there was going to be a scene.

"Oh?" Matt said mildly. "And, please, the name is Matt. Surely you remember, Jason?"

Jason leaped from his chair, furious. "Farraday, if you think Alexandra's going to stay under your roof, while I'm out there in some far removed guest house, then you're very much—"

"The sleeping arrangements for my guests are my decision, Randolph, not yours."

Alexandra rose and put a restraining hand on Jason's arm; he looked ready to throw a punch.

Matt's eyes rested on her coldly for a moment, then he turned to Jason. "Of course, you're not obliged to stay at Vista del Lago if it doesn't suit you." His voice was laced with sarcasm.

"You're right. It doesn't suit me." Jason bent down to snatch his briefcase. "We'll stay at a hotel."

Jason was heading for the door when Matt's voice stopped him in his tracks.

"Leave here, Randolph, and you can forget Fortune's Lad."

"What?" Jason was stunned.

"There are other bidders." Matt's tone was matter-of-fact.

Jason's gray eyes turned a dull slate color, his clenched fists showed white at the knuckles and his body stiffened as if he were ready to strike out. Alexandra's hand tightened on his arm instinctively, and when his arm suddenly sagged as he turned to look at her, she could sense the swift, unmistakable rearrangement of his priorities.

"Alexandra, I won't have you staying here, not if you object. Do you understand?"

"I'll be fine." She understood only too well.

"Good," Matt said, as if nothing had happened.

She met his eyes. Under the dark lashes he was laughing at her. He had good cause. Jason had just traded in her dignity for a piece of horseflesh. As she walked out of the study holding Jason's arm, Matt called after them.

"What's the matter, Randolph, don't you trust her with me in the same house?" It was very soft, like a purr.

Alexandra spun around. "Stop it, Matt!" Those were the first words she had spoken to him directly.

"I'm going to marry her," Jason said tautly. "Of course I trust her."

Then you're a fool, man. Matt didn't say a word, but she could read the silent comment in his amused glance as it flicked from Jason to her and back again.

After Jason left for the stables with Matt, Scott had a word with Aoki, then picked up her suitcase, offering to show her the way.

Scott was less talkative now, and as they walked through the hallways she realized that he was feeling awkward at having witnessed the scene in the study. She was grateful for a spell of silence—she needed to collect herself.

She'd been mistaken about Matt. He hadn't changed at all, only his circumstances had. In a few blunt words, he had just cut through Jason's six-generation veneer, right through to the bone. And he'd cut through her own hard-won defenses.

Only for a moment had she been taken in by the expensive clothes and surroundings, and the aura of power that had made him seem so different. Before he'd even sat down, she had seen the hard sculpture of muscles under the slacks, the predatory stride across the room. She was thoroughly shaken. It made no difference whether he wore cashmere in a rosewood study or patched jeans in the bluegrass. His raw sexuality remained intact. It had telegraphed its destructive message to her, making her conscious of every nerve ending in her body.

She smiled at Scott, trying to dispel his embarrassment.

"I knew Matt once in a . . . a former life. He and Jason have always rubbed each other the wrong way. It's nothing to worry about," she said lightly. "But I'm sorry you were subjected to that."

Scott laughed. "I've seen feelings run high before over a very special thoroughbred." He shrugged, and again made reference to the Devil Winds stirring up tempers.

He led her past an elegant sweep of stairs for a brief look at the layout of the house.

"There's a party tonight, by the way," he said. "A grand gathering of the racing set. Matt usually has a big get-together before the Oak Tree Meet. It's at eight-thirty, and if you'd like to rest until then, I'll have dinner sent up to your room about seven."

"Sounds great," she said, cringing at the idea of a party with Matt as her host.

The house was built of adobe and stone, Scott informed her, long before frame houses were thought of. The eighteen-hundred-acre spread surrounding it was all that remained of a once huge Spanish land grant.

"The original house was over a hundred and twenty years old," Scott explained as he led her up the staircase. "Matt found it rotting away and riddled with termites. It would have been a lot cheaper to raze it and put up a modern custom house, but he fell in love with it just the way it was. Spent a fortune renovating and restoring. He gutted the floors and most of the interior walls to lay plumbing and wiring—and *voilà!* Only the foundations and the basic floor plan remain."

It was magnificent. Rugged, massive and enduring-looking, like the authentic home of a conquistador.

"It looks as if it's been here just this way forever," she said, admiring the cream plaster niches filled with garden flowers and small sculpture, the stippled plaster arches, the oak plank floors covered with rugs.

Scott grinned with personal pride. "Remarkable, isn't it? You're looking at a great restoration job. When Matt does something, he does it right."

She could think of several replies to that, but none that Scott would like to hear, so she simply nodded as she followed him down the second-floor gallery.

"Your room," he said, opening the last door.

Alexandra caught her breath. She was looking into a private haven of pale smoky lavender and gray. She walked in on a cloud-gray carpet thick enough to sleep on and saw a wide canopied bed. Through a casement window she could see cypress trees, flowering shrubs and the glint of water. An archway in the far wall led into a sitting room where the muted lavender theme continued, warmed by shades of persimmon and burnt orange.

It was delicious, sensual . . . she remembered receiving a similar impression when she first walked through the showrooms of Fratelli Conti. Scott left her to discover the private bathroom for herself. It was tranquil and huge, encompassing a walk-in closet and a dressing area. This wasn't a room, it was a luxurious suite.

And she might as well enjoy it. She ran a bath and sank into the deep warm water, trying to soak out the tension that made her muscles stiff. She closed her eyes and let the water lap over her breasts, but not even the warm water calmed her. Alone, with no further obligation to make conversation, nothing she did could prevent her mind from returning feverishly to Matt.

She had seen him, spoken to him, and although they hadn't touched—not even a handshake—sensations that had mercifully faded after five years were inflaming her again. She'd forgotten that furry quality to his voice when they made love. She clapped her hands over her ears as if she could block out the sounds she heard in her head.

It's not hot water you're craving, princess, it's this . . .

How eagerly she had once drowned herself in his touch, his scent, the very sight and sound of him. She bit her lip and forced herself to remember how he had dumped her like an old pair of shoes, and that she hated him. It was an antidote she'd used often. But this time it wasn't working.

Furious, she pushed herself out of the tub and into a cold shower. She gasped as the hard needles of spray stung her skin.

"Forget him . . . just forget him!" she said out loud through chattering teeth. "I'm going to marry Jason, and I'm going to make him happy." *And I'm going to be happy too*, she insisted silently. *Jason will be the only lover I'll ever desire.*

She dried off, slipped on a nightgown and slid between the cool sheets. Her watch showed it was close to five. She felt drained, but she had a while to recover before she had to face anyone. Her eyes closed in bottomless exhaustion.

She awoke feeling chilly. She wasn't ready to open her eyes, but she was aware she was uncovered. She stretched out an arm to pull up the blanket and her fingers touched something warm. A hand . . . a hard set of knuckles. Instantly she was wide awake.

The bedside lamp glowed softly in the dark room. Matt Farraday stood near the foot of the bed, taking in her scantily clad body. She understood instantly that he had pulled off the covers to look at her. She yanked at the sheet but he held it back, bunched up in his fist, while his eyes traveled curiously up the length of her until they met hers. It was a dispassionate, almost clinical stare that froze her.

"You're still a beautiful woman," he said with detached admiration. "Even more beautiful. You grew up some."

"Yes, a long time ago. When you weren't around." Once she found her voice, she was out of the bed in a flash and reaching for the terry robe she had thrown on a bedside chair.

He snatched the robe away from her, then held it out so that she could slip into it. As she wrapped it around her, his body and arms walled her in. Through the cloth, she could feel his heat warming her back. His hand stroked the side of her neck and slid slowly down toward her shoulder, under the strap of her gown.

"Not that long ago," he whispered in her ear. "Don't think I've ever forgotten."

"Well I have." She twisted away from him. "I've forgotten everything, except that you were never notable for being a gentleman."

"Like Jason Randolph the Third?" he said, and she was glad her sarcasm had stung him.

"Exactly what do you think you're doing, sneaking into my room like this?"

"My housekeeper tried to bring a meal to you, but you were still sleeping." His face was expressionless. "She's tried twice since. Scott said you'd be down at eight-thirty. You're my guest; I was concerned." He grinned suddenly, his eyes distilling an intimate message. "You were never less than punctual."

The allusion was mortifying, just as he had intended. Once, he had only to name a time and a place and she would have been there waiting for him.

"Since when were you so concerned about my welfare, Matt?" The words were icy, but her voice was tremulous.

He reached out, entwining his fingers in her tousled hair, pulling her close, then pressing her face into his chest until she could hear his pulses roaring. "Ali, I never meant—" His voice became halting and rough. "I never dreamed I'd have the chance to—"

"The chance to use me again? Well you won't. Ever!" She was shocked at the treachery of her body. It still responded to him, but with an effort of will she thrust him away from her. The racing pulses she heard were her own, she realized now, not his. Her legs felt rubbery, and she groped for the bedpost.

"You were a grown man who took advantage of a silly little schoolgirl who'd led a very sheltered life. No, Matt, you won't ever get that chance again." She forced herself to continue. "As you say, I grew up. I'm not a sucker for any man. Not even one who's memorized all the erogenous zones, so forget it."

"That's not the way I remember it, but that's hardly the point." He made no attempt to recapture her in his arms, and his expression had turned to granite.

"There are other guests in my house, including your fiancé. He expects you to put in an appearance, and so do I," he said very quietly before he left the room.

She sank down on the bed after he had gone. Matt was right about one thing; for the sake of appearances, she would have to get dressed and join the guests downstairs. That was the least she could do for Jason, now that she had idiotically talked him into this trip.

It seemed a mammoth task just to make a simple decision. She fussed with her clothes and changed three times before she settled for one of her own designs. It was a silver-gray crepe de chine, simply cut, but dressy because of the plunging neckline and the diaphanous effect of that particular shade on the fabric. She had designed it with candlelight in mind, and it worked perfectly, even though Fabio had pronounced it too costly to mass-produce.

As she dressed slowly, she could hear the muted sounds of door chimes and low, muffled greetings. The greetings grew louder as more guests arrived. Laughter rang out in explosive little bursts. She procrastinated further, fiddling with her hair, finally smoothing it back tightly into the heavy chignon she'd worn that morning and adding her emerald drop earrings. After a long inspection in the mirror, she was forced to admit that she had run out of excuses. She left her room reluctantly.

The best way to cope with this ordeal was to put distance between herself and Matt. First thing tomorrow, she would call her friend Carla Minton and arrange to stay with her in Los Angeles. She could make some excuse to Jason—she wanted to see Carla's design studio, tour the garment district—something, anything.

No, it wouldn't work, she decided, descending the

staircase at a snail's pace. She could get away with a day trip, but a longer visit was implausible. Los Angeles was only a two-hour drive; it would be too blatant. She'd simply brazen it out somehow. She would grit her teeth and keep her bedroom door locked, she thought as she dragged her feet down the stairs.

On the west patio, the guests stood drinking and talking in small clusters. She heard a booming voice above the general buzz, coming from a portly man in a pale blue dinner jacket.

". . . sixteen hands, I swear to God. Great gait, great conformation. Perfect manners. You won't see a colt like him in another hundred years."

Alexandra watched his small audience, two women and four men nodding eagerly. As she skirted the intent little group, she wondered if it was Fortune's Lad they were discussing. Jason had used the same awed hyperbole when he first described the colt to her.

Animated cliques were mushrooming all over the patio and breaking off to form new combinations as she wove through the elegant festivities looking for Jason.

So this is how he lives . . . all this gaiety. How could she have imagined that he was hurting too, all these years, avoiding relationships? What a romantic idiot she was.

Looking around, she saw there was hardly one female present who wasn't absolutely gorgeous. Under the glow of hanging lanterns moved the svelte, golden bodies crowned with glossy hair, posing charmingly, laughing, mingling. Some sat drinking at tiny candle-lit tables with red cloths. The fabled glamour of Southern California unfolded before her like a well-mounted movie.

For a scruffy foundling raised by dirt-poor farmers, Matt Farraday had come a long way. He was a latter-day king holding court. And if tonight's scenario was a sample, no one would guess that he was not wealthy from birth.

She saw a vaguely familiar face, then recognized Aoki, in formal black attire tonight with a white ruffled shirt. He seemed to be in charge of the comfort of the guests and directed the crew of waiters and bus boys with the sternness of a samurai general.

The patio was on two levels. Below the huge area where she stood was another stretching toward an elaborate swimming pool. It was built to resemble a natural grotto, with outcroppings of porous tufa stone and boulders of hollowed Mexican bowl rock from which water cascaded.

Heavy oak beams were cantilevered out from the house's tile roof, forming an arbor over the upper level. Overhead hung colorful baskets of flowers and greenery.

She located Jason near the bar. He was talking to a young woman whose pale blonde hair did more to clothe her upper torso than did her white sequined gown.

"Ah, at last, Alexandra," Jason said. "I was beginning to wonder what was keeping you."

"Just vanity, pure and simple."

The blonde extended a smooth, manicured hand. "Toni Dodd," she said, and flashed a dazzling smile outlined in glossy coral.

"Hello. Alexandra O'Neill." They shook hands.

"I know. I've already heard a lot about you," Toni said.

Alexandra noted the wide, cornflower blue eyes and the speculation in them. "You have? I'm surprised." She took Jason's arm, smiling at him. "And flattered. Usually Jason doesn't talk about anything but horses."

Toni beamed. "Then I'm afraid tonight's no exception. It wasn't from Jason I heard about you."

Could Matt have talked about her to this blonde sex symbol? The thought was disarming, and suddenly the night seemed balmier, the air less hostile.

"'S'matter of fact, it was Scott Maddox who told me about you," Toni went on.

"Oh, I see." Alexandra heard her voice come out flat.

"Disappointed?" The wide blue eyes were suddenly as busy as a calculator at tax time.

A quick glance at Jason's face told Alexandra that he wasn't registering the undercurrents. "No, of course not. Why on earth should I be disappointed?" She made it decisive, then wondered if she'd overdone it.

The blue eyes looked innocent. "No reason I could possibly think of." She flashed an electric smile, then trained it on Jason. "I'm dry as a bone in the Mohave Desert, darling. Would you mind getting me a drink?"

"My pleasure." Jason raised an inquiring eyebrow. "You look like a champagne drinker to me."

Toni threw back her head and laughed huskily, the heavy blonde mane tumbling lushly onto her golden shoulders. "Then I'm sorry to say, Jason Randolph, you don't know as much about women as you think you do."

Alexandra had to admit she was a magnificent female—flashy, but gorgeous just the same. Jason looked positively bewitched. It was extraordinary— Toni Dodd was so blatantly aggressive, she was just the type he usually abhorred. But she was glamorous, and even Alexandra could tell she exuded a primal earthiness that would magnetize any man.

"I drink Scotch," she was saying. "Straight. I like strong drink and strong men." While she spoke, her attention drifted across the patio.

Alexandra followed the direction of Toni's gaze. Matt was emerging from a French door. So that was it; she was a fan of Matt's. They were probably well matched.

"Alexandra likes champagne."

She found Jason's remark oddly disparaging, as if she were being compared unfavorably to this blonde torpedo. *This was stupid;* she was getting paranoid. Seeing the adoring expression in Toni's eyes as they fixed on Matt was upsetting.

"Your Jason's a nice man," Toni said after he left for the drinks. "I guess what you'd call a true Southern gent. You don't see many of his kind in racing these days. You find the hustlers and glamour boys, men who go for the thrills of the track. He's a rare breed."

"Randolphs have been involved with racehorses for over six generations." Alexandra knew it sounded stuffy. "They're old Kentucky—roots, bluegrass tradition—left over from *Gone with the Wind*—that sort of thing." She tried to make it sound humorous, faintly ridiculous, but was suddenly embarrassed at the way it all sounded, especially to someone as earthy as Toni.

"Real blue bloods, huh?" There was a hint of cynicism. "Well, that's just terrific. My own roots are one generation removed from Cleveland. And I don't mean Shaker Heights, babe. The crummy part of Cleveland. Ever hear of Dodd's Discount Drugs?"

Alexandra nodded. Who hadn't heard of Dodd's? They were to be found in shopping malls and on Main Streets everywhere.

"That's daddy." Toni's grin was not especially proud. "He's Dodd's Discount. He started it during World War II. What you'd call an American success story."

"I used to be a regular customer when I was at school. There was a Dodd's close by," Alexandra said. "That's a huge network your father built up. I'm impressed."

"I doubt it." Toni's smile was fading. "How could people like you and Jason possibly know what it means to come up the hard way? You've had it all from the beginning. So have I," she conceded with a shrug, "but I've seen my father start from nothing. Like from ground zero, and really kill himself for it. That's the difference between us. People like my father and Matt Farraday . . . those men pay their dues, believe me. And I understand them."

Alexandra struggled to hold her tongue. The idea that Matt, of all people, had paid any dues was ludicrous. God only knew how he had acquired Vista del Lago, but it certainly wasn't from "paying dues" in life. But it was no concern of hers, she remembered, watching Jason approach carefully with their drinks. If Toni appreciated the kind of man Matt was, more power to her.

"Roger Petty's here," Jason announced with excitement.

She followed his gaze toward the bar where she could just glimpse the diminutive figure collecting a crowd of admirers. The forty-year-old jockey had made racing history, taking more consecutive stakes than anyone on record. It was just a one-year triumph, of course. Over the long haul, Johnny Longden and Willie Shoemaker still reigned. But the victories were still fresh in the mind, and word was out that Petty had at last come into his own. He was willing to take chances, had years of experience and, most important, the scuttlebutt was that he needed money. It was a dynamite combination for a jockey —not just skill and daring, but a pressing need to win.

She caught sight of Matt again, talking to an elegant silver-haired man who was strangely familiar. It teased her for a moment, then she remembered. Matt was hobnobbing with Steve Mitchell, the movie star. Mitchell owned two of racing's top stallions and had made more money on them in two years than he had in his entire movie career, which in itself was considerable.

It was obvious that Matt had cultivated all the right people. She had already recognized an industrialist, whose face was familiar from photos in *Time* and *Fortune*. Sitting at one of the tables was a songwriter whose musicals were smash hits all over the world. Of the sixty or seventy guests, not all were international celebrities, but they all looked wealthy and successful. And they were bound together by the common bond that only the wealthy could afford—a passionate involvement in racehorses.

Alexandra was admiring Steve Mitchell's famous profile when Matt turned suddenly and their eyes met. For just one heartbeat she could have sworn that he was paying some kind of tribute to all they had once meant to each other. But it was only a moment.

"Will you excuse me?" Toni said. "Matt is probably wondering where I went." She touched a light farewell on Jason's arm, flashed another glossy smile and left them.

Jason barely noticed. His eyes were glued to the jockey. "Alexandra, I'd really like to corner Petty for a few minutes and talk about—"

"Fortune's Lad," she finished for him. His thoughts were already on getting Petty to ride for him. It was easy to read his mind. "Go ahead, Jason." She smiled at him. "I'll mingle."

"Don't you want to come and meet him?" he asked politely.

"You just go ahead and do your thing. I'll be fine."

Jason's arm hugged her shoulders. "You'd tell me if you objected to me going off and talking shop at a party?"

"Jason, really!"

"I know." He grinned.

They had gone through this before, about her managing her own life, sparring around the fact that she had a career in suspension but no intention of dropping it permanently. She might be marrying a Southern gentleman, but she wasn't about to surrender her individuality completely. In spite of their similar upbringing, temperamentally she was far from the traditional Randolph wife, and Jason had a rough time accepting it. But he was making a noble try, and she appreciated it.

She lifted her head to receive his kiss, then straightened his bow tie. "Go get him, Jason."

Alexandra sensed she was being watched, and as Jason left, she turned to scan the patio behind her. Matt's eyes were trained on her and looking fierce.

She turned away and picked up a canapé from a passing waiter. She had to be mistaken. What right had he to glare daggers at her when she kissed her fiancé? What possible cause? But the look had been so raw, so open. Was it remotely possible that he still cared for her?

You'd have to be a moron to believe that, she thought, as she watched Toni sidle up to him. Matt's hand slid around Toni's waist in a familiar, possessive gesture that spoke of a very intimate relationship. Standing beside him in all her glittery blondness, she was a dramatic contrast to his dark, tough virility. They would have beautiful children together.

Once she had lain in Matt's arms, playfully depicting the children they would have one day. They would argue hilariously over ridiculous names, giggling over their silliness, two people enchanted with each other, like a man and woman hopelessly in love.

That's sick, she thought, maudlin. She had to get away. She set her glass down on a waiter's tray and dodged through the groups, catching fragments of chatter.

"Sudden Force . . . we snatched it up just one step ahead of the Kellermans," a woman said.

They were familiar words. Sudden Force was an $18 million stallion. Jason owned one of the shares, and had been delighted to pay $200,000 for it. Already the stud had sired runners who'd earned $5 million. "And that's just the beginning of the bonanza," Jason had crowed.

Alexandra threaded her way to the lower level where it was less crowded, skirted the poolside where the musicians were returning after a break, then headed into the cool darkness of the grounds beyond. As the patio lights receded, she slowed, picking her way carefully over a gravel path. It was quiet here in the crisp night air, and she began to relax.

She had walked perhaps a quarter of a mile when a man's dark shape loomed up in her path. He stopped suddenly, as startled as she was, then came closer.

"Miss O'Neill? Is that you?"

It was Scott Maddox. "Hi," she called back. "I was just taking a stroll."

"Is the party not a total success? I was just about to join it."

"Quite the contrary; it's the perfect gala occasion," Alexandra said. "As a matter of fact, everyone's having a marvelous time."

"Except you?" It was too dark to see his expression, but she thought she could hear undue concern for her welfare.

"Nonsense. Of course I'm having a good time," she said quickly.

"Sure," he said, coming close enough so that she could see his rueful half smile.

"Of course. I just needed—"

"To get a breath of fresh air?"

They both laughed at the cliché. She would rather have been left alone, but she couldn't help but like Scott. He didn't exude power or charm; he was natural, and his concern for her was genuine.

"Come on," he said. "I'll walk you back. We don't want the coyotes to get you." He took her elbow lightly.

"Are there really coyotes?"

He grinned. "Sure. California's got nature and tradition, just like Kentucky. We've got coyotes, foxes, old missions, Spanish treasures—and I'm sure you've already run into a few of our famous California wolves up there." He inclined his head toward the house.

She glanced in the same direction. Somehow the pun wasn't especially funny. It made her think of Matt's hands and the suggestive way they moved over Toni's silken hips. "Look, I don't mean to sound antisocial, but if it's all the same to you, I'd sooner stay out here for a while."

"Why?" It was blunt, unsmiling, as if he didn't like fencing and wasn't about to be put off easily.

Alexandra sighed. Scott was a young man who didn't play games. "Okay, if you must know, I don't want to go back in there because there's someone I don't want to see."

"Matt?"

"Why do you say that?"

"An educated guess." He gave her a knowing look. "I got my clue from the way you two reacted to each other in his study. Jeez, you could curl your hair just standing between you two. Talk about high voltage!"

"Oh come on, Scott, there wasn't—"

"Miss O'Neill," his voice cut in urgently.

"Alexandra, please."

"Okay, Alexandra, listen—I don't just work for Matt, I'm his friend, a good friend. I know him like I know myself, and I'd do anything to help him."

She didn't like the sound of this. She had left to get away from Matt. "I'm sure you're a dear friend to Matt, but I'd rather not talk about him right now. If you'll excuse me." She began to walk away, but he called after her, pleading.

"I don't want to talk about it," she insisted.

"You've got to." He followed her, making it sound like a matter of life and death.

She stopped. "Why must I?"

"Matt's acting wild again." Scott's face was weighted down with anxiety. "Maybe you didn't know, but for a while he had a real problem. He was very depressed, not eating, not sleeping, working too hard and driving too fast, as if he was bent on destroying himself."

It was hard for her to imagine Matt Farraday with any real problem, any weakness he couldn't control. He was nothing but a perfectly tuned instrument for self-gratification, unhampered by feelings of conscience, guilt, caring. How could anything ever bother him? "Since when did Matt have a care in the world?" she said cynically.

"It started about two years ago. Something was gnawing at him and he wouldn't talk about it, wouldn't admit that anything was wrong." Scott raised an arm and kneaded the back of his neck, frowning. "It was just when he had it all together, at least outwardly. Everything a man could possibly ask for."

He shook his head slowly, staring down at the gravel path. "He pulled himself out of it eventually. It took him months. At least I thought he had. I hadn't seen him down for over a year, until—" He broke off and let out a sharp breath.

"Look, to be honest, I'm really worried about him. When he found out you were coming out here, he changed. It was like an overnight thing. The moods came back. I know he's tried to shake them, but he's irritable and angry and generally unpleasant. Then he'll try to make up for it. He's a great guy, really. The strongest man I've ever known.

That's why I worry. Whatever this is, it's cut clear to the bone."

"I'm sorry, but it doesn't concern me."

"Alexandra, please!" He was shocked at her callousness.

"I'm sorry, Scott, but you make it sound as if there were something I could do about it." She shrugged. "He's surrounded by adoring friends. Me, I'm only an acquaintance from his Kentucky days, that's all."

"Yeah."

She couldn't fool him for a moment. She cursed herself for being so transparent. There had to be some privacy, some dignity to her life. She looked down, avoiding his eyes, and twisted the diamond ring on her fourth finger. "Scott, if you imagined you felt any vibrations this afternoon, they were merely your overactive imagination. I've neither seen nor heard from the man in five years. We had a passing acquaintance."

"Some acquaintance," he said caustically.

"Will you mind your own business!" The man was infuriating.

"This isn't something you can walk away from, Alexandra. He's a human being and there's too much at stake. You know him well. Better than I do, I think, no matter what you say. He's a man who has everything. I want to help him, but I can't until I know what's really bugging him. What is it?"

"I really couldn't say," she said icily. "Matt's a different man now. He wasn't quite so well set when I knew him."

"What's that got to do with anything?" It was Scott's turn to get angry. "I know, if you care for him at all, you could get—"

"But I don't, Scott. I don't care for him in the

least. And I don't care for this conversation. Enough!" She shook him off and ran back toward the bright lights of the patio.

Jason was still huddled with Petty. He put an arm around her as she came up and introduced the jockey.

"Roger was just telling me about his last race on Sudden Force. A wonderful story."

Across the room, Alexandra could see Toni wrapping her supple body around Matt's, moving to the seductive Latin rhythm of the five-piece group playing at poolside.

She smiled at the jockey. "Mr. Petty, I'm thrilled to meet you, but please forgive me. We've had a long trip and I'm exhausted." She kissed Jason's cheek. "Would you mind?" she whispered. "I need some sleep."

Jason kissed the top of her head. "No, no," he said hurriedly then turned to Petty. "Don't go away. I'll be right back."

"There's no need for you to leave, Jason." She could see how reluctant he was to lose his advantage with the jockey. "I'm quite capable of fighting off the dragons all the way to the second floor. Besides," she added, laughing, "I wouldn't dream of disrupting this *tête-à-tête*."

Jason took her hands. "You sure, now?"

"Of course."

After they said good night, she made her way back into the house, declining would-be dance partners with as much grace as she could and breathing a sigh of relief as she mounted the stairs to the second floor.

This time, she locked the bedroom door behind her. In the bathroom, she splashed cold water on her face. As she patted it dry, she stared into the mirror above the basin.

It wasn't the same face Matt had known. It had been rounder, softer then. Shadows stressed her cheekbones now, emphasizing the fullness of her lower lip and the size of the widely spaced eyes. Right now they had a wild look, overbright, as if she were lit from within by desire.

She had cheekbones now, and Matt had black moods. *That's the way the world goes.* She removed her earrings, then let down the heavy coil of coppery hair, attacking it viciously with her hairbrush. *Well, everything changes. The world moves on regardless.*

But her mind kept revisiting the recent conversation with Scott Maddox, like a tongue probing a painful tooth. How worried he was about Matt and his moods. What did they stem from, anyway? Success turned sour? No more worlds to conquer? Too much, too soon?

She tugged at her hair until her scalp hurt. *Moods.* She could tell Scott a thing or two about melancholy, about long walks alone when she wished she could walk off the face of the earth. She knew enough about black moods to last a lifetime. And she was finished with them. She stopped brushing her hair for a moment. Her eyes accused her in the mirror. But she wasn't finished with Matt; the chemistry was still there.

It was just an unhappy quirk in the way their respective bodies were put together that made them mutually attractive. At any rate, that's all it was on his side. On her part, she didn't believe that for a second. But if he could drool over her body and not give a damn about her feelings, she certainly wasn't going to bother about *his* feelings.

Jason had been so right, not wanting her to come.

She'd insisted. And look at her, reduced to mush, aroused in a way she could hardly remember feeling before. Well, it was a passion grossly misplaced. Those feelings rightfully belonged to Jason, not that two-faced predator in custom clothes. This ambivalence toward Jason wasn't fair; it was treachery.

She forced herself to sit down calmly and review her future. That was the secret—the future would be her salvation. She pictured her wedding, the guests, her father's happy face. She saw Jason, the Chantilly lace train that belonged to her grandmother, and she thought of their wedding night . . . and the image in her mind grew fuzzy. She could see Jason, but she couldn't see herself. No matter how hard she tried, she could not see herself in that picture.

Chapter Three

Alexandra undressed slowly and picked out a filmy black negligee, then had second thoughts about it. Quite likely Jason would come in to say good night before he retired. She wouldn't want him to get the wrong idea. But of course, he wouldn't; he was Jason, not Matt.

Through the window, she could see the house-lights reflected on the black surface of the lake, a calming view, removed from the bustle of the patio party on the opposite side of the house. She sat in an armchair, gazing at the night, trying to think of anything but Matt.

She must have dozed off. When she heard the rapping at the door the night had paled to a violet-gray. Jason had come to say good night. A little dreamily, she went to the door and unlocked it to let him in.

But it was Matt who walked in, kicking the door closed behind him.

Her mind was slow with sleep; before she could react, he reached out for her swiftly and brought her body close to his.

"Alexandra," he breathed close to her ear, and buried his face in her sleep-tousled hair.

Her name on his lips was a caress, and she felt a deep response, as if he had kissed her. "Matt, no," she said. "Please."

"I had to come," he whispered, and his voice caught. "I couldn't help myself."

"This isn't right," she pleaded, unable to bring herself to pull away from him.

"Yes it is," he said fiercely as he pressed her closer. "It's as right as anything in this world is right." His lips began to slide down the smooth column of her neck.

She arched back and looked up into his face. In the dim moonlit room the deep blue intensity of his eyes looked velvety black.

"Jason might come," she said.

"Then let him come . . ."

She stiffened in his arms, afraid of her longing to stay in that flaring circle of desire. Beyond that circle lay cool sanity, predictability . . . the safe world of her father and Jason. In Matt's arms, reason stopped. She trembled, wanting him so intensely that it was all she could do not to cry out, *Yes, yes! Please love me. Don't ever stop. Don't leave me ever, ever again.*

Her arms felt leaden as she pushed him away, and the air around her chilled her skin. She turned away, hugging her arms to ward off a sudden, bone-deep chill. What a monumental effort it was to release herself from Matt's touch—not a physical effort, but a profound inner struggle. It wouldn't go away, not ever, she realized, until she could face it squarely.

She turned to face Matt and spoke as deliberately as she could. "Jason is my fiancé. I'm going to marry him. How could I respect myself if I—"

"If you let me make love to you?" His eyes slipped down from her face and swept hungrily over her slender length draped in the misty fall of chiffon. He took a step, closing the cold gaping space between them.

"No!" She could feel his arousal, hard against her as he pressed her to his body warmth.

"Yes, Alexandra. Please stop playing mind games with yourself. You know—"

"They aren't games," she protested, "not any kind of games." But she lowered her eyes from his, afraid the bewildered uncertainty she suffered would show in them.

"Oh yes they are, my love." Firmly, gently he tilted up her head with a finger at her chin. His eyes were melting her bones. "I know because, you see, I've spent five years playing them myself. Yes, mind games. I know all about the fine points of rationalizing, insisting to myself that I didn't really feel what I felt, didn't really want what I was sick at heart from wanting." He shook his head lightly and frowned as if he were brushing off a dream. "But it doesn't work, does it? It all boils down to . . ." He faltered as his fingers ran lightly over the swell of her breast, and his voice hoarsened with pleading.

"Don't marry him, Alex. Don't, don't."

It was the same as it had always been, she thought, suddenly noticing how her arms were wound about his neck. She loosened them. When he touched her, spoke that way, she became his toy, his fool, drinking in every moment. Even the pain was a sweetness.

"Don't do this to me, Matt. Don't talk anymore, don't try to persuade me. I'm too confused. I don't know anymore what's right and what's wrong. Not when you deliberately—"

"Is this right?" He bent his lips to her mouth until they met with a tentative feathery touch. She felt him shudder against her, then something wild broke, some ravenous, long-suppressed hunger. It resounded in the depth of her being, becoming an answering hunger of her own, making her forget their separate identities, making of them one volition, one organism.

He lifted her and laid her down on the bed. And she watched him undress, loving him so much that tears began to gather, blurring her vision. He lowered himself to her side, and with his fingers traced a slow path across the planes of her face and body, as if he were reassuring himself that she was truly there, truly welcoming him. She reached up and encircled his neck with her arms, pressing him closer until they were locked in a timeless kiss that demanded nothing for a long, blissful moment, just the holding, the mutual touching.

"I have never stopped loving you," she said at last.

At the sound of her words, his stillness was broken and passion erupted in him, tensing his sinews and spilling over into the soft urgent sounds deep in his throat. "Alex Alex Alex Alex . . . Oh, how I've wanted you."

His tongue warmed her skin, his lips lingering at her nipple, then claiming the rest of her. He lifted the chiffon, uncovering her thighs, and parted them.

She sighed deeply and shuddered as the pleasure

she took in his touch mounted swiftly to a tormenting need. As much as he took, she wanted to give. She arched up to him as he crushed his mouth against hers. Crying out her name, he buried his flesh in hers, thrusting again and again until the cries of their passion mingled in an ultimate explosion of pure joy.

Later she lay listening to his breathing grow quiet. His hard, smooth chest glistened with moisture. She sensed that some spell had broken, but she clutched at it, reluctant to lose that elusive completeness. Already it seemed less real, more dreamlike.

Matt's eyes were closed as she laid her face over his heart. "Matt, I love you. . . ."

She spoke softly, not wanting to wake him, and dimly she remembered she had said it earlier.

But he had not said he loved her.

Her heart constricted with pain. What was it he had said? He wanted her. Yes. *I've wanted you.* Matt had never mentioned love. Those were only her words, and now she felt them choking in her throat. She rose from the bed and looked down at Matt's sleeping, sprawling form. *You are dangerous, Matt Farraday. Look at you, lying there with that careless, splendid body. Even sleeping, anyone would sense that charm, that powerful persuasiveness that turns on like heat to melt whatever it touches. Who wouldn't fall in love with you? You make it too easy . . . but then you—* She turned away abruptly.

What an absurd idiot she was, she thought as she bathed and dressed. Stupid, gullible, unforgivably naive. She was willfully hurting herself.

She sat by the window, waiting for him to wake. He wasn't to blame, she decided, if he approached life differently. He was what he was. He had spelled that out for any fool to understand when he'd left her five years ago. She couldn't blame him for taking pleasure in her body when she offered it. She could only blame herself for self-deception.

A slight sound made her turn toward the bed. Matt was stirring, reaching an arm over the cold sheet under his body. Slowly he opened his eyes, then sat up abruptly when he saw her by the window.

"I think you'd better leave now," she said coolly.

He leaned forward, frowning. "What's wrong?"

"Nothing."

"Alex? What is it?" He began to reach for his clothes at the side of the bed.

She swallowed the lump of grief that swelled in her throat as she watched him dress hastily. He stood bare-chested, fastening the waistband of his slacks, when she managed to speak again.

"This was a mistake, that's all. Now it's best you go and we forget the whole thing."

She saw the blurred confusion in his eyes in the predawn light as he reached for her shoulders. "Wait a minute. What are you saying? I don't get it. What is this? Weren't we—?" He broke off, his gaze turning toward the bed as if he were no longer sure the night had taken place.

"Yes, I know. We had sex on that—"

"We had what?" His head reared back in an involuntary movement of shock. He stared at her as if she'd said something quite irrational. "Alex . . . we made love," he said, as tentatively as if he were asking.

She shrugged, and her words came out clipped and dry in the effort to suppress the wild sobs trying to wrench loose from deep in her lungs. "Whatever, if you want to get into semantics—"

"I don't want to get into anything but what's going on in that head of yours."

"Please, Matt. Just leave."

Get out. For pity's sake go before I break down and bleed all over you and melt while you tell me how wonderful I am, while you console me and lure me deeper and deeper into this intolerable pain.

"I'm not leaving you, Alexandra. Not until I know what this is all about," he said quietly.

Oh, how could she stand it! What could she tell him? What did he know about this all-encompassing emotion that made her want to weep with joy when she so much as heard his voice? She was just a desirable woman to him. A choice pleasure he wanted until he was sated. She must stop demanding a reciprocation, stop hoping, stop expecting. Her eyes caught the tousled sheets on the bed. To him that was an end in itself. It was enough.

From somewhere, she dredged up a resolve as ungiving as steel. "I don't want Jason coming here and finding us together," she said harshly.

It was as if she had slapped him. He almost staggered, then instantly steadied himself. She saw granite replace the sensitive, vulnerable features. His lip curled in deliberate irony. "Jason," he repeated.

"Did you think a bout of sex would change everything?" she said dully. It was easier to cope with Matt when his wounds were decently covered. They were only carnal disappointment, she remembered. He would recover much faster than she. "Sex never cemented our relationship five years ago. Why should it now?"

Matt's eyes glinted as sharply as broken glass. "Perfect," he said. "Alexandra and Jason. The Kentucky bluebloods—wed . . . bed . . . and dead.

In each other's arms. They'll be very cold arms, Alexandra."

She shook her head. "Very faithful arms, Matt, holding me always. Jason happens to love me."

"Loves you, does he?" Matt seemed to consider this with the cool detachment of a biologist at a microscope as he gathered up the rest of his clothes and slipped into his shirt. He buttoned it slowly. "We both know what Jason loves, or I thought we did. He loves Windermere. He loves being a Randolph. And he loves that horse he's come to buy. There's no passion left over for a woman in his life."

He tucked in his shirt with exaggerated care, then sat on the edge of the bed and reached for his socks. She stood stiffly by the window watching him, cold under the heavy long robe.

"That's where you and I differ from Jason," he said blandly. "Passion is what we are all about. It's in our natures, as much as needing to win is in Jason's. You can't walk away from that fact, Alex. And you won't be able to expend it in Jason's bed. He'll have little use for it."

She sat down again abruptly, her knees buckling with fear that this might be true. "Would you suggest I expend it all in this bed?" she said, gesturing contemptuously to the disordered sheets behind him.

His eyes sought out her face for a keen, searching moment, then he shrugged. "Not for me to say. You have to make up your mind about what you really want."

What you really want. As if she were choosing between two flavors of ice cream. Despair inched up, seeping into her flesh like a slow, icy flood. Jason might know nothing of passion, but what did Matt know of love? "I want you out of here," she said roughly.

He stood, his jacket in one hand, his shoes in the other. "No you don't," he said. "Not really."

"Get out, Matt. Please, please, get out!"

"You're a very lucky woman, Alexandra," he said, his hand on the doorknob. "You have wealth and looks and youth. You can afford to change your mind, play your games. But I'm not a poor kid off the farm anymore. I don't have to beg for anyone's scraps."

The sky outside was pale peach. Matt was gone, but the bruised fullness was still on her lips, and his male musky scent lingered in the room. A tidal wave of disgust engulfed her at the thought of the orgiastic night. Matt's hard, thrusting body, her own ecstatic cries . . . his sexual expertise, so practiced it was second nature to him.

Her reflection glanced back at her from a mirror against the wall. Her hair was a wild auburn mane, and the eyes were too bright. She had craved Matt's body only a few hours before; she couldn't pretend otherwise.

What a fool she was! All these years she had romanticized her physical hunger for Matt because, where she came from, it was unthinkable for a "nice girl" of seventeen to crave a man's body as she had. The taboos were everywhere, from her teachers' undertoned warnings about "urges that must be controlled," to her father's moralistic deluges on conduct befitting a young woman of her social position.

Well, she could give it the right label now. What she had felt all this time was the great social equalizer. Plain old lust, on her part as much as Matt's.

Nothing cosmic or transcendental. Put the right two chemicals together, shake them up, create a bit of friction, and step back for the fireworks, folks. But shooting stars don't last; they burn out in the stratosphere. And you don't see them in the daylight, she thought bitterly, glancing at the empty place in the bed where Matt had slept.

He'd simply taken her again, literally and figuratively. For a few hours she had confused all that tumult with love, permanence.

Crumpled at her feet lay the robe where it had dropped the night before. She'd made herself no different than that—a piece of soiled laundry. But not anymore. Stooping, she picked it up and laid it carefully across the bed. In future, she'd take much better care of herself.

How many women, she wondered, had Matt lain with on those same nights when she had tossed alone in bed, loving him so intensely that no other man could reach her?

Jason had been so patient, graciously tolerating her rebuffs when she had gone into her pristine Southern belle routine. God, he deserved more from her than this two-faced treachery.

She would start fresh with Jason and be everything he hoped she would be to him—and everything he deserved. The enemy was not Matt, she knew that now, but her own fantasies and the stubborn carnal gnawing deep within herself. The fantasies were gone for good, and as for the lust, she would arm herself against it.

She would never lay her hurt on Jason. Confession might be good for the soul, but only the soul of the sinner, and she must think of Jason's well-being from now on.

* * *

It was past ten o'clock before she had the courage to go down and face them. She wandered into room after room and was beginning to think the whole house was empty when she caught sight of Scott through the breakfast room French windows, which led to a small sunny patio. Scott sat outside at a round glass table, drinking coffee.

"Good morning," she said, joining him. "I was beginning to think I'd been completely deserted."

"Hi!" Scott glanced at his watch. "You slept well."

"Very well." She was surprised how easily the little lie came.

He put aside the legal pad he had been writing on and took a cup from the tray on the table. "Coffee?"

She nodded, and he poured from a silver urn. "They've gone to watch Fortune's Lad run laps."

"Yes, of course. Jason's been anxious to see the wonder horse put through his paces."

"You missed breakfast, but Mrs. Gonzales will fix you something. What would you like?"

She declined, and Scott smiled, giving her a questioning look.

"All right. What?" she demanded.

He raised his eyebrows innocently as she set down her coffee cup.

"You're doing it again," she told him. "Reading my mind."

"I am?" He poured himself some more coffee. "Well, let's just say you have very revealing eyes. Don't ever play poker."

"Thanks. I'll remember that."

She sipped her coffee through a slightly awkward silence.

"Thank you, Alexandra," he said finally.

"For what?"

Scott's eyes lit with pleasure. "Matt was up early and he got more work accomplished before nine this morning than he's handled in months. He also gave me the go-ahead to break ground on the new stables. He's been putting me off for over a year. So"—his smile was genuinely affectionate—"I want to thank you. You revitalized a man who was floundering around only half alive."

Alexandra shrugged. "I'd like to be able to take credit, but I had nothing to do with—"

"Everything!" Scott leaned toward her. "You have everything to do with Matt."

She shrank away from him coolly. "You're over-stepping the boundaries, Scott, and I don't care how devoted you are to him. Stop trying to include me because, like it or not, I'm definitely not a part of Matt's life. Do you understand?"

He looked at her, not flinching. "Do you?"

"I came here to keep Jason company. I am going to marry him." Her voice stayed decisive.

"Then why the hell did you sleep with Matt last night?"

She felt the color leave her face and she took a breath to deny it.

"Don't," he cut her off. "I know you were with him. I *know*, all right?"

"Did he tell you that?" Her eyes were stinging. So Matt couldn't wait to tell his crony.

"Is that what you think?" Scott sounded shocked. "If you could really believe that, then—"

"I'd be right on target. It would be very much in character with the man I know."

"Lady, you don't know a damn thing."

It was so harsh, she was taken aback.

"I went to find him after the guests left. He seemed so down earlier in the evening. He tried to hide it, but he never fools me. I was going to see if I could lighten him up with some of the horse gossip I picked up during the party."

She looked up at a slight rushing sound and saw a large black bird circle, then swoop away into the blue. She envied the soaring freedom of it, and the coffee tasted bitter on her tongue. "My God, I hope he pays you enough. What you do for that man goes above and beyond the call of duty." Her voice was acid, but it didn't seem to touch Scott.

"I've told you," he said, "he's more than a boss. He's my friend."

"Well bully for you and for Matt." She got up abruptly. "I'm going to take a walk or something."

Scott took her wrist. "Please, I didn't mean to be offensive."

"Well, you were."

"I'm sorry. Matt hasn't said a word to me about last night. I told you the truth. I went to his room and he wasn't there. I hunted for him. All the horses were in, the cars all parked. There was only one place he could have been. With you."

"What about someone else?" Alexandra said. "Like Toni Dodd?"

Alexandra noticed the flare of resentment in his eyes. She had finally touched a nerve.

"No. Not Toni. Not this time, anyway. Toni came to me last night. She came looking for Matt."

"I see." Alexandra sagged. "So Toni knows too."

"I've no idea what she knows," Scott said flatly.

She groped for words, some justification. "Scott, listen, I can imagine what you're thinking, but—"

"Please. Spare me the speech. I don't make judgments, okay?" He sounded weary. "I just see what I see. A classy lady doing some kind of con job on herself, and I don't know why, but—"

"I know why," she cut in, "and it's no con job."

"You're in love with Matt," he said stubbornly.

"Let me ask you something, Scott," she said after a pause. "How many women has Matt been involved with since you've known him?"

He shrugged disinterestedly. "A few."

"Quite a few?"

"He's not a monk," Scott said grudgingly.

"Including Toni Dodd?"

He hesitated. "I couldn't say."

"Come on, Scott! You owe me one."

"They've been . . . physically . . . involved." The words seemed to choke him.

Alexandra turned her face away to protect herself from this man who read her thoughts so easily—and cared so much.

"Physically involved," she repeated flatly, shocked at how much the knowledge stung. She'd always known she was neither the first nor the last of his affairs, but there was a much sharper edge to thinking of Matt making love to a woman she'd met.

She let her face smooth over before she turned to him again. "Why doesn't he marry Toni?"

Scott didn't answer.

"Maybe because he doesn't want anything from her but what he already has? She's wild about him. I saw it last night. She'd marry him in a minute."

It was a while before Scott met her gaze. "Is that what you want from him. Marriage?"

"I want nothing from him. Not anymore." *Not ever again*. "What happened last night"—she gave a cool shrug—"it was just something that happened."

"It meant—"

"Nothing. Absolutely nothing."

Scott nodded silently. But she wasn't sure he was satisfied. Somehow, convincing Scott had taken on supreme importance. It was like one more brick in the wall she had to build between the past and what would be her future with Jason.

"Oh!" He touched his forehead. "I almost forgot." He delved into his hip pocket and brought out a small beige envelope. "For you."

She took it from him without comment and opened it. There was a single sheet of notepaper. "Ali, I'm not good at words. My apologies. I'm blunt and sometimes I overstep the mark. But how can we kid each other now? We're right together. We always will be. I understand things are difficult for you with Jason around. Meet me this afternoon at my place near Del Mar at four o'clock. We can talk there. Take the white station wagon." There was an address, directions and, at the bottom of the envelope, a car key.

Her hand shook as she struggled to fit it back inside the envelope. How dare he! Was he so sure of her that he expected her to sneak to him behind Jason's back when he beckoned? Rage must have shown in her face.

"Whatever's in there, I gather it doesn't suit you," Scott said. "Subtleties are not Matt's style. He never had the background—"

"Don't tell me about his background!" she shot back.

"Mornin'" The patio door opened.

They both turned toward the cheerful voice.

"Well, aren't you two the lazy ones? Still at breakfast." Toni Dodd swung toward them, her slim legs tightly encased in white jeans. Under the sun-bleached hair, the dusty glow of her tanned face made her eyes seem incredibly blue.

"I've been up since the crack of dawn," she said. "Matt called at some ungodly hour and told me to swing by the architect's first thing and pick up the stable plans." She brandished a roll of blueprints in the air, beaming. "We're finally gonna get started, Scott."

He grinned at her. "Yeah, he told me."

So they all worked together cozily on this project. Toni was more than horseflesh to Matt; she was neatly woven into his life.

"Look, you two," Alexandra said quickly, "I've poked around enough this morning. I promised to visit a friend in L.A. This looks like the right moment."

Scott started toward the house. "I'll have Aoki drive you up."

"No, thanks anyway." Her thumb pressed against the key in the envelope. "I'd prefer to drive myself. Nice to see you again, Toni."

Toni looked up from the plans she had already spread on the table. "Same here," she said cautiously. "I expect we'll see a lot of each other the next few days. I'm always here."

Alexandra nodded, decoding the full message. "That's what I understand."

"Any messages for Jason?" Scott asked.

"Yes, of course," Alexandra said after a moment's hesitation. "Tell him I'm sorry I missed him. I'll be back early this evening." She glanced back at Toni. "And give Jason my love."

As she passed Scott on her way into the house, she saw his eyes glaze over with cynicism.

Chapter Four

Alexandra was grateful for the loan of the car, at least. It was a relief to be doing something mechanical like driving. Just to be behind a wheel, to examine a freeway map, restored her feeling that she was fully in control of her life. She wasn't in the mood for swapping feminine confidences with Carla Minton, she decided suddenly, passing the northbound ramp that would lead her to Los Angeles. Instead, she turned the Mercury wagon into the southbound entrance of the freeway and headed for the Mexican border. In less than an hour, she could be at the U.S. border. The thought of leaving California behind, leaving the country even, seemed very attractive.

She let her mind empty as the warm wind roared in through the open windows and the golden hills and glimpses of bright water slipped by her right window.

At the border, an ugly collection of bureaucratic sheds, seedy parking lots and garish commercial buildings bore the pretentious name of National City. To Alexandra it seemed more like a marker that ended the affluent life than a political boundary. There were no plush homes to be seen as she approached, no beautifully landscaped greenbelts or bronze-mirrored corporate structures. There was nothing but squat industrial plants, box houses and eyesores. On the far side of the chain link fence lay a world that made National City look like heaven.

After the guard waved her through, she followed the signs leading to Tijuana and what seemed to be its main boulevard, Avenida Revolución.

She found a car park and began to stroll. Street vendors called to her, some teasing her with compliments in broken English. At every corner stood a woman or child with a colorful mass of tissue paper flowers, each bloom like a huge balloon nodding on a long wire stem.

After a little exploring, she discovered the bazaars, narrow sunken alleys reached by steep, worn steps, just off the main thoroughfare. They were fascinating and much more colorful than the upper-level shops. In one of them, she found a comparatively clean cafe and ordered a burrito. She enjoyed the finely shredded beef and savory beans laced with a mildly hot sauce inside the crisply fried tortilla wrapping. Fortified by the meal, she threaded her way through stalls of novelties, leather wares, brass goods and tourist junk.

She haggled for a white, hand-embroidered peasant dress, and after ten strenuous minutes the dress was hers. Three stalls down, she found the same dress marked forty pesos less than she had paid. The streets and alleys of Tijuana diverted her for hours.

They were gay and noisy and dirty, and not very different from the suqs of Marrakech. She was surprised when she glanced at her watch. Four o'clock.

Alexandra enjoyed a small moment of triumph. She had successfully kept Matt out of her thoughts for over four hours. At this moment he would be waiting for her in Del Mar. How would he enjoy waiting for a no-show lover? she wondered. It would never occur to him that maybe she simply wouldn't come.

Would he be hurt? As she nosed the car out of the town and back onto the San Diego Freeway, she savored the picture of him standing forlorn at a window.

Or would he be furious? These days, very few people dared to stand up to Matt Farraday it seemed, not if they wanted a chance of dealing with him. Well, she didn't have to worry about that. Matt held no financial hold on her.

It dawned on her at once that this wasn't quite true. Matt could perhaps exercise control over her by proxy. He owned a horse that Jason wanted more than he'd ever wanted anything in his life. She was committed to Jason, and that meant being committed to his priorities. She had to start identifying with them, trying to understand them.

A mile from the Del Mar Racetrack exit, Alexandra coasted, her foot letting up on the gas pedal. Matt's apartment was nearby. She hesitated and thought of turning the wheel into the exit lane. It would be so easy. And why not? This was the eighties. She'd play his game, take what *she* wanted and then leave him. Where was it written that a woman wasn't entitled to as much sexual satisfaction as a man?

No sooner was the thought completed than she felt hot with shame. *Jason*. It wasn't a question of new morality, of women's liberation. This had to do with trust, integrity. Commitment.

Her hands were slippery on the steering wheel as she accelerated past the exit. She drove fast all the way back to the rancho, her mind busily trying to still the churning desire inside her.

It was four-thirty when Aoki let her in the front door.

"Mr. Maddox is in the library, if you would like to join him," he said with a tiny bow.

"Thank you, I will, as soon as I've changed." Her shoes were dusty from her walk through Tijuana, and her slacks and blouse were clinging limply to her skin.

She had showered, and was stepping into a jersey jumpsuit when she heard the knock on the door.

"It's Jason. Can I come in?"

She hurried toward the door, pulling up the long zipper as she went.

When she opened the door, Jason hurtled past her and into the room.

"Where the hell did you go? I've been going crazy waiting for you to get back!"

"I went for a drive," she said, closing the door and realizing that he hadn't even looked at her. "Didn't Scott tell you?"

"No. That is—maybe he did." He turned to face her, his whole bearing agitated. "I don't remember. I've been preoccupied. . . ."

Alexandra went to the dressing table and sat down to brush her hair. In the mirror, she saw him coming toward her, eyes bright, his usual complacency stirred into something resembling feverish excitement.

"What is it, Jason? Are you all right?" She twisted in the chair to face him.

"I'm far more than all right."

"What do you mean. Has something happened?"

"Nothing yet . . . oh . . . everything."

He was full of frantic energy, at her side for an instant, then bounding off across the room toward the French doors.

"That explains a whole lot!" Alexandra shook her head. "Why don't you start with the nothing, then move right along to the everything. That way, perhaps I'll have some clue as to why you're acting like a jack-in-the-box."

"Everything I've hoped for, Alex, everything I've worked for is starting to come together."

Ah, the horse. What else could stir Jason so but his passion for winning? For a moment she had a picture of Matt, sitting on the edge of her bed, impersonally pointing out Jason's deficiencies. "Is it the horse, Jason?" she asked softly.

"Yes. Fortune's Lad. Oh Lord, what an animal! And he's going to be mine."

"I'm glad for you." She wished it meant more to her.

"Be glad for *us,* Alex. You're going to be Mrs. Randolph soon, and when we walk through a crowd, there won't be a man or woman in Kentucky who won't envy us."

"Yes," she said quietly as she turned back to the mirror, "glad for both of us." Her eyes looked strained. Suddenly she was looking past them, into the life that lay ahead: Mrs. Randolph Jason, dressed to perfection, a paper-doll woman walking into the future on the arms of a paper-doll man, the two of them socializing with the Kentucky horse set . . . a whole population of frozen-faced, one-dimensional mannequins. Smiles always in place on all the faces, and hers the brightest smile, because she had the most to rejoice in. After all, she was Mrs. Jason Randolph III.

She dabbed away the moisture seeping into her eyelashes and blinked before Jason could notice. Through the mirror she saw him still pacing off the jubilant excess energy and smiled. She doubted he would notice if she were wearing two heads at the moment.

"We'll have it made," he was saying, pounding one fist against the other. "You know, things haven't been the way they used to be in my grandfather's heyday. I've been witnessing the gradual change since I was a small boy. The elegance, that great margin of comfort—it's been floating away, piece by piece. But I'm going to get it back. Windermere's going to have some of that true splendor again."

He stopped behind her, peering at her reflection in the mirror with narrowed eyes. "You're a very beautiful woman, Alexandra. Perfect. I want you to stay beautiful always and take the best possible care of yourself. I don't care how much it costs. You'll be a Randolph, a standard-bearer in a way. But I'm sure I don't have to tell you that." He gave a smile of utter satisfaction. "O'Neills understand all that. You are your father's daughter."

Yes, she thought, she did understand completely. She was being cast in a social role that would endure for a lifetime. Why should it panic her? Jason was right. She was well cast, perfect for the role by birth and by breeding. It was well within her grasp. Her hand shook, and the diamond on her fourth finger caught the light with a harsh, cold brilliance.

A shrill ring sounded in the room, and as she went to the bedside telephone, she knew who it would be.

"Why didn't you come, Ali? Why didn't you come?" The warm dark timbre of Matt's voice made her stomach tremble. She could feel Jason's eyes on her and for a moment she held her breath.

"Where are you? Can you talk? Are you in your room?" he demanded.

"Yes."

"Please Ali, we have to . . . will you let me . . . will you for God's sake say—"

"Oh, hi," she said crisply. "Jason's right here."

"Really." The urgent warmth in his voice had vanished. "Jason in your bedroom? Then, of course, I understand why you couldn't make it over here."

She heard him exhale a quick, harsh breath.

"You're a surprising lady, you know. I underestimated you. Or should I say overestimated?" His tone was cutting.

She felt a need to defend herself, but Jason was beside her, listening. "It's not exactly the way you—"

"Let me speak to him," Matt cut in.

She held the phone out to Jason wordlessly, then went into the bathroom and stood running cold water over her wrists.

When she returned, Jason was off the phone and waiting for her, a new urgency in his demeanor. "Farraday's taking bids on Fortune's Lad," he said frowning.

"You mean, right now?" Alexandra was startled. There was supposed to have been a meeting with all prospective bidders, a formal presentation, and a few days to watch the trials. "But it wasn't supposed to be for—"

"I thought so too," he put it. "Something's made

him change his plans. He just informed me he's taking two bids this evening."

"Oh, Jason." She could imagine how he felt; Jason was a planner, not one to act on impulse. Matt's plans would force him into a premature decision.

"I don't like it," he said sourly, "but there's nothing I can do about it."

"He can't manipulate you like this. If the horse is so great, why would he want to force the bidding?" She hoped faintly that he would take a stand against Matt, call his bluff. She longed to see a sign in Jason that there was some principle in him, some passion or even stubbornness, something that was more important to him than a horse.

But Jason simply stared at her in utter disbelief. "I clocked him today."

"And he ran well," she said flatly.

"God! He didn't run, he flew! His name should be Pegasus."

"There are other horses, Jason. Father says there's always another—"

"There's only this one for me," he snapped, as if she had insulted him by suggesting he'd settle for less.

"Then you're going to bid tonight with the others."

"Do I have a choice?" Jason asked in surprise.

She went to the French windows and opened them. Over a distant ridge she could see a faint darkness billowing into the sky. A fire, perhaps.

Matt was pulling Jason's strings, and Jason was allowing it. It was a despairing thought.

"We always have a choice," she said quietly.

"Not in this case. I do what Farraday wants, or I lose Fortune's Lad. That's no choice at all."

She couldn't look at him. This was Matt's spiteful way of getting back at her because she hadn't come to him today. But she couldn't tell Jason that; it would destroy his pride, shatter their relationship. That was exactly what Matt would like. Matt had them both where he wanted.

"I can't go myself this evening," Jason said suddenly. "I'm going to write out the bid and have you take it to him. He's at an apartment he keeps near the track. I've got the directions."

When she turned, Jason was opening a desk drawer, looking for notepaper.

"Please, Jason. I'm exhausted. It's the jet lag."

"It'll only take a few minutes. It's not far." He was jotting figures on a sheet.

"You can send Aoki. He'll know the place."

Jason frowned in irritation. "I'm not going to trust one of Farraday's people to handle something this crucial. It's got to be you."

"Why can't you take it yourself?" She was determined not to go to Matt on any errand.

He stopped writing for a moment. "I met Ross Phillips at the track today. Remember him?"

"No." Alexandra couldn't remember anyone or anything at the moment. She could think only of how idiotic she'd been not to go and face Matt at four o'clock. She could have spelled it out that there was nothing further between them, not now, not ever.

Jason's face became animated. "Phillips used to train for Greenlake Farms in Winchester. He feels the same way I do about Farraday. We're meeting at six for dinner and an interesting little chat."

"You're passing up placing your own bid for a social occasion?" She stared at him, confused.

Jason gave a quick smug grin. "Hardly a social occasion. He knows something about Farraday's past, and how he came by all of this." His head moved, a darting movement that suggested the house and the acreage that lay beyond the window.

"Let's face it, if I've got something on Farraday, I've got leverage. The other bids won't matter then. He'll be obliged to let Fortune's Lad go to me . . . at my price."

She struggled with a spasm of disgust. "That's blackmail."

"I'm prepared to bid fairly," Jason said, unperturbed.

"Holding up Matt's past? That's fair bidding?"

"What is this?" He looked faintly amused. "Are you defending him against me?"

"No, of course not, but—"

"But nothing! This is business. How the hell d'you think Farraday got all this? By playing little Lord Fauntleroy?"

"I've no idea."

"Well you soon will. I'm going to find out tonight."

Alexandra clenched her hands. "Jason, is it because of the horse, or is it something else that's driving you to such lengths to dig up the dirt on Matt?"

Jason was busy transferring the figures he had jotted down onto a fresh sheet. He checked the figures once again, signed it, then slipped the sheet into an envelope and sealed it.

"I could tell you it's not your concern, but I have more respect for you than that. It's the horse . . . and more." Jason rose from the desk chair and faced her intently. "Farraday and I had a deal. We made it a few years back. It's my opinion he's not keeping his end of the bargain."

"Which was?"

"That's my concern," he said gently.

"We're going to be life partners, Jason. Doesn't that count for something?"

He glanced at her briefly, then held out the envelope. "You tell me, Alexandra. Doesn't it count for something with you? My parents were life partners. That certainly meant a lot to my mother. She was always at father's side, always loyal. A constant support he could bank on. She took care of her end of the partnership."

She had resolved only that morning to be everything Jason hoped she would be, she remembered. Was she failing already? "What was her end, exactly?" she asked.

Jason's brows were raised in surprise. "She was wife and mother and hostess, of course. She made Windermere a warm, beautiful haven for her husband and children and guests."

Irritation creased his face. "I'm surprised you have to ask."

"Jason, I've never really thought about it in that way before. We need to—I want to discuss it with you."

"Well, your timing is off. We'll have to talk about it some other time."

"When?"

"What?" He glanced at his watch and made for the door.

"I said when, Jason."

"Oh, for heaven's sake, Alex—"

"Yes, when?" she insisted. "I mean, should I make an appointment for some time when you're not clocking horses or at the races . . . or investigating Matt?"

"Alex, what's got into you? This isn't like you, this . . . this—"

"Streak of independence?"

"I'd call it touchiness, myself."

"Touchiness!" Suddenly she wanted to laugh. Anger seemed to pound in her ears and waves of rebellion were roiling up under her ribs. And he saw it as touchiness. Why did everything come out diluted, with Jason. Eyeing him critically across the room, she thought even his coloring seemed watered down compared to Matt's stark vitality.

The angry turmoil gave way suddenly to shame. She was acting this way because of Matt, because she hadn't resolved her ungovernable feelings yet. Finding fault with Jason, making too much of going to Matt's apartment, were ways of camouflaging her own shortcomings. She was disappointed in herself and was taking it out on Jason.

"I—I'm sorry, Jason. I don't know why I'm acting this way."

He gave a quick, easy smile. "You're forgiven." He gave her a light peck on the cheek. "Now I have to run."

"Jason, do you love me?" she asked suddenly as he stood in the open doorway.

Did a light crease of impatience cross his features, or did she imagine it?

"Alex, haven't I told you before?"

"I don't know. I can't remember." She thought hard. Love seemed a passionate, full-bodied idea, somehow remote from Jason's nature. Just the sound of it in her head carried resonances she couldn't associate with him.

"Well, of course I do, silly girl." He squeezed her arm briefly. "I'll check to see how it went when I get back tonight. Wish me luck."

"Good luck, Jason." From the eager light in his eyes, she knew his mind was back on the horse.

Alexandra stepped out of the elevator into a lush paneled entry hall and found herself facing large walnut doors. She swallowed hard and pressed the bell. Matt Farraday's apartment seemed to occupy the entire top floor of a luxury six-story building.

It was a while before the bell was answered, time enough for her to have second and third thoughts about agreeing to run Jason's errand. She caught a fleeting expression of surprise on Matt's face when he finally opened the door. He stood blocking the doorway and stared.

"Jason insisted I come," she said quickly and showed him the envelope she held in her hand. "He wanted me to give you this. The bid you suddenly needed."

There was a movement behind Matt, and she glimpsed Toni Dodd.

"Hello, Alexandra." Toni's voice was offhand. "What a surprise!"

"Jason just asked me to—"

"You don't need to explain," Matt interrupted. "Are you coming in?"

She shook her head and thrust the envelope at him. "I just want to drop this off. Mission accomplished," she said and started toward the elevator.

He shrugged. "Suit yourself. I thought you'd want to know the outcome."

She hadn't even thought about that. "Yes, of course. If you're going to decide right now."

He didn't extend another invitation, but simply

turned back into the apartment, leaving the door wide open for her to follow.

The blueprints she'd seen that morning were lying on a coffee table. Matt swept them up and began to roll them as he spoke to Toni. "You know the specs as well as I do now. I've got a meeting in the morning, so why don't you talk to Colfax for me?"

"Whatever you say, boss man." Toni smiled up at Matt admiringly. The smile faded as she glanced at Alexandra, who began to feel more and more like an unwelcome intruder.

"Well, I guess I'll be running along." Toni sounded reluctant as she tucked the roll of plans under one arm and backed toward the door. "I'll be home, just in case you want to go over any more details before tomorrow."

"Thanks," Matt said. "I'll keep that in mind."

He waited until the front door closed behind Toni, then gave Alexandra a cool look of evaluation. "Jason's getting careless with his property," he said.

"I'm nobody's property." Alexandra tried to match him in detachment. "Jason had a business dinner this evening. He didn't trust this bid to anyone else."

Amusement pulled at Matt's lips. "You, on the other hand, he can trust implicitly in every way."

She held out the bid envelope, refusing to react. Finally, he took it from her, tossed it carelessly onto the low table between the sofas, then shrugged and headed for the bar at the far end of the room.

The furnishings were impeccable, she noticed, his taste running toward the modern and cool. Glass, smooth teak and walnut surfaces, leather chairs with chrome frames, nothing sentimental or fussy. A bold painting on the ivory wall looked very much like a Jackson Pollock to her.

Matt returned with two glasses of sherry, but she hesitated to take the one he held out.

"Go on," he coaxed, "even the Russians and the Americans have been known to share a glass or two together."

She blushed slightly as she took it, knowing he must think her ridiculously prudish in contrast to her performance the night before. She took a sip, wishing he would get on with it so she could get out of his apartment. "What about the other bids? Do you have them already?"

He nodded silently. He seemed to enjoy keeping her in suspense.

"And?"

"I haven't opened them yet." He turned to a desk by the wall, took something from a drawer, then returned, throwing two more sealed envelopes on the table beside Jason's.

"Well?"

He sank down on the arm of the sofa and swirled the sherry around in his wineglass. "In good time. Don't you know that rushing business is not the classy way to do things? I'm sure Jason knows that."

She set her glass down and faced him squarely. She was tired of playing mouse to his cat's paw. "What kind of a deal did you make with Jason?" she asked quietly.

Matt looked slightly off-balance for the first time. He drained his sherry to cover it, but she knew she'd found a vulnerable spot.

Just when she wasn't expecting it, he threw back his head and laughed. "So he told you we had a deal, did he? That is a surprise." But there was no laughter in his eyes as he returned to the bar.

This time he poured straight Scotch.

"Jason said you haven't kept your end of the bargain," she said.

"Oh, I've kept it, all right. Far too well and far too long." He stood over her and swigged down half the Scotch in one angry gulp. "What do you see in him, anyway? No, wait. I can guess." He took another quick swallow of whiskey before he continued.

"It's the Randolph position in society. Yeah. And the money. A lot of money," he said lightly. "And yet even with all that, it surprises me that Jason would be enough for a woman like you. I always thought you had too much fire to settle for that."

"Settle?" Alexandra folded her arms defensively. "No one else in their right mind would say I was settling by marrying Jason Randolph."

"That's only because they don't know you. Not like I know you."

He wasn't baiting her anymore. There was no innuendo in his tone, she realized. He was quite serious. She had felt used this morning . . . but hadn't she equally used him? It was time to make herself unmistakably clear.

"Look, Matt, what happened last night—"

"Yes, what did happen last night? I'm not sure myself anymore. Perhaps you'd be so good as to spell it out for me."

"It was a moment of weakness," she said firmly. "It won't recur."

"No, you're right. It won't," he said, biting off the words.

"I'm relieved you understand that and accept things the way they are."

"I understand, all right. But who said anything about accepting things the way they are? I don't. I can't accept your marrying Jason."

She caught the regret in his voice and it touched her, almost made her believe . . . No. Hadn't she learned her lesson by now? He hated the idea of her commitment to Jason only because he wanted her available, without having to make any commitment of his own. "You have to accept it, Matt," she said slowly. "You have no choice."

Matt left his drink at the bar and came to rest opposite her on the facing sofa. Elbows on knees, he leaned forward in thought. "Why don't we talk about choices, Alex?"

He made it sound like some kind of game, twenty questions or charades. It was just something to kill time or break the ice between strangers, she thought. "What do you mean? What kind of choices?"

"The everyday choices people make that may not seem momentous at the time, and yet gradually take on a pattern, maybe tally up to a complete lifetime in the end."

"Is this a trap?" Suddenly Alexandra felt wary.

He laughed and shook his head. "No. It's not a trap, pretty lady. I'm just"—he shrugged—"just trying to make civilized conversation with you." He frowned suddenly. "No, that's not it either. Let's just say I'm trying to get inside your inscrutable head, since . . ." He paused to tilt his mouth and look at her with a smile half sad and half humorous. "Since the rest of you is off-limits from now on."

"Okay, I'll play. Choices." She looked at him expectantly, still a little wary, unsure why she was agreeing to this.

"You made a choice to come out here with Jason, and I'm sure it wasn't because Jason was so keen on the idea. Why did you come?"

"Because—" She hesitated, hearing the words

forming. . . . *I came because Jason is the man I'm going to marry and I wanted to be with him.* No, this time she had an intense desire for the raw truth, for her own sake even more than Matt's. "Because I wanted to see you," she said quickly, before she changed her mind.

"Thanks for being honest," he said, but there was little pleasure in his face. "How do you find me, now you've seen me?"

She found herself examining the carpet. "Your circumstances have changed, of course. But I think you're basically the same . . . in the ways that count."

"And that choice to come here," he pressed. "That was just the beginning of other choices, wasn't it? A lead-in to other choices?"

It was a mistake to have agreed to this grilling. It was going to get her into trouble. "I don't know what you're talking about."

"Yes you do, Alex."

She stared at a painting on the wall and tried to empty her mind. She didn't want to think. She didn't want to go on with this.

"You came out here because you weren't sure you were doing the right thing in marrying Jason. That's the real reason you chose to come."

"Oh, I'm sure, all right. The date's set. Everything is planned to the last detail."

"Did you make all those plans, by any chance?"

She only hesitated a split second. "My father made the wedding arrangements, if that's what you mean. It gave him a lot of pleasure, so I let him go ahead. I think he'd made them all in his dreams a long time ago."

"Yes, I know exactly when he made them," Matt said quietly, then went to the bar and returned with a glass of ice water. He sighed deeply as he perched on the arm of the sofa. "I don't suppose he ever mentioned that I called once. After I left Kentucky."

Her heart seemed to lurch in her ribs. "Once? Only once?"

"I spoke to your father. He said you'd left for Italy." Matt looked aggrieved at the memory.

He should have told her. Things might have been so different if she'd known that. Or would they? Hadn't Matt made it clear that what they had between them was pure passion? "My father told you the truth," she said defiantly. "There's no need to make it sound sinister."

"Sure, that part was true. But he also told me you were engaged to Jason. I don't believe you were. Not then. Not the way you felt about me."

The way she had felt about him, the small deaths she had suffered day after day when he left, she would never let him know what that had felt like.

"Oh Matt, you are so monstrously sure of yourself, aren't you?"

"I needed to be. I thought it was a mutual feeling. I could never have committed myself to another woman."

Sincerity made his eyes a dark midnight blue and her heartbeat was so wild she struggled to breathe. He was saying all the right things.

"Then why?" she demanded, clutching at the raft that would stop her from drowning in this hopeless feeling. "Why didn't you call me again? Why didn't you write?"

"Because I was not as sure of myself as you seem to think, Alex. Because your genial bluegrass daddy made me feel like an ugly smell in the salon, a distinctly annoying embarrassment that threatened to hinder your grand progress through life."

He rose and started toward her, then restrained himself. "Alex, Alex." He shook his head. "We might as well have come from different planets. You've always had the best life has to offer. It came to you on silver platters, all the way up from childhood." He began to move restlessly about the room, pausing to touch his own expensive treasures as if to confirm their existence.

"I couldn't help my background, Matt."

"That's not what I meant. But you had eyes and ears of your own, girl. A mind of your own."

"I use them."

When he turned back to her, there was a kind of patient despair in his features. "You bend them," he whispered.

This wasn't fair. She'd gone to the schools her father had picked out, but what choice does a child have? She had a circle of friends based on her schools and her environment. "Matt, this is nonsense. My father was a single parent and he simply did his best by me."

"He orchestrated your whole life."

"So? All parents do that."

"But a child should grow up to be her own person."

"I am my own person."

"Not if you marry Jason." Matt's face was an inch from hers. "You aren't choosing Jason, Alex. Your father's choosing him, just as he chose your school and doubtless influenced your socially acceptable career. This is a final choice. It should be yours alone."

"Final choice," she said, trying to deflect him.

"You make marrying Jason sound like going to the electric chair."

Matt's face darkened. "Don't be flip, Alex. You don't love the man."

She stood up and moved away from him. There was something claustrophobic about his nearness and his words. "You can't possibly know what's in my heart."

He caught her arm fiercely and drew her back to face him. "Maybe I'll never know what's in your heart, but if what happened between us last night is a barometer of your feeling for Jason—then I know that much. You don't love him, Alex. Don't tell me last night was just a weakness. You wanted it, you chose it, and you meant it as much as I did."

Yes, she thought. That much was true. They both meant it in their own way. But what it meant to him was: *this is what I want for now, for as long as the feeling lasts.* That's exactly what all his professions had meant five years ago.

"I'm tired of this game, Matt," she said, releasing her arm from his grasp.

Matt suddenly sank to the sofa looking deathly tired himself. "All right. We'll play Fortune's Lad. Is that what you want?"

"Fine. That's what I'm here for," she said grimly, taking her seat across the low table.

"Sure," he said, and gave a brief nod.

They shared a moment of silence before Matt sat on the edge of the sofa and began to open the three envelopes. One by one he read the offerings, then let them drop back on the table. He leaned back and stared at the ceiling.

"Well? Who has the highest bid?"

"Read them yourself."

She bent to the table and read them, then sank down on the sofa. "Jason's the lowest."

There was no triumph in his face as he looked at her. He simply nodded agreement. "Jason blew it."

She tried to think of Jason, of what this would do to him. The horse had completely possessed him, but the other bids were astronomical. Even Jason couldn't have dreamed of figures like those.

"There'll be other horses," Matt said with an indifferent shrug. "Other horses . . . other women." He gave a tired smile.

"There's only one horse for Jason, and you know it."

"Why, Alexandra. I can hardly believe what I'm hearing. You actually seem concerned about him. Could I have been wrong all this time?"

She leaned forward across the coffee table. "Please, Matt. Give him another chance."

"That wouldn't be fair to the other bidders."

"Oh, come on, Matt. Nobody knows how to run a horse like Jason. You've got to have some—some—"

"Pride in my own bloodstock?" He seemed vastly amused. "Some loyalty to my beloved former boss? You must be kidding. But okay, suppose I give him another chance to bid. What's in it for me? What do you think might twist my arm?"

Alexandra kept silent, wondering for a moment what kind of dirt Ross Phillips was dishing up over his dinner with Jason and loathing herself for thinking of it.

"You?" His eyes were contemptuous. "Would you offer yourself to me, just so Jason could have his pony run a race?"

"No. I'd never do that."

"Not even to uphold the Randolph record?"

Something flamed briefly in his eyes, then faded, his face closing over. It was as if for a moment he had touched some elusive truth.

"It never occurred to me before. Could last night have something to do with Jason's wanting that pony? Would you go that far to help him get it?"

She gasped. Was he really capable of thinking that? Or was he just being spiteful because he couldn't get what he wanted. "Of course not."

"I'm sorry," he said quickly, and had the grace to look ashamed.

"Just tell me what it takes for Jason to have another chance on bidding. In plain language, what do you want in return?"

"Plainly?" He gave a quick grin. "In one word— you."

But the grin faded quickly, and she could see that under the humor he was in earnest. "My God, you really mean that."

"Of course I mean it. How many times do I have to tell you I want you? Why should I pass up the one chance to have you?"

Why should it shock her? she wondered. Hadn't she told herself over and over that she was no more than a sexual choice to Matt? Why should he be so fussy about the circumstances? And then, of course, it would be a case of glorious one-upmanship for Matt.

"Yes. You'd like that, wouldn't you?" she blurted out. "To rub Jason's nose in the fact that you've beaten him for once?"

Matt didn't answer. Instead he rose and went to the desk across the room that stood against a heavily paneled wall. "There's something you should see," he said, reaching across the desk and sliding aside one of the panels. Behind it was a wall map of the

United States. Small thumbtack flags in red and green studded seven states.

She followed him to the map and stood at his shoulder as he explained.

"Each flag marks the location of a business holding of mine. Some are wholly owned, some are only interest holdings, but they're all mine.

He slid the panel back. "So you see, I don't feel the urge to best Jason Randolph. There's no need. He's past history as far as I'm concerned."

"Thanks for the lesson, professor." Alexandra collected her purse and headed for the front door. "I'll tell Jason, and we'll leave in the morning."

"Alexandra!"

She didn't turn.

"Alexandra, I don't expect you to come to me because of Jason; I want you to come because it's what you want. You know you do. For once, before it's too late, do something you honestly want, not what your father wants or what Jason wants."

His voice followed her to the open door.

"You play at being a woman. Why not be one, Alexandra?"

She left, slamming the heavy door.

Chapter Five

The rancho was quiet when she got back, for which she was thankful. Mr. Farraday would not be in for dinner, Aoki explained, and since Mr. Randolph and Mr. Maddox were also gone for the evening, Mrs. Gonzales had suggested she might like a tray in her own sitting room.

She picked guiltily at a perfectly pan-fried trout and fresh asparagus, then set the tray outside her door on the caddy, barely touched. Her appetite had vanished.

Downstairs, she prowled through a surprisingly well-stocked library, hoping to find distraction in a book. Nothing looked interesting. Instead she poured herself some brandy from the side bar and went back to her bedroom, the scene that lay ahead of her weighing heavily on her mind.

Jason had lost Fortune's Lad, and she was going to have to break it to him. He was so demonic about that horse that she dreaded it, but she couldn't stop dwelling on it. It was better than dwelling on Matt's accusations. An uneasiness seemed to tease her nerve endings every time she let herself hear Matt's voice again.

You play at being a woman.

She changed into a light wool robe and paced the room, phrasing and rephrasing sentences that would soften the news about Fortune's Lad. Nothing seemed to lessen the impact of the message. Jason had lost his wonder horse. Nothing she could think of would make that palatable. She began to resent being the messenger of such news, fuming at having to guard it hour after hour until he came.

It was past eleven when he rapped at her door. Jason's face was flushed, and he kissed her lightly as she let him in. He threw his jacket on the bed and spoke in a rush.

"Phillips came through. He gave me the lead I wanted." He paused and looked at her as if he expected a cheer.

She managed a watery smile. "Jason . . . the bid . . ."

"Damn, I almost forgot about that. Can you believe it?" he said chuckling. "I almost forgot."

He was in a high, crackling mood, almost exalted. She hoped it would help him through the bad news.

"Jason," she said softly, "of the three bids, I'm afraid yours was the lowest."

He looked distant, but the smile was still on his face.

"I'm truly sorry, Jason." It was almost as if he hadn't heard.

"Yes, it's too bad about that. . . ." His voice trailed off.

She had the feeling he was rejecting it, refusing to

let the finality of it sink in. When she gave him a consoling hug and laid her face on his chest, she sensed his total preoccupation. There was no response from him.

"That's too bad about the bid," he repeated, extricating himself from her embrace and stroking his chin, as he did so often when something was brewing. He looked up with a quick, bright grin, as if he had just remembered she was in the room. "But it's immaterial now. It doesn't amount to a hill of beans. Not after what I've learned tonight."

"Jason! Matt's selling the horse to the highest bidder. That's something you can't change. No gossip from Phillips can alter that fact."

His eyes gleamed as he finally focused his gaze on her. "I can nail Farraday with the stuff I have. Ruin him, Alexandra. That'll stop him selling the horse to anyone else."

She could almost see his mind working quickly, accurately, a laserlike instrument of destruction. She saw the unmistakable jubilation in him. A sudden sense of danger made her recoil, as if she were herself threatened with destruction by the act of participation. There was something ugly in him that made her shudder. She wanted no part of it. She didn't give a damn about the horse. It was *their* horse, *their* stupid grudge against each other. Why had she ever allowed herself to get involved? she wondered in disgust.

"It's going to take several days for the sales contract to close on the Lad," Jason was saying. "That's all the time I need."

"Time to do what?" She sank down heavily on the nearest chair, completely drained.

"I'm flying to Chicago tomorrow. The plane

leaves at six A.M. I'll pack now and spend the night in L.A. near the airport."

"Chicago!" Jason would hardly leave her here, but she noticed he had said nothing about her traveling with him.

"I'm going to see a man who's handled several banking transactions connected with Farraday's holdings. Phillips knows him—the same man put together a merger for the owner of Greenlake Farms."

She stared at him in silence, trying to quell the queasiness in her stomach.

"We're talking big money deals," he went on. "The word is"—he paused dramatically—"Farraday's on the board of Kenicrest Mills."

It was a familiar name to her. Anyone would know Kenicrest. Jason was waiting for some kind of reaction.

"That's not against the law, is it?" was all she could think of.

Jason expelled an impatient breath. "No, but he's not registered as a board member. It's obviously a blind, and I'm going to find out why he doesn't want his connection made public. But everyone knows there's a certain unsavory element that's got its claws deep into the steel industry."

Unaccountably, Alexandra felt a moment of relief. Perhaps because it all sounded so preposterous. "If you're talking about organized crime, Jason, then you'd have to include almost any big industry. You're talking rumors, unfounded rubbish, just like the sensational headlines in the tabloid press. You have no basis whatsoever for concluding that Matt's involved in anything illegal."

"For God's sake, must you always be so naive?"

Jason clenched his hands in frustration. "How the hell do you think a man gets all of this so fast?"

He loosened his tie with an irritable tug, then thrust his hands into his pants pockets and stood over her. "You've been so sheltered, you think the world's all roses and rainbows. Well, it isn't. I'm going to do my best to shelter you from some of life's harsher realities when we're married, but you aren't going to be living in a bubble!"

"You have no right to say that." She was shouting. It was the second time that evening she'd had that same accusation hurled her way, and it was doubly painful this time. "I've been working, supporting myself, these past years. I know very well what the world's about."

Jason gave a humorless grin. "I'll just bet you do."

"What does that mean?"

He shrugged. "Whatever you want it to."

They eyed each other like wary antagonists before he spoke again.

"I'm sorry, Alexandra." His tone was more patronizing than apologetic. "We should have spoken before about this. I've always let it go by because—well, I hoped the whole topic could be avoided." He lifted his hands as if to say it was regrettably beyond his control now.

"The fact of the matter is, you've been sheltered and coddled your entire life. Not that it's your fault, of course. If I'd been your father, I'd have done the same. And if we have a daughter, I'd hope to raise her that way," he added quickly, then paused, his mouth tightening.

"But for you to persist in claiming you've been supporting yourself, as if you'd clawed your way up some ladder of success, is utterly ridiculous. And annoying."

"I have been working," she said icily. "I've paid my own bills and bought my own clothes—"

"You went to the most expensive schools, had the finest training available. You had what amounts to automatic entry into any firm you chose. Who wouldn't take you?"

"I have talent."

"You have privilege!"

She turned her eyes away from his scornful look and felt the sting of tears. "You're just too insecure to have a wife who's independent."

"You're wrong," he said quite calmly. "I just don't want a wife who's unrealistic."

"All right! You just tell me what your idea of reality is." She rose from the chair, hugging her arms tightly about her in self-defense.

Jason gripped her shoulders intently. "Reality, Alexandra, is what my trip out here is all about. I want that horse—no, I've *got to have* that horse." He spoke with slow deliberation, as if he were teaching her to read from a child's primer. "I thought I made this clear just hours ago. Weren't you listening? Don't you understand?"

"Apparently not." The distancing coolness that washed through her reflected in her voice. "Spell it out for me."

A small sound of disgust came from the back of his throat, and as he spoke she noticed his hands nervously clenching and stretching. "Running Windermere takes money. Since my father's time, the costs have skyrocketed. Your father was like mine—a man caught halfway between the gracious past and the tough reality of the present. They had the luxury of dipping into the very last of the old money. I have none. There's nothing left except the hustle. So if you want our children to grow up the

103

way we did, then I'm going to have to fight to survive. And that means fighting tooth and nail for the sure money-makers like Fortune's Lad."

"Thank you. That was quite a speech."

Moving away from his grasp, she went to the windows to look out at the night, but found herself simply staring at her own reflection. She was startled at the bitterness she saw.

Jason had always refused to discuss anything too serious with her, shying away from financial matters as if money were too vulgar for mixed company. By turns she had been amused and irritated. Now she understood it thoroughly. He thought she was a twit, a spoiled brat who wouldn't understand. Her father had kept the truth of his finances from her too, still refusing to discuss it even now. Her father . . . Matt . . . now Jason. Dear God, they couldn't all be wrong!

"Jason, I appreciate your leveling with me," she said quietly, and turned back to him. "I still say I've been supporting myself, and I do believe in my talent. You're right, I did have every advantage in getting into a top fashion house. But you can't hold my father's good intentions against me. No"—she put up a hand to ward off Jason's protest—"you don't, I know that. The thing is, I do understand now why you need the horse. I thought it was just some sort of compulsive ego trip. Now I see it's not that. But I can't believe anything's worth stooping to blackmail. If that's the price of the horse, it's just too expensive."

Jason took a step toward her. "Let me decide that."

"No! As your wife, I'd be living off the proceeds too, remember."

He tilted his head and pierced her with his shrewd gray eyes. "Is that what's really bothering you?"

"Of course. What else?"

"You're afraid of knowing the truth about Farraday."

"I'm not involved. Why should I care what—"

"Because you've always seen him as some sort of heroic figure and you don't want that destroyed. You're going to have to decide, Alexandra. Either you're going to be my wife and be with me, or—" He stopped, not needing to finish, then added, "You can't go on straddling the line forever."

He had every right to say that to her. Guilt and remorse washed through her. "Jason, you know I'm for you." She should go to him now, show him she meant it by putting her arms around him. A warm, honest physical gesture would cement their unity. But somehow she couldn't touch him, couldn't even raise her arm.

"Then help me now," he whispered urgently. "Stay here and divert Farraday while I go to Chicago."

Quickly, she looked into his eyes for a sign that he didn't mean it; she found he was deadly earnest. "No! I want to go with you, Jason."

"Please, Alexandra, try to understand." His fingers tightened on her upper arms. "I need you here. I'm not a fool. I know Farraday is still interested in you. But I do trust you implicitly, you know, and it will amuse him to have you here. . . . And it serves my purpose to have him amused while I'm gone. It won't be more than a couple of days."

She sagged a little, and Jason smiled at her, taking her limpness for acquiescence. "Just tell Farraday where I've gone and why, and that if he does anything about those bids before I get back, I'll be leaking his connection with Kenicrest Mills to the *Wall Street Journal.*"

"Jason, I'd feel like an accessory. I don't want any part of this."

"You're doing nothing wrong, Alexandra," he said wearily. "You're just telling Farraday the truth for his own good. That's all I'm asking you to do. Is that too much?"

"When will you be back?" she asked faintly.

"Soon as I can." He glanced at his watch and sighed. "There isn't much time."

After he left, she shivered. What had happened to Jason, the charming, soft-spoken gentleman of candlelit dinners and hazy afternoon walks by Windermere Lake? He could be harsh, determined, even ruthless. She didn't know him any longer.

And Matt. After all these years, did she really know the first thing about him? Did she know anything? Was it possible that she really was the pampered, sheltered ninny they claimed she was? What was happening suddenly? She had come to California in search of solutions, for the sake of future peace of mind, and suddenly destructive fingers were raking at all the givens that lay in the center of her world, threatening all the assumptions upon which her life was built, unraveling her very identity.

Late into the night she searched for answers to questions she never dreamed existed until a few hours ago.

The grass was still covered with a netting of morning dew when she went out in search of Matt. She didn't relish the meeting, but she had a message to give him. She had failed Jason so many times, in so many ways; she wouldn't fail him again.

In the stables, she found Scott in faded jeans and a work shirt. The strange-looking bandana around his forehead was dark with perspiration.

"Working hard already?" she asked as he hoisted a saddle from the back of a dappled mare.

"You bet." He took the saddle to a bench to inspect its underside. "I'm gonna break this baby if it's the last thing I do." He walked back to the mare and gave her a light slap on the rump and a push toward a young groom who was mucking out the far stall.

"Take her out, Miguel."

The slender boy dropped his rake and nudged the gleaming mare through the open stable doors and across the courtyard where a chain link fence encircled the paddock. As soon as the boy swung open the gate, the mare lifted her head and cantered out to the grass.

"Stubborn gal," Scott said, shaking his head at the mare's flying tail. "But she's gonna be worth it."

For a moment, Alexandra had the odd thought that it was Jason saying that, not referring to a horse, but to her. She felt an inward spasm of rebellion.

"Do you know where Matt is?" she asked.

"With the architect," Scott said, bending to examine a saddle strap. "They're over by the new site for the stables."

"Thanks." Alexandra turned to leave, then changed her mind. "Scott, what do you know about the two other bids on Fortune's Lad?"

"Matt took bids?" He looked up in quick surprise. "That's news to me. He wasn't going to open the bidding for at least another week. We have plans for the showing first, and— He took bids?"

"Murchison and Felix—no, *Feliz*, I think," she said.

Scott was laughing.

Alexandra looked at him curiously. "What's the joke? Jason didn't think it was so funny."

"Those two jokers!" Scott was still laughing as he shook his head. "Slickos, the both of them. They pull this stunt all the time."

"What stunt?" she demanded.

"Manipulation. They submit these preemptive bids, way out of line. The owners are so delighted, they jump at the offers, then something always snags to keep the deal from closing. They've got it down to a fine art. They keep the seller dangling for so long, the other bidders drop out. Then they come in for the kill. The seller's worn down to a frazzle by that time, sick and tired and just longing to see the rear end of the horse. Often he'll settle for half what he could have gotten on a legitimate bid."

"But why would Matt bother with them, if he knows they're con artists?"

Scott motioned to a stable hand to hang up the saddle and walked her into the courtyard. "He just wants to get them out of the way so when the bidding starts in earnest, they can't bitch that they weren't given a fair shake. That's another of their little scams. You'd be surprised how much damage that kind of thing can do to a breeder in this business. Matt'll just run a credit check on them, and that'll be that."

Outside the sun was warm on her face and painfully bright. She reached into her purse for her sunglasses. "But any owner could do the same thing, Scott. How come they ever get away with it?"

"These dudes are pros, and the pros always cover their tracks. It's pretty hard to get the real scoop on their credit. But Matt's got his ways." Scott bounced his eyebrows up and down implying deep mysteries and gave her a Groucho Marx grin.

She didn't feel like laughing. Matt's life was too mysterious, too guarded not to be hiding something. "What do you mean, Matt's got his ways?" she asked rather sharply.

Scott paused, and she thought he was avoiding a straight answer, but he was just choosing his words. "Matt's a shrewd businessman. He keeps extensive records, cultivates useful friends. He believes in networking."

Alexandra turned to face him. "I'm not sure I know what you mean by that."

Scott took her elbow. "Tell you what," he said. "Why don't you ask him? Here he comes."

She looked up to see Matt and Toni side by side, crossing the paddock and approaching the court-yard. Matt was dressed in work clothes, the sleeves of his shirt rolled up to the elbows. Toni, as always, looked impossibly glamorous in cream twill jodh-purs. The two were deep in conversation, unaware of her until they entered the stable area.

Alexandra watched his expression change several times: from surprise, to obvious admiration of the way she looked in a strapless sundress, to a kind of contemptuous amusement.

"Hi. We're going up to Santa Anita. The Lad's running in the fifth race. I would have thought Jason would want to see it, but I hear he's left."

"Yes. He was called away on some business," Alexandra said. "He'll be back." Matt looked amused at that, and she wondered if it was because he thought Jason was so disappointed he couldn't face anyone.

Toni didn't seem disposed to leave Matt's side.

The rest of her message would have to wait, she thought impatiently, until she could talk to him in private.

"That's a real shame," Matt said in a guileless voice. "Jason would've enjoyed the meet."

Alexandra felt a sudden irritation at Matt's detached amusement and at Toni's hovering presence. Why was she always nursing heavy messages, waiting on the convenience of others?

"Matt, I need to talk to you privately, if I may," she said brusquely. "There's something I need to—"

"I have to take these back to my study," Matt cut in, brandishing the rolled-up plans and turning away quickly, as if he suddenly remembered he was pressed for time.

"Afterward, then?" She moved forward insistently, although he was making it clear he wanted to avoid being alone with her.

"I'm going to Santa Anita." He glanced at his watch.

"Then if you wouldn't mind, could I talk to you for a moment in your study?" She made her tone crisp and impersonal. "It will only take a moment. I won't delay you."

She became aware of Toni and Scott, as openly absorbed in the exchange as spectators at a heated tennis match.

Matt faltered, then said with a great show of reluctance, "Okay, but make it quick. I'm going to be late."

He forged ahead with monstrous strides toward the house, while Scott bent his head in conversation with Toni and led her back into the stable.

Alexandra followed Matt at a distance, making no attempt to catch up with his deliberate breakneck speed. She would give him Jason's message all right, but she had no intention of getting into another slinging match with him.

The hall was cool and dim, and their footsteps on the terrazzo floor made a brisk, dispassionate sound. Alexandra quickened her pace involuntarily as the distance lengthened between them. She was beginning to feel awkwardly like a small dog at his heels.

Matt's study was not the office she and Jason had seen when they arrived at the ranch. It was a secluded, smaller room in another wing of the house.

"Why the duplication of facilities?" she asked him, looking around the room.

Matt went to a wall of built-in cabinets and unlocked a door to reveal an orderly system of shelves and special storage compartments. He ignored her question while he went to a teletype machine in the corner. He tore off a printed message, glanced at it, then folded it and slipped the paper into the hip pocket of his jeans.

"I have a couple of secretaries who work adjacent to my office. This is a private place for my eyes only." Matt raised his brows in cool inquiry, as if she were a solicitor and he had just been called to the front door to answer her nuisance call. "What can I do for you?"

The chill in his voice destroyed her composure and she began to stammer. "He—Jason—he's—he wanted me to tell—Jason's—"

"Look, I don't have the time or the inclination to hash over Jason with you. I don't want to hear it. If you've got business on your mind and it's urgent, just get on with it. I have to change and get to the track." Matt turned his back on her and struggled to get the set of plans into a drawer already overfull.

He was right, she should just spit it out. She was

so flustered she could barely speak. She would make a fool of herself if she didn't calm down. As she watched him, suddenly absorbed in shuffling plans, opening several drawers, removing contents and rapidly rearranging them, she prepared the words carefully in her mind so that she could deliver her message succinctly and be done with it. She wouldn't let him intimidate her again. She took a deep breath.

"Matt," she began as the door flew open and Toni burst into the room, breathless and radiant.

"Sunstreak's started labor!"

Matt darted for the phone.

"Scott's already called the vet," Toni said.

"Okay. Then let's go." Matt started toward the door, then stopped and pounded his forehead. "Santa Anita! Damn, I forgot. Toni—do you mind? I can't put off the—"

"Hey, no sweat, Matt," Toni cut in. "Scott's with her now and the vet's on his way. We're covered."

Matt put his arm around Toni's shoulders and gave her a squeeze. "I know how much this means to you."

"And to Scott," she said. "Don't forget, it's his mare too."

Matt grinned. "Got a name picked out?"

Toni nodded. "It's a surprise for later." Then she turned to Alexandra with a friendly grin. "Sunstreak's my mare. She's been stabled here at the rancho. This is my first foal. Damn if I don't feel like it's a baby or something." She dipped her head sheepishly. "I guess it's pretty ho-hum stuff for you, Alexandra, but I can hardly keep my feet on the ground. And you should see Scott—the expectant father!"

Alexandra found herself warming to Toni for the first time. "I've seen my share of foaling," she said.

"On a horse farm it happens a lot, but it's always special."

Toni beamed at her softly. "Where I was raised, we gave birth to discount coupons and special promotions." She raised her hand by way of farewell and darted out of the room.

"Hey, make sure you bed her down in the new double stall," Matt called after her, but she was already out of earshot. He followed her, calling back to Alexandra over his shoulder. "Be back in a moment."

Matt was gone for a long time, long enough for Alexandra to get restless and start pacing the study. She began to examine the bookshelves. They were crammed with marketing and finance volumes and books on horse breeding. She was puzzled when she noticed a second wall of books that seemed out of place. It was devoted to standard classics in literature, biography, history, music, art appreciation. She scanned the titles, her eyes roving curiously from floor to ceiling. Henry James and Balzac kept company with a life of Clarence Darrow and art books on the Louvre and the Prado. *A History of Ancient Greece. The Development of the Symphonic Form.* Opera librettos. Durant's *The Story of Civilization, The Complete Works of George Bernard Shaw,* Tennyson, Byron, Robert Frost. *Mozart—His Work and His Genius.*

Had Matt bought up a library to add tone to the decor? No, this was his private sanctuary; he'd said no one came into this study but him. She stepped back and narrowed her eyes at the copious collection. Taken in sum, it was a comprehensive course in the liberal arts. The kind of cultural education that was the domain of the wealthy. He had been painstakingly trying to improve himself, self-administering the schooling she took for granted. Could that be it? How much could he possibly have covered? Did he plan to read it all?

She was touched by the thought as she moved on to another wall of shelves. Leather albums were all neatly labeled. GUNNY'S ENGINE, POWER HOUSE, BLACK WIND, LUCKY LADY. She drew out one, then another, riffling through pages of photographs, documentation of pedigrees, meets, victories and defeats. Each one held the life history of a racehorse.

At the end of the shelf was a much older album, its leather binding a faded red and worn with handling. It bore no label and she pulled it out to examine it. It was a scrapbook too, but filled with newspaper clippings from Kentucky—the *Clarion*, her hometown's local daily, and the weekly *Times* of Fayette County. She noticed a date: almost five years back, soon after Matt left.

Fascinated, she looked at the grainy black-and-white photographs—a lazy summer pasture, a Christmas card shot of the Cumberland Gap in a thick blanket of snow, long double columns cut from the social page and carefully folded and pasted. She opened them out and scanned them quickly. Here and there were news items mentioning Laurelwood, her father, herself.

She turned the pages slowly, realizing he must have been homesick, must have at least missed her. Had he actually subscribed to these small-fry papers after he left?

On a page near the middle was a two-column clipping. The headline read, "Off to Italy," and the article bore a small photo of her, smiling a little stiffly into the camera. She remembered her embarrassment just before she left for Livorno that her father should have informed the *Clarion*, given them the snapshot, then sprung the article on her . . . all that hokey stuff about the talented daughter, the illustrious O'Neills. To think Matt had read it! How would she have felt, she wondered, if she'd known that at the time? And how had Matt felt reading it? She turned the page, then another. The rest of the book was blank.

Matt glanced at his watch as he hurried back into the room. As he looked up he noticed the scrapbook in her hands and, under the deep tan, the color beneath his skin seemed to fade.

"Matt, why did you leave me?" she heard a small voice plead. "Why did you run out on me like that, just when your father needed you? When I needed you?"

His body tensed and a dark flush rose slowly, deepening the taut face until it reached the hairline at his forehead. His eyes stayed on the album and his knuckles showed white on tight fists. He was ashamed of weakness, she thought, ashamed of sentimentality. Her discovery was a humiliation to him.

Without a word, he took the book from her hands and closed it. Beside the desk stood a wastebasket. He looked down at it, his teeth clenched beneath his jaw, as if he might toss the scrapbook into it. Then he walked back to the album shelf and replaced it.

His back was to her, and under his shirt she could see the tension in his shoulder muscles. "I think it would be a good idea if you'd pack now, Alexandra. Would you please pack Randolph's things, too? Call him. There's no point in his coming back here, really."

Infinite regret clutched at her with a sharpness that caught at her throat. "Matt, I'm so sorry. I didn't mean to pry. Truly I—"

"It's all right," he said sharply. "It's just that it's pointless to wallow in what's past. That's reserved for the senile, isn't it? It makes much more sense if you just leave Vista del Lago as soon as possible. We'll both be better off."

He left the room before she could think of anything to say, anything that could push past the painful constriction in her throat.

Alexandra stared down at the armful of Jason's soiled laundry she had just collected from the cabana. The shrilling of the princess telephone by her bed summoned her out of a slight daze. Dropping the clothes on the carpet she reached for the receiver, feeling like Pavlov's dog. It was Aoki.

"Your flight is all arranged, Miss O'Neill. Four o'clock. If you would please press the housekeeping button when you have packed, I will come and collect your suitcases and drive you to the airport."

Tell Matt where I've gone and why. Keep him distracted Alexandra.

Pack your things. Leave as soon as possible.

Call Jason and tell him not to come back.

Press the housekeeping button when you have packed.

The male exhortations chased each other through her head until they were jumbled and meaningless. How blindingly simple it was. The men in her life pulled her strings and she jumped.

A swift surge of rebellion rose up through her nervous system. In a few minutes she was speaking to Aoki again. "I'm ready now. Don't worry about the suitcases; I'll meet you downstairs." She hung up before he could protest and hurried from her room.

Aoki waited for her by the limousine in the

driveway. "Your bags, miss?" he said, looking confused as she hurried down the steps without them.

"I won't be needing them," she said, and stepped into the passenger seat. As they drove off, Alexandra leaned forward and opened the glass partition. "By the way, we're not going to the airport," she said firmly. "We're going to the races. Santa Anita."

"But this is not what Mr. Farraday told me this morning. I am sure," Aoki said, pulling out a memo he'd written to himself.

"There has been a change in my plans." Her tone defied argument.

When they pulled up at the track, Alexandra dismissed Aoki firmly and paid for general admittance. It was two o'clock, she noticed. The meet had started an hour and a half before.

The Turf Club was a luxurious private restaurant and lounge open only to members who paid a steep annual fee to view the races with the elite, the horse owners, famous trainers and, here at Santa Anita, the sprinkling of movie stars. Even Alexandra couldn't talk her way into this club. But when she asked for Mr. Farraday, she was told he'd left for the backstretch ten minutes ago.

The backstretch was a familiar world to her. As a young girl, she had accompanied her father behind the scenes many times. This unique world of grooms and trainers had always been exciting to her—and jarring. The accommodations for lowly staff were dingy, the wages unbelievably low for the hours and work put in. But it was understandable. Anyone who lasted in the backstretch had horse blood in their veins. When "their" animal won, all the drudgery made sense, and for a brief moment they felt a part of the glittery life their employers led on the "front side."

Security at Santa Anita was as tight as at the Derby, she discovered. But her father's name still meant something in the racing community. After a brief hassle and a request for identification, they let her through the barrier.

The backstretch was just a huge stable housing a series of barns, and this one wasn't so different from the backstretches she was familiar with in the East. There were accommodations for hundreds of horses and perhaps twenty-five hundred people who worked the area.

There seemed at least that many employees scurrying around as she hurried past stacks of hay and clotheslines of laundry along "shedrow," dodging the cats and dogs underfoot.

Passing the tack rooms, she saw racing equipment hanging beside the personal effects of grooms who made their homes in rude cubicles. Many of the workers were Mexican, and she noticed a few women leading sweating horses back to their stalls.

Alexandra hadn't been part of the scene for years now, but she'd forgotten nothing, she realized in a sudden rush of nostalgia. After a race, the horse would be cooled out, which could take up to an hour. First there were a few gulps of water for the animal, then a careful bathing with alcohol and liniment wash to draw out the muscle tension. Then the horse would tread on the mechanical walker until its body temperature returned to normal.

And of course, there was the pecking order. Owners, like Matt and Jason, were at the top. Next came trainers, beneath them the grooms, and then the lowly stable hands and trainees. Owners never discussed a horse with the groom, although in many cases the groom knew his animal better than anyone. Etiquette ordained that the owner consult only with the trainer. But a few feet ahead, she saw a clear breach of etiquette.

Down on one knee, Matt Farraday was stroking the bandaged leg of a filly and speaking intently to a dark-skinned groom. When they parted, they were both smiling, but Matt's smile faded when he caught sight of her.

"You're supposed to be on your way to the airport," he said.

"I wanted to talk to you before I left." She tried to sound firm but was horrified at the shake in her voice.

"We're both talked out," Matt said flatly, and his face creased with weariness.

"Please, Matt." She caught hold of his sleeve. "Don't freeze me out again. For once, can't we just meet on neutral ground?"

He shook his head as if she were a hopeless case. "You're just like Randolph, aren't you? You just hate to lose. You'll be a wonderful wife for him."

She gulped down the huge lump that suddenly lodged in her throat. "I can't lose something I never really had."

Matt glanced at his watch. "That's right. Look Alex, this is bad for both of us. I've got a race coming up so I can't take you to L.A. International. You can call a cab from the clubhouse. You can still make that flight."

"I don't want to make that flight," she whispered.

Matt gritted his teeth and lowered his voice as a group of stable hands jostled by him. "I meant what I said. I want you gone. You and Randolph. I can't handle— It's for the good of everyone concerned."

"Matt, I'm tired of doing what everyone else wants. There's something I want. . . . I wanted to come here and set things straight."

There was the faintest softening of his mouth and eyes, but it was gone in a moment.

"Jason went to Chicago," she said, lowering her voice as a jockey in silks and a knot of shirt-sleeved men came within earshot. "He wanted me to tell you something and I said I would."

Matt shrugged. "I'm not interested in anything Randolph has to say. Good-bye, Alexandra."

"You've got to know, Matt."

He started to walk away and she threw one word after him.

"Kenicrest!"

Matt froze, then turned back. "What did you say?"

"Jason knows about Kenicrest . . . and he's going to use it against you if you sell Fortune's Lad to any other bidder before he gets back."

A curtain of ice came down over his expression, and his words became clipped and businesslike. "Good for Jason. Thanks for the message, Ali."

He was striding away so rapidly, she had to run to catch up with him. "Look," she said, "I don't know what you have to do with Kenicrest and I don't care. The message is from Jason."

"Fine."

"It was an obligation. The last one."

Matt stared straight ahead. "What does that mean?"

"You said some things yesterday that made sense. I'd never seen myself that way, but you were right. I was privileged and pampered and . . . it was very hard to see what was happening to me and what I'd become." She stopped, not sure she was making sense or what exactly she was trying to say. She was groping. "I've been dancing to everyone else's tune.

I have to strike out and find my own tune, I guess," she finished lamely.

"Is that it?" Matt seemed to be waiting for more. She nodded.

"Then I'm very glad for you. I hope you'll be happy. But why tell me?"

"I just wanted you to know," she said miserably.

Matt gave a brief dry sound, approximating a laugh. "Why?"

"Because . . ." It was no longer clear. It had seemed so crucial this morning that she confront him, that Matt should know she'd learned something about herself. But her resolution was blurring now. She searched for words, but her motives were suddenly indefinable.

"You want independence? Take it, Alex. It's all yours," he said, sweeping his arm in an arc. "You want to break with Jason? Fine. What's stopping you? I doubt you'll go that far, but either way—it's got nothing to do with me." He glanced at his watch again. "You can still catch that plane."

"Not very well," she said, feeling absurd. "I haven't packed yet. I left everything at your place."

Matt's look changed from disbelief to exasperation. Then he lifted her chin and forced her to look at the indignant accusation in his eyes. They were burdened with pain. "Pretty damn sure of yourself, aren't you?"

She reddened painfully. She hadn't thought it out very clearly, but she had envisioned a more sympathetic response from him. Not that he'd fall all over her, but she had expected to neutralize all that harsh defensiveness in him, to hear him say "let bygones be bygones." She'd botched it completely.

When she saw him grin suddenly over her shoulder, she turned. A groom was leading out a feisty young roan.

"Fortune's Lad?" she asked.

Matt nodded. "I'll drive you back after the race," he said, not taking his eyes from the horse, "and this time, please pack before the morning. Aoki will take you to the airport tomorrow."

She watched him turn to the groom and refocus all his attention. He had put her out of his life for good. The sight of his turned back became blurry as her eyes filled with tears.

The remainder of the meet and the drive back to the ranch with Matt was an ordeal for Alexandra. Matt aimed the white Ferrari down the freeway like a bullet. It certainly wasn't Fortune's Lad that had brought on his dark mood. The horse had won handily. After the win, while Matt collected back-slapping congratulations and dollars, she sat alone at a table in the Turf Club for almost an hour until he came and muttered, "Let's go."

Matt's frozen profile above the leather steering wheel clearly stated that he was inaccessible. Even the car's engine discouraged conversation, screaming down the highway in fifth gear. And for added insurance against the risk of her attempting to reach him, Matt slipped a cassette into the tape deck and turned the volume up full blast.

Oh, that noise! Did he have eardrums of steel? But he seemed oblivious to the shattering sound, not even blinking at the deafening clash of cymbals. Gustav Holst—it had to be—such virile music, the orchestrations by turns fulminating, then somber, then wildly adventurous. Under different circumstances she might have thrilled to it. She never knew he had a taste for symphonic music. She had assumed he hadn't, simply because he had dropped out of school at fifteen, then she remembered the wall of books in his study. So he really had made that enormous effort to . . . Oh, what did it matter, anyway? *What did she really know anymore about this local-boy-made-good?*

She closed her eyes and reminded herself that she was seated beside the man who had once held her gently in his arms, professing an undying love for her. . . . A man of integrity. Five years before, he had prided himself on that. He must have said it more than once, because the words had always stuck. *When a man's got nothing, Ali, all he can cling to is his integrity—his personal honor. I can promise you that.* It was why she resisted Jason's slurs on his character. Matt's personal honor was a fiction she'd clung to longer than Matt had.

An interminable fortissimo poured through the speakers, and Alexandra's nerves began to scream in protest at the relentless blare of brass and drums. She reached for the eject button and pressed it. Blessed relief. Matt didn't react to the sudden drop in noise level; he was deep inside a thick shell of indifference. No act of hers could register with him.

The void that followed was hardly better than the din, except that at least now she could think coherently, and after a while she began to talk aimlessly, as if for no other reason than to establish that she was in the car, a passenger, a human being with the faculty of speech.

"Your Del Mar apartment is very different from the rancho. You have some very contemporary paintings," she said, remembering the harsh portrait of a woman's face in a famous pop art style. "Where did you acquire the taste for Warhol?"

Matt scowled through the windscreen. "Maybe I

didn't. Maybe I had a decorator come in and tell me what should hang where."

She doubted that. Matt didn't take kindly to being told what to do. It was hard to imagine anyone imposing their taste on him in his own home.

"Do you like it?" he asked.

"If you want the truth, I find it rather chilly."

"Chilly." He contracted his brows slightly above the polarized sunglasses. "You'd prefer hazy pastoral scenes, I suppose. Or maybe a fat Henry Sargent depicting the good life for posterity. As I recall, you'll find one in your new home when you move in to Windermere."

He was right, Alexandra realized. There was a Sargent in Jason's library. "You took in a lot more than I thought," she said, showing her surprise.

"Yes'm," he drawled. "Ah surely did. Some of us hired hands, we got eyes big as the moon. We see a powerful lot, even from the back door."

"Come on, Matt. It wasn't like that," she retorted, irritated. "The Randolphs never abused their people. They treated them as equals. Those horror stories died out years ago."

"Did they really, now? Too bad my father didn't know that. I don't recall him getting invited up to the big house. I don't recall your fiancé asking me in for a brandy. The only times I walked through the Randolphs' hallowed halls were times when Jason found it inconvenient to come out back. And there I'd stand, hat in hand so to speak, one of your precious Sargents staring down at me, while Randolph fished around for his list of chores for me to do." He spoke lightly, humorously.

"You had a job. Jason was your employer. What did you expect?"

"I'd expect what *my* employees expect. Human consideration. I'd expect to be offered what it's taken organized labor in this country fifty years to fight for—just minimal guarantees that there'll be something to fall back on when they're no longer young enough and strong enough to sweat out one more buck for the big cheese. Just a little insurance when the back breaks in return for a lifetime of backbreaking work."

"That's nice union rhetoric."

"That's the truth."

It was pretty sanctimonious, she thought, for a man who'd run out on his dying father. A man who'd become one of the despised landed gentry himself. "So how did *you* manage to get where you've gotten?" she said spitefully. "Through the milk of human kindness?"

Matt revved the engine impatiently while it idled in a traffic snarl. "How many times have you slept with Jason?" he asked casually.

She colored and looked away at the stream of traffic going in the other direction. "That's none of your business."

"And how I got my money is none of yours!" he said smoothly.

"That's a different kind of question, and you know it," she said hotly. "Anyone would be curious about a man accumulating so much wealth in five years. I can't be the first one who's asked. Do you ask them all who they've slept with and how many times?"

"I tell 'em to use their imagination. It's what you're doing anyway. I know exactly what you're thinking."

Alexandra folded her arms tightly and scowled through the windscreen. "You don't know the first thing about what I'm thinking." From the corner of her eye she saw his smug, contemptuous grin. "All right then—what am I thinking?"

"That I've done something heinous to get it."

"Heinous! Strong word. Also sophisticated for the Matt Farraday I once knew." It sounded like the ultimate snob put down, and she regretted the remark as soon as she'd said it.

"You never knew Matt Farraday."

"No," she said softly. "I guess not." She was beginning to feel that the deafening symphony was definitely the better of two evils. She was sorry she'd ever opened her mouth.

"Putting it more simply," he was saying, "since my new vocabulary distresses you, you think there's something dishonest about the way I make a living. And from you, that's rich."

It made her sound like the pot calling the kettle black, and she couldn't help the astonishment that spread over her features. Was he implying *she* was dishonest? But she wasn't going to say another word. Perhaps he'd shut up and play some more "music to split ears by."

"Yeah, that's rich," he persisted. "Honesty can be a fascinating topic. For instance, is it strictly honest to marry a man you don't love? Is it dishonest to sleep with a man you really—" He broke off abruptly and slipped into second gear as the traffic began inching forward. "You don't have to answer that. I apologize. It's obviously none of my business anymore. You've made that clear."

Alexandra reached out, pressed the cassette back into the tape deck and pushed PLAY. For the rest of the ride the tumultuous Holst drove out all painful thoughts.

The front driveway of the house was a scene of

bustling activity as the Ferrari screeched to a halt. No one had bothered to mention there was another party scheduled at the ranch. But of course, if she had followed orders, she would have been on her way back to Kentucky by now. Three caterer's vans were parked in a row, their side doors open as men in waiters' uniforms lifted out covered trays and hurried into the house.

At the front steps, two men were unloading tables and chairs from a truck. They stopped to make way for an enormous cake carried by two men. There was something elaborate on top of the cake she couldn't quite make out.

Toni must have been watching out for Matt's car. She hurried down the steps just as Matt stepped out, looking very distressed, her eyes rimmed with pink.

"Did something go wrong with Sunstreak?" Matt asked quickly.

Toni shook her head. "She's fine, she had a beautiful colt. Matt, I've gotta talk to you."

"Is Billy Reynolds here yet?" Matt looked around at the activity in front of the house.

Walking a few steps behind them, Alexandra heard the name. Reynolds was another top jockey.

Alexandra slackened her pace until there was a discreet distance between them. Toni looked desperate to talk to Matt, but at the front door, Matt patted her shoulder and darted into the house.

Toni looked so abject as she leaned against the wall in the entryway that Alexandra's heart went out to her.

"Hey, it can't be that bad," she offered tentatively.

"Bad?" Toni buried her head in her hands rather theatrically. "Not bad? It's the worst, the absolute worst."

"Is there something I can do?"

Toni shook her head. Her mascara was smudged, and under the surface tan her face was drained of color. The blue eyes turned on Alexandra, half desperate, half beseeching. Her lower lip trembled, then her face seemed to crumple and she began to cry.

"Matt put in a bid for a horse last week," Toni managed between gulping sobs. "Carry On. It was a winning bid, too. It should have gone to him. But he's lost it now."

So Matt can lose out on a bid too, Alexandra wanted to say. *Big deal.* But Toni was beside herself. It didn't seem appropriate. "Oh," was all she managed to comment.

"No, no, you don't understand. I got the horse!"

Alexandra led her to a wooden settee in an alcove and sat beside her, at least minimally out of the traffic pattern created by the frantic caterers. She fished in her purse and offered Toni some tissues.

"I want to be known as a serious buyer, so I submitted a good bid," Toni said, dabbing her eyes, "but I never thought—" She crumpled with sobs again so that her words were lost.

"Hey, Matt's in a raw mood right now and you caught the brunt of it," Alexandra said sympathetically, "but he can't hold a fair bid against you. He's a businessman, Toni. Fair's fair."

"But that's just it. It wasn't fair." She seemed to be somewhat calmer as she stood up and wadded the tissues in her right hand. "I knew exactly how much Matt was offering for Carry On."

"I see," Alexandra said, acutely embarrassed by this confession of shady dealing.

The sudden wincing expression on Toni's face

made Alexandra turn. It was Matt. The controlled anger on his face was formidable.

"Please," Toni whispered, "let me explain."

"Save it. This isn't my day for a party. It's your bloody celebration—so have at it!"

He turned on his heel and, within seconds, was gunning the Ferrari down the drive.

"Rah, rah, for me," Toni said, ignoring a fresh stream of tears. "I won."

Misery loves company, Alexandra thought with a rush of feeling. "I know what you mean, Toni. Sometimes getting what you thought you wanted is the pits." She watched, feeling helpless as Toni wiped her face with the backs of her hands and threaded her way through the caterers to the outside.

The festivities had a twofold purpose, Alexandra learned. They were to celebrate the Lad's first race and, apparently much more crucial, Matt's acquisition of Carry On. Matt had been confident of winning on both scores, Scott confided to her, recruiting her help with last-minute arrangements before the guests started to arrive.

"What will you do if Matt doesn't show up?" she asked him, as they watched the trucks disappear from the front driveway.

Scott shrugged. "They'll start coming within the hour. What can I do? The show must go on, I suppose."

"Is there anything else to do?"

When Scott shook his head, she excused herself. She had no intention of attending the party. She'd had enough events for one day.

After a shower, she sat by the French windows in

her bedroom, too exhausted to start packing. The sounds of the guests made her feel unutterably alone, abandoned by Jason, unwanted by Matt.

Odd snatches of conversation floated through the open window. She listened as Scott explained Matt's absence. ". . . sends his regrets. He was called away at the last minute. A sick relative . . ."

How unfailingly loyal Scott was, always willing to front for Matt, even lie for him. Matt seemed to inspire devotion in all the people he used and abused. No, she wasn't going to dwell on that anymore. She roused herself and began to pack. Her suitcase was out and she was folding her clothes when Scott knocked at her door.

In spite of his impeccable dinner jacket, there was an anxious, ruffled look about him. "Alexandra, it's a charade down there. I'm smiling like a fool and I can't even think straight anymore."

"Matt's a problem child," she said, turning back to her packing. "I don't mean to sound indifferent, but he's your problem, not mine." Matt had made it quite clear he wanted her out of his life.

"It's not just Matt. It's Toni. I'm really worried about her. She's got herself a heap of trouble and I'm partly to blame."

"You?" Alexandra turned in surprise and found his blond boyish face ravaged with anxiety. "I can't believe you'd do anything to sabotage Matt."

"I didn't. Not directly, but getting that horse became all-important to Toni because I talked up Carry On's potential."

Alexandra felt like patting his tousled head, he looked so much like a choirboy in hot water. "That's hardly a reason for you to feel so guilty."

"There's more to it."

She smiled. "I'm listening—if unburdening is going to make you feel better."

He started, then looked faintly embarrassed. "Yeah, well, it's not my story to tell."

"Toni's story?"

Scott nodded. "Toni's not really tough. She's got this act, but she couldn't begin to take care of herself the way you do."

"Me?" Alexandra found herself laughing for the first time in what seemed like weeks.

Scott failed to see the humor, staring at her with a baffled expression as she sat on the bed surrendering to such gales of laughter that her eyes began to water.

"I'm sorry, Scott," she said when she was able to speak again. "Private joke. It's just that for the past couple of days I've been accused of being anything but strong. According to some, I'm spineless, shiftless, hopelessly pampered and spoiled—quite incapable of the least little decision."

Scott's blond brows rose an inch. "Sounds like you could use a new fan club. I haven't known you long. I can only tell you what I see and—well, I feel an undercurrent of strength in you. Quiet, latent maybe —but it's definitely strength."

"That's a new tune. I like it." She grinned suddenly. "All right you silver-tongued rogue; you just sweet-talked me into hostessing your party."

His tense face sagged with relief. "Thanks, Alexandra. I won't be gone long, just long enough to find out why Toni's not answering her phone."

"Don't worry, Scott. Take as long as you need." She gave him a wry smile. "Just remember that all's well back at the ranch. I'm the tower of strength, remember?"

He gave her a thumbs-up sign as he turned to leave, then stopped and hurried back to give her a heartfelt hug. "Thanks, Alexandra. You're wonderful."

Scott could no more hide his feelings from her than she could from him; he was hopelessly, painfully in love with Toni. "Listen Scott, why not take the whole night off. I'll manage," she said, recognizing the desperation she saw in his eyes. "You need to, don't you?"

Scott flushed. "Yeah. It shows, huh?"

Only to a fellow traveler on the same road, she thought. But she said only, "I just took a guess. Good luck, Scott."

Chapter Six

𝒜lexandra woke to the sounds of chairs scraping against patio tile, heated discussions and the jangle of a broom sweeping up some broken glass. The night seemed to have passed in moments. She opened her eyes and registered the noise floating up through her window; the clean-up crew was busy removing the debris of last night's party.

The evening was still vivid in her mind, as if it had only been moments before. She had gone down to the party to help Scott out and had risen to the occasion, wafting through the guests like the lady of the manor, charming and amusing them all to distract them from their host's glaring absence.

Stretching lazily, then lying back on the pillows, she savored the small satisfaction of having been useful for a few hours. Ever since she'd arrived in California, she'd felt like a fifth wheel. But the party had taken ingenuity, tact and a touch of inspired invention to keep all the guests diverted. She knew she had performed well. Once she had gotten into her stride, it wasn't difficult. In fact, she realized with utter surprise that she had rather enjoyed the role. She sat up, ignoring the faint ache at her temples. Perhaps she shouldn't be surprised at all, considering she was bred to be the "lady of the manor."

She lingered in bed, remembering that she was all packed except for her nightgown and toilet articles. There wasn't much to do before Aoki took her to the airport.

"Coming, Aoki," she said in answer to the tentative knock on her door, and slipped into a robe.

But it wasn't the chauffeur. "Please, Alex," Matt said, holding up a hand in truce, "before you say anything, I just want to thank you for what you did yesterday."

Matt had a clean, laundered look about him, scrubbed and pressed and chastened, almost as if fresh clothes and a morning toilette could cleanse away the suppressed anger of the previous day. His mild manner kept Alexandra from making any quick retort.

"I appreciate your stepping into the breach like that," he went on, avoiding her eyes. "Running out on my guests was unforgivable. I won't try to excuse it. I've never run away from responsibilities, but yesterday . . ." He stopped in mid-sentence.

At least he had the grace to do that, she thought. *No, Matt, not you. You never run away from your responsibilities.* But some inner wisdom told her to let it pass. No more recrimination. "I didn't mind helping out," she said pleasantly.

"I hear you were magnificent," he said, and she knew he was just expressing grateful recognition that although she could have gone straight for the jugular, she hadn't.

"You didn't just help out—you *made* the evening. You were beautiful, charming and altogether a delightful hostess, they tell me."

Alexandra dipped her head in silent acknowledgment of the compliments.

Matt stood there awkwardly, like a schoolboy not knowing what to do with his hands. "That scene yesterday with Toni—it wasn't losing the horse that sent me off like that. It was just this awful sense of—"

"Betrayal?"

Matt nodded, grateful that she understood.

"Maybe you deserved to be betrayed, Matt. Maybe you had it coming to you." It was a blunder. A familiar pain shot up behind her ribs without warning and she turned aside to fiddle with her suitcase before it showed on her face. "Everything's packed and ready to go."

"I'll tell Aoki." His voice was soft.

"Same flight as yesterday?" she asked briskly, moving about the room to collect her toilet articles.

"Yes . . . yes. Same flight, same time."

"I'm booked on it?"

"Yes—booked. Of course."

He sounded fragmented. When she turned back to face him, bracing herself for a quiet, friendly parting, Matt was staring at the two flight bags, side by side on the carpet.

"You're taking Jason's things with you, I see."

"No, as a matter of fact, I'm not." She had no idea why she said it, and he looked at her, as confused as she was.

"I've packed what he left behind," she explained, "but I've no idea what his plans are. He didn't say where he'd be staying, so I can't reach him to get my instructions or follow yours." She shrugged, realizing her voice had risen harshly. "And when I'm not programmed—well, I do nothing. Sorry."

Matt gave a heartfelt sigh. "So am I," he whispered.

"I mean I'm sorry I can't reach Jason, sorry I'm acting like a shrew—" She took a deep gulp of air to eliminate the tremor in her voice. "Sorry for just about everything in my whole misbegotten life."

Matt glanced at his watch. "Yes, well—we live and learn. Have a good trip."

He left quietly without a kiss, a handshake, a farewell speech. *We live and learn.* Just a tired cliché and he was gone.

As she closed the door after him, the thought "finished business" ran through her mind. *So this is really how it ends. No drum rolls or shouts. No acrimony. It ends quietly, the passion burned away, leaving a great big empty space.*

On a sudden impulse, she threw the door open again. The hallway was empty. She stood looking at the space he had filled only moments ago. *Please hold me! Please love me,* she wanted to shout. But she stood there silently.

"What do you mean, Aoki? Are you crazy?"

Alexandra stood fuming down on him in the front entryway. But although her voice crackled with irritation, the little Oriental looked unperturbed, as if the insane comings and goings of this household had no power to disturb his rocklike serenity. "I have no instructions to take you to the airport today," he repeated tranquilly.

"But you *must* have. Mr. Farraday confirmed it just an hour ago." Alexandra felt alarmingly close to tears. "My bags are all ready for you to pick up from my room. He just forgot to mention it, that's all."

"Mr. Farraday does not forget, Miss O'Neill," Aoki said with infuriating certainty.

Alexandra took a deep breath. "You're quite right, Aoki, Mr. Farraday does not forget." She reached for the phone.

"I'm sorry," the reservations clerk replied to her question, "your name is not on our seating list."

"Okay, then put me on now," Alexandra snapped.

"I'm sorry," the voice came back pleasantly. "That flight is completely booked."

She slammed the phone down, feeling as if she were coming apart at the seams. It was a small thing, she told herself, she could correct it easily enough, but suddenly she couldn't cope anymore. She was getting paranoid, a rising sense of manipulation all around her like a gossamer net about to be drawn tight. For an insane moment she suspected Matt and the airline of a dark conspiracy against her.

Aoki stood, hat in hand, calmly waiting to be dismissed. "Stop it!" she yelled at him. "Stop that . . . that infuriating calmness! You know very well what's going on here. You stand there like some kind of tranquil Buddha while this lady here turns into a crazy person. I'm coming unglued! And your boss is to blame—you know that, don't you?"

"Perhaps, Miss O'Neill, it would refresh you to take the station wagon and drive away from here for the day . . . down the coast. It's very soothing."

"Down the coast?" Alexandra echoed distractedly.

"Up the coast?" he offered, as if he wished to cover his bases.

It flashed on her that the serene chauffeur was as

desperate as she was, searching for options that would get this lunatic houseguest out of his hair. He held out a set of car keys. "To be alone with one's self, it is a way of receiving wise counsel," he said solemnly. As she accepted the keys, a brief look of relief escaped his eyes. He gave a little bow and left her quickly.

In her hurry to leave the madness behind her, she gunned the station wagon's engine down the private road as if it were Matt's Ferrari.

Alexandra watched Carla peer over her menu, dark eyes darting from table to table in the crowded Beverly Hills restaurant, and thanked her lucky stars she'd been able to raise her friend on the spur of the moment.

"You look like a spy," Alexandra said. "An obvious one."

"Huh?" Carla lowered the menu. "Isn't this fabulous? Look at them. Over there—the one with no hair and the bushy eyebrows?"

Alexandra followed her friend's gaze. The man was seated next to a woman with lots of hair and almost no eyebrows. "What about him?"

"What about *them*," Carla corrected. "Alex, you been living in a nunnery or something? Don't you read any rag journals, scandal sheets? Don't you know a hot item when it's sitting right under your nose?"

"Oh." Alexandra had been too filled with relief at finding Carla free for lunch to get excited about the celebrities ranged about them.

"You're not into all this Hollywood glitz, are you?"

"I guess not," Alexandra said apologetically.

138

Carla swirled her martini. "What's to be sorry about? If I had your talent, your background, everything you've got going for you—then maybe I'd be paying more attention to the glamour in my own life too."

"Hey, don't give me that." Alexandra raised her glass and clinked it against Carla's. "You've got a great career—here's to it. And no more false modesty."

Carla grinned sheepishly. "What can I say? You're right. I've made it, babe; all the way to the top. Well—it's not Paris or Rome—but who cares! The climate can't be beat, my money's my own and—"

"And your life's your own," Alexandra finished, feelingly.

"You better believe it! But then, the same's true for you."

"Not quite." Alexandra frowned and turned her attention to the waiter. After they had made their choices, she continued quickly, speaking in a monotone.

"I quit Conti. I went home to Kentucky. I'm scheduled to be married in two months."

Carla said nothing. She seemed to be waiting for more.

"Well? Don't I get a gasp? An ooh, an ah? A little congratulations?"

"I'm waiting," Carla said, and replaced her wire-rimmed glasses with a rather serious expression.

"Yes, I can see you're waiting. For what? I just shot the works. Getting married. It generally calls for a hip-hip-hooray."

"Scheduled to be married? What kind of statement is that, for crying out loud? You didn't say the magic words yet, kid."

Alexandra pressed her fingers into a crusty dinner roll and began to shred it with careful concentration. "No, I didn't, did I?"

In the pause that followed as the waiter returned with their Cobb salads, Alexandra felt a sharp pressure on her lungs. She was drawing perilously close to the edge of hysteria, making statements to Carla that she wasn't sure had any meaning.

"Oh Carla," she said when the waiter had left, "I'm falling apart."

"Yeah? You look pretty okay to me. I'd say you're good for a few more miles," Carla joked gently, then stopped and gave a searching look across at her friend. "Okay. You're the expert on you. If you say you're falling apart, you're falling apart. I suppose it's to do with the fact that you just announced your wedding like you were planning chicken for Wednesday night. No name, no stars in the eyes, no glowing description. Nothing. I'd say you've got big trouble, kid."

Alexandra felt a slight lightening of the pressure in her chest as she nodded. "Have you got your violins ready?"

"Always. Violins, credit cards—never leave home without 'em." Carla's grin faded. "So shoot, Alex. What's with this marriage?"

"It's a long story, Carla. . . . I think it's the story of my life."

With an infinite sense of release, she found herself unrolling her life like an endless carpet stretching back to her adolescence. Her affair with Matt when she was seventeen, his desertion, the years spent trying to forget him, her father's financial problems and how Jason seemed to be the ultimate solution—except that she couldn't bring herself to love him sexually.

She sat back exhausted after the long recital and looked at her untouched salad. She wasn't hungry, but she felt lighter and saner than when she'd first sat down at the table. "I think they call this catharsis, Carla. Thanks for listening."

Carla glanced at her friend's untouched food and grinned. "In Hollywood, they call it getting your act together."

"So what am I going to do now, friend?"

"Hey, sweetie. You're going to have to answer that one. It's your life we're talking about, not mine."

"Please?"

Carla opened her mouth to say something, then changed her mind. After a moment's silence, she said, "I listen. I don't talk."

"But you know what I should be doing, don't you? Those are answers I see jumping around in those shrewd black eyes of yours."

"What you see is probably mascara—" She broke off, as if weighing choices, and when she spoke again her voice was very gentle. "Honey, I can see you're hurting and all mixed up, and I could give you all kinds of obvious advice. But it wouldn't help. You've got to know what you want and go for it. And I think you do know what you want."

"What?" Alexandra leaned forward, goggling at Carla as if the woman had just spoken in tongues.

"Mmmm . . ." Carla's lips curled. "I see you got the message."

"Matt said almost the same thing to me. That I should listen to myself and lead my own life for once."

Carla cocked a delicate black eyebrow. "A wise man! He can't be all bad. Oh boy, you've got me sounding like a fortune cookie!"

141

"Oh Lord, have I ever been a chump!" Alexandra muttered fervently.

"We're all capable of chumphood. The cure starts when you recognize it." Carla winked reassuringly, as if her friend's moment of truth was hardly apocalyptic.

"All I've ever done is what other people expected of me or taught me to expect from myself. It's like I've drifted through life on autopilot. I'm so used to it, I don't even know what I really want. I thought I was pretty hot stuff in Rome, building up my career, in the thick of all the parties and excitement and glamour. But what did I do when the first little problem came up? I didn't examine it, overcome it, or even try to work it out. I just threw up my hands and quit."

Carla gave a big sigh. "All right, enough with the hair shirt. You want advice? Big mouth here will give you advice. I think you don't know what you want 'cause you don't know who's doing the wanting anymore. You marry this Jason—or anyone else for that matter—and it's not going to solve any problems. Who's gonna be walking down that aisle? Daddy's little girl? Jason's dream of the perfect companion? Miss Bluegrass? Miss Finishing School? But the real Alex won't be there—because, babe— that lady's been out to lunch her whole life."

Impulsively, she reached across the table and squeezed Carla's hand. "Thanks, smart lady. Someday maybe I'll grow up and be just like you."

"God forbid!" Carla rolled her eyes.

"So listen, keep in touch?" Carla said as they waited at the front entrance for their cars.

Alexandra gave her a bear hug, half crying and half laughing.

Carla returned the friendly squeeze, then climbed

into her green M.G. "I think you just made a decision. I heard something rusty just go *clunk!*" She tapped a forefinger against her temple. "So tell me already. I can't stand the suspense. What are you gonna do?"

"This lady's going south, and she's going to do some heavy housecleaning. She's going to give Daddy's Girl the heave-ho. She's going to dump the Southern gentleman's perfect fiancée, scheduled to bloom into the perfect wife. Then maybe, when there's a nice clean space, it will be filled with the one and only genuine Alexandra O'Neill, whoever she may be."

"Oowee," Carla squealed, delighted. "Sounds like you're gonna need one big broom. Right on, kid!" Carla started her engine, then turned it off again. "Wait up. You left out one name."

"Matt." Alexandra's smile vanished. "Well, whoever it was who fell in love with Matt Farraday, that wasn't the real me either. The only thing lasting in that relationship is the way my body feels. He turned me on—and I guess he always will. But it doesn't seem to be enough, Carla. Not for me, and not for Matt either."

Carla's eyes lit with frank pleasure as she followed the graceful progress of a Hollywood Adonis in open-necked sports shirt and tight jeans, who crossed in front of the M.G. with a sidelong glance at the occupant.

"Well, each to his own, Alex," Carla muttered, her eyes lingering on the graceful form as he strode down the sidewalk toward the stop lights. She turned back to face Alexandra, eyebrows shooting up innocently as she revved her motor. "Sometimes bodies are . . . more than enough."

By the time Alexandra drove through Vista del

Lago's gates, it was past ten o'clock. She had spent the afternoon at the L.A. County Museum of Art on Carla's recommendation. The costume exhibit absorbed her for several hours, and after she left the museum, she had found her way to Little Tokyo. A sight-seeing stroll, a solitary dinner in a quiet sushi restaurant, and she had felt calm enough to return to the ranch.

The house seemed to be locked up for the night, no lights at the window and the front steps shrouded in darkness. Before she rang the front doorbell, she decided to try one of the French doors. It looked as if everyone was sleeping.

She worked her way quietly around the house, finding everything locked until she came to Matt's study. The glass door swung on its hinges, and as she reached it, a hot gust of wind slammed it shut.

No sooner had she opened it again and stepped inside, than it struck her as a foolish thing to do. In the faint moonlight from the window, the room was shadowy and somehow menacing. She heard a slight movement from somewhere in the pitch-dark center of the room and held her breath. Instantly a lamp lit up.

"I thought that must be you," Scott Maddox said.

"Scott!" She sank into the nearest chair, listening to the thumping subside in her chest.

"Sorry to scare you," he said. "I didn't think you'd come in this way."

"I know. It was dumb, but I didn't want to wake up the house with the door chimes." Scott looked as if he'd just lost his best friend. "What are you doing anyway, sitting all alone here in the dark?"

"Thinking."

Alexandra smiled. "Not exactly happy thoughts, I take it."

Scott's mouth turned down at a morose slant she'd never seen before. "Not particularly."

"To do with Matt?"

He stood up, and as he moved aimlessly around the room, emptying an ashtray, reshelving a couple of books left lying on the coffee table, he looked bone-weary. "Yes, Matt," he said at last. "I made the mistake of trying to talk some sense into him. The guy has a very thick skull at times."

"Don't we all, at times?" she asked fervently.

"I suppose. But Matt's a tough case—and the one I have to deal with every day." He shook his head despairingly. "I beat my brains out trying to—" He sank back into the chair opposite her with a defeated sigh. "I'm beginning to wonder if it's worth the effort."

"Why do you care so much?" she asked, knowing his distress was genuine.

Scott examined his fingernails. "I've known Matt less than five years. I've known my brother for twenty-three years and I don't care about him this much." When he looked up, the genuine hurt on his face surprised her.

"We worked to build something here. The two of us. He made me feel a part of it—more like a partner than an employee. Oh, I know he's got bigger fish to fry than this. Financial holdings that make Vista del Lago just a spit in the ocean. Mostly he handles all that himself. But this is what he seemed to care most about. His heart was in this ranch, and that's why I've stuck by him. But now . . ."

Alexandra leaned forward attentively. He was finding it hard to talk about. She didn't press him.

He raked his fingers through the coarse blond thatch and sat holding his head. "I'm at the point where I don't know if I can take it anymore. Those moods of his . . . when he's hurting so much and I can't reach him. Oh, it's not just the verbal bloodbaths I get for trying. I know that means nothing. It's what he's doing to himself. Sometimes he's like the walking dead."

He stood up stretching his limbs with a stiffness that told her he'd been sitting in Matt's study for hours, brooding. Then he jammed his fists deep into his pants pockets and went to stare out of the dark windows. "The man's got everything, for crying out loud. Look at this place. What more does he want?"

"New worlds to conquer, maybe?" Alexandra offered.

Scott folded his arms and sagged against the window frame. "I used to think that too. I don't anymore. I believe it's less tangible. . . . Peace of mind?" He turned to look over at Alexandra with a faintly mulish set to his chin. "You won't like this I know, but I still think that his peace of mind's got a lot to do with you."

She gave an involuntary smile at his expression, half stubborn, half wary. "It's all right Scott, I won't bite you this time. Last time you said that I got furious because I was so mixed up myself. I even hoped you might be right. Now I know better. If there was anything there, it's gone. He said as much. He's asked me to leave."

Scott's eyes rolled up to the ceiling. "You think you're mixed up! He's a very complicated man, Alexandra. I can't figure him, but I know he's lost on some level. Completely lost and drowning." He came closer, frowning intently. "Asked you to leave, did he? Said it was over between you?"

"Yes," she said in a dull voice. "He gave me the

impression that it was the sensible thing to do. He's probably right."

Scott nodded his head. "Sensible. Sensible and practical. And absolute baloney," he muttered. Pushing himself away from the window wall, he began to pace nervously, punching a fist into a flat palm. "That would do it. This latest explosion. Boy, was it ever a dilly." He came to rest and leaned over her chair anxiously. "He was so down, so low tonight, I began to wonder if he would do something to harm himself and—"

"Suicide?" Alexandra jumped out of the chair. "Oh, Scott, you don't mean suicide?"

He paused, his face solemn. "I don't mean he'd take a gun to his head. But still, he's driven his car fast before, so fast he was asking for it. He's taken turns too fast, had a couple of blowouts—and if he hadn't been in the desert, he'd never have walked away. I think he's dangerously cheap with his life."

"Scott, find him. Talk to him."

He threw up his hands angrily. "I tried. We got into this argument. He changed the subject, turned it around to Toni's getting that horse. He went into this song and dance about how I conspired with her against him."

"He surely doesn't believe that of you?"

"No, of course he doesn't. I know that," he said testily. "But he'll use anything as a red herring to keep from admitting the real issue—what's really eating him up, what's making his life a misery and everyone else's too. Everyone who cares about—"

Scott stopped abruptly and dropped into an armchair. His voice had risen with anxiety, but when he spoke again it was low and dispirited. "Alexandra, I tried to talk to him about you."

She closed her eyes for a moment. "And that made things worse."

"Yes. He didn't want to hear it. Said it was over. Only it isn't. It can't be, because he can't let go."

"He's got to let go."

"Will you level with me for once?" Scott strained forward in his chair, his eyes narrowed and pleading. "Don't you care about him at all?"

"Yes, of course. I care about him. But I can see that Matt's right. Too much has happened. There's too much hurt between us and . . . I'm not much good to anyone until I straighten out my own feelings. Not just about Matt. . . . About a lot of things."

Scott nodded unhappily, as if the truth were a bitter pill.

"He went out," he said, looking out into the darkness beyond the window. "That's my immediate concern. There's a bad storm forecast. Sometimes there are flash floods through those gullies, heavy mud slides after a hot dry summer."

She gave a brief laugh. "Are you suggesting he doesn't have the brains to come in out of the rain? Are you hinting I should go pull him in?"

"Would you? You've no idea how dumb he can be about his safety when he gets like this." Scott's expression was as soulful and pleading as Oliver Twist's as he rose and turned his sandy-fringed, round blue eyes on her. "I'd go myself, but he's too furious with me already. He'd never listen to reason."

"He won't be overjoyed to see me either," Alexandra commented wryly, walking toward the door. "Where do you think he went?"

Scott stared out toward a group of foothills. The moon still shone, but dark clouds were moving swiftly toward it. "I'm almost sure he went out to the shack. It's this tumbledown place he likes to hide out in." He smiled to himself. "He thinks I don't know about it. It's just a dinky old collection of scrappy old boards on the far edge of the property. Should've been razed long ago. It sits in a kind of bowl, a clearing surrounded by rocks."

A shack, Alexandra thought. Yes, it was hard for Matt to give up the past.

"There's a path. If you took one of the horses, it wouldn't take you more than twenty minutes," he said hopefully.

"All right," she said. "For you, I'll go."

"Thanks. That's a load off my mind," he said fervently and started out the door with a grateful hand on her shoulder. "But you're not really going for me. You're going for that lunkhead."

"I'll take it from here, Scott," she said, waving him away. "I know where the stables are. Go get yourself a night's sleep and stop worrying. . . . I'll take over."

I'll take over. It wasn't a phrase she'd ever had much occasion to use, she thought, as she threaded her way over the gravel toward the outbuildings behind the house.

The wind had torn open the barn door. It swung back and forth, its hinges creaking with every gust. One stall was empty. Faintly she remembered seeing a gray quarter horse the day before. Matt must have taken it.

She took a saddle from the tack room and threw it on the friendly dappled mare in the third stall, as Scott had recommended. She looked down at the pencil-slim skirt she wore. She had dressed for her flight home in a lightweight gray suit. In spite of the churning she felt inside, the outfit had remained cool and crisp through the long day, like a fragile shell of discipline holding her together. She slipped off the blazer and tossed it aside, then, with a sigh of regret, she grasped the hem of her skirt and ripped first one side seam, then the other, ruining the loose linen weave, but giving herself enough freedom to ride.

Cantering out toward the dry hills beyond the compound, she took what seemed in the moonlight to be a well-used equestrian path through the flat-lands. The hot wind whipped around her, making the air bristle with electricity. What was it Scott had said—the Santa Anas? *Yes, the Devil Winds,* she remembered with a little thrill of exhilaration. The name was apt.

When the trail ended in tall grass and clumps of tinder-dry tumbleweed and scrub, she paused and listened. But the only sounds were the wind rustling the grasses and the brittle snap of twigs as small creatures scurried through the undergrowth. Ahead loomed rolling hills, but some trampled grass suggested a horse had already crossed them and she spurred the mare forward in the same direction.

Her hair rose and fell, then whipped across her face as the crazy Santa Ana changed directions. The mare whickered nervously as the sky darkened. Scudding clouds were obscuring the full moon. Alexandra slowed the pace to a walk as they entered a narrow ravine littered with crackling chaparral. Beyond the gully lay a flat expanse of scrubland, stretching all the way to the distant foothills.

She reined in again, scouring the desolate landscape for some sign of the shack and beginning to question her memory. Scott had given her simple directions, but she couldn't quite recall them. The mare pawed the ground nervously, and Alexandra became aware of a new sound and a growing dark form to her right. Suddenly the mare raced forward, neighing in recognition. It was the gray quarter horse missing from the stable, saddled and riderless. He frisked around the mare, balky and agitated, then broke into a runaway gallop toward the ranch. With a sudden vision of Matt lying somewhere under the sky, injured from a fall, she turned the mare in the direction from which the gray had appeared to her right.

A deafening clap of thunder suddenly terrified the mare; it reared, whinnied and began to turn in skittering circles. Alexandra dismounted and stroked its withers, coaxing it forward with a firm pressure on the reins until it quieted and obeyed.

They were skirting an outcropping of smooth rock that formed a head-high wall, when suddenly the mare let out a screaming whinney and bolted, wrenching the reins from her hand. She spun around to see a dark shadow slithering away. A lizard? A snake? A squirrel? The light was so deceptive it was hard to tell. Whatever it was, it had lost her mount for her. She stood paralyzed for a moment, wanting to bolt for safety like the horse, then gradually calmed herself with a growing sense that Matt was close by, needing help.

She followed the path beside the rocks until, after a few hundred yards, the terrain gradually flattened out. A straggly stand of trees became visible and, beside it, the outline of a shack. A light shone from a small square window, and as she came closer she could hear sounds inside. Limp with relief, she hurried forward.

Remembering how he had looked only that morning, she was startled at the change in Matt. In the yellowish light behind him, his face was hollow-eyed, gaunt and unfocused. A tautness in his facial muscles made her think of someone who had just risen from a haunted, sleepless night. He stood holding the door open, too stunned by the sight of her to say a word.

"There's a storm brewing, Matt. Come back to the house with me?" she said.

He gave her a strange look, as if she were an apparition, then glanced at the sky as her words slowly registered. A distant boom of thunder seemed to snap him together. "Ah—Maddox sent you out here?"

He turned back inside and she followed him in. An old kettle was steaming on a rusty wood-burning stove in the corner of the room. A chipped kitchen table, two chairs, and a cot against one wall were the sum total of the furnishings, except for a plywood shelf on the wall near the stove. He went to the shelf. It held a few canned goods and staples. "Coffee?" he said, taking a jar of instant coffee and two mugs from the shelf.

"Matt, can't we just go?" she said.

He fished around the shelf for a plastic spoon, then brought the two cups to the table. "Did I say I was leaving?" He busied himself with the boiling water and the jar of instant in a long, stalling ritual.

"No, you didn't, but Scott tells me the flash floods can be very sudden and you—"

"Oh, come on, Ali!" He stopped stirring and threw down the spoon. "You fell for that?"

"He's genuinely worried about you, Matt. He—"

"He wanted to throw us together."

She took a breath to argue with him, then suddenly clamped her mouth shut. All of a sudden it was perfectly obvious, she realized, feeling warmth rise up her cheeks.

Matt handed her a steaming mug with an eloquent tilt of his mouth. *Now, really,* it seemed to say, as if her gullibility were pitiful. "I suppose he told you we had an argument. There are times when he really gets to me and—I walked out on him. This is typical—his way of getting in the last word . . . sending you as his spokesman."

Thunder boomed again, a little closer. "The storm's genuine enough," she said, and set down her unwanted coffee on the stained formica.

"No doubt about it," Matt said, turning one of the chairs from the table and straddling it. He leaned his arms on the chairback. "Marble told me that. I untethered him when he started to spook and gave him a pat on the rump. He knows the way back to his stall."

"My horse bolted too. I guess I'll have to walk back—and I don't plan on walking by myself," she said firmly.

"Then you'd better plan on staying here." He grinned. "That would please Maddox no end."

Was there nothing more than matchmaking behind Scott's anxious protests? She felt a sense of anticlimax that it was just an elaborate hoax. Then she saw Matt's grin fade and the grimness was still there. Scott might be a meddler, she decided, but he hadn't done all this strictly for his own amusement. Matt did look lost.

"Matt, you came here to hide out, to escape from things," she said, wondering why she said it. "What good could it possibly do?"

He stood up and opened the door to look out. A rush of wind filled the room and dry leaves slid across the floorboards. His dark hair lifted as his bulk filled the doorway, and the cream cotton of his shirt stretched tight across his back as he flexed his broad shoulders.

"You can't run away from yourself, Matt," she said quietly, feeling the weight of his despondency like a heaviness on her lungs.

He turned, closing the door and leaning against it. "When you get right down to it, coming here is more like facing it than running from it, wouldn't you say?" His eyes traveled over the bare room. "What does it remind you of?"

"Your place in Kentucky?"

He nodded. "I used to stable some horses near Vista and sometimes I'd ride out this way. One day, I came across this hovel. That was long before I bought Vista del Lago. It's *why* I bought it, if you want to know."

He'd bought a vast tract of land because of this pile of junk? But he had always despised poverty. Her mind flew back to the damp smell of dogtooth violets and lush summer grass, Matt's face dappled with light filtering through the foliage of the beech tree under which they lay. *I'm going to climb up out of all this, Ali. We'll live in a house with white marble floors—so bright and shiny they'll knock your eyeballs out.*

"There's something about this, isn't there?"

His voice jerked her back to the present and to the acid irony in his smile.

"A certain . . . well, a primitive kind of honesty . . . very basic."

She watched him move trancelike about the room, pausing to touch the cheap furniture with a strange mixture of affection and contempt. He seemed withdrawn, retreating into an unpopulated world where nothing and no one could touch him.

"We had a table much like this," he was saying.

"And just three chairs. The Farradays didn't do much entertaining. . . ." When he glanced up at her, it was the first indication that he was fully aware of her presence.

"Sometimes I'd imagine what it would be like to—have you visit. Beautiful, fascinating and very, very rich Alexandra O'Neill."

His face was calm now, but the slight distortion of his voice made her think he was slowly carving himself up inside.

"Don't, Matt," she said. "That part of your life is over. You have so much now."

"I knew you'd get to see it after I left," he muttered. "Tell me Ali, what did you think of the shack I called home?"

"What does it matter? It was you, not your—"

"I used to dread your seeing it. We met on your turf all the time—our whole relationship was built in your world."

"Stop it, Matt. People are people. What does it matter now?"

"Sure." He stood, feet apart, thumbs hooked in his belt, like a spunky kid, frightened inside and defiant on the outside. "People are people. There are the rich people and the others. I wasn't any of them then. I was sub-others. My bed was like this," he said, turning to the cot. He sat down on the threadbare blanket and the chicken wire beneath the thin mattress groaned.

"Sometimes when I got home from being with you, I'd try to re-create the scene, only I'd relocate it here on my bed. I'd scrunch up my eyes and try to see those smooth white shoulders, try to feel all your silky warmth moving beneath me. It never worked. And I knew it was because it was impossible. It was—"

"Matt," she pleaded, "what's the point of all this? You have everything you want now. Millions of people are born into poverty, and only a fraction ever get to have—"

"I have nothing," he said flatly.

"My God, Matt. You call that—that Taj Mahal nothing?"

In the flickering light, something seemed to flare behind his eyes. "Ali, Ali. Are you so blind you can't see what matters to me? Do you really think it's material?"

Her mind reeled. *A huge country mansion, Ali, darling. And a swimming pool and million-dollar horses in a stable of my own.* It had driven him fanatically for five years and now he had it all—and more than he could have dreamed of. What in God's name was he saying?

"You went after it all with a vengeance, Matt. If none of it matters, why did you bother?"

His head moved and entered the circle of yellow light from the kerosene lamp that hung overhead. A nerve jumped in his temple, then stilled. "For you, Ali. So you wouldn't ever have to sleep in a bed like that one. I wanted you for keeps, as my wife, as the mother of my children—the whole stupid, romantic works. That was the dreamer in me. And the practical me knew it was hopeless. I used to torment myself because the rational part of me knew something the dreamer couldn't face up to. It knew that every time I kissed you, every time we made love, you were just a kid playing games—bored with the perfect childhood and not quite ready for the perfect womanhood, amusing yourself with a spicy little adventure before you settled down with the first Jason Randolph who came along."

She stared at him in open astonishment, her mind

spinning backward, back to their loving. How could he have imagined for a moment that she was playing games? How did he dare suggest that? Her mouth was open to protest when she heard Carla's voice again. *You don't know what you want 'cause you don't know who's doing the wanting . . . the lady's been out to lunch her whole life.* Her sense of reality rocked dangerously. Perhaps . . . could it be that Matt was right? Finding yourself, wasn't that the cliché she'd heard on all sides, ever since she'd come back from Europe? Was she ever going to be her own woman, knowing exactly what she wanted and who she was?

A guttural sound of derision came from his throat. "Nobody ever died of love. But there were times, Ali, when—it hurt so much . . ."

She walked toward the cot and involuntarily held out her hand to him. In wonder and compassion she saw real hurt in his eyes, old hurt, buried and hardened beyond excision. She was not the only one who had suffered five years of desolation. "Matt, I loved you," she whispered.

"Loved me?" A fleeting smile touched his features. "Wanted me, yes. I was a first—a new kind of trophy. But if I'd stayed, I'd have found out, wouldn't I? It was a lark for a summer, something to giggle about in the fall with your fancy school friends. Not exactly a way of life."

"That's not fair," she said, wondering for the first time in her life if perhaps it was true. Her mind seemed to be playing tricks on her.

"I know you Alex." There was a hint of gentle mockery in his voice. "Oh Lord, my dear, do I ever know you and your silky kind of life. You even grew tired of your glamorous job in Rome—a dream job in a dream city for a girl like you. What happened?

Did a real-life problem come up? Is that why you threw it all away and hurried home to the nice insulated cocoon and the life you were bred to live? No, don't tell me what's not fair."

She dropped her eyes and tried to dodge the inescapable shreds of truth. But he was twisting it. *She had loved him.*

"Tell me something, Alex—and answer straight from the heart for once if you're capable. If you'd had to make a choice then between this or Windermere"—his eyes swept contemptuously over the room—"what would it have been?"

"That's hardly a valid question. Well, I—"

"The plain truth, Alex. Is it so hard to say?"

The wind had dropped suddenly, and a lone cricket in the corner sang out, almost deafening in the unearthly silence.

The truth, she thought, trying to search her heart. What was the truth when she was seventeen? The question had no meaning. "I think . . ." She spoke slowly, falteringly. "If I'd been forced to choose then, I might have chosen Jason. Oh, I don't know. I never even thought about Jason then; he was just a neighbor. It's what my father would have wanted. I'd been raised to do what came easily and naturally, what was expected of me. I was still a child, and I was raised to walk a smooth path."

"And my path wasn't smooth," he said gently.

"I think I'd have lost my way. You were flint-hard and tough and fascinating to me. But to have married you then . . . it would have gone against my whole background, my idea of the world." She paused, wondering if that was the truth and, if so, where it was suddenly coming from. "I loved you totally, hopelessly. I was never playing games. But at seventeen, perhaps I didn't have the equipment for a step like that, not the courage or the decisiveness." The admission stung her with humiliation, and an edge of bitterness crept into her voice. "How will I ever know? I never had to face that crossroads, did I Matt? You never gave me the opportunity to find out."

He ignored the cut, wrapped tightly in his own hurt. "My God, I put you on such a pedestal. Everything I've ever done since was only to—" Turning his head away, he broke off abruptly. "What's the point?" he muttered.

God help me, I did love him and I still love him, she thought, her heart suddenly burgeoning with feeling. She took a step toward him, longing to comfort his pain and hold him.

"Matt, we missed something wonderful, missed it by inches. I was too young, too spoiled. You were too drastic—too much too soon for me. But so help me, I did love you, and I went on and on loving you, and hurting so much because I thought—"

A sudden lightness seemed to buoy up his body and transfigure his face. "Let's start again, Alex. Here. Now."

He came forward, sweeping her into his arms and off the ground, swinging her in circles as sounds of joy rose deep from his throat. *"Ali! Ali!"* When he set her down on her feet, he cupped her face and searched her eyes, laughing at what he saw.

"You love me—you *do* love me! Jason be damned. The whole bloody world be damned, Ali. You belong to me."

She kissed his eyes, his nose, then gently laid her mouth on his. *Is this me at last,* she wondered, *knowing who I am and what I want? I love him beyond life itself. And this is so right. . . .* Tenderly, slowly, she began to unbutton his shirt.

Even when they were naked he stood unmoving before her, his eyes transfixed by hers. "Alex, I love you so much. Oh God, how I love you."

"Yes, darling. Yes." She took his hand and led him to the bed.

He knelt beside her and swept his gaze over her body in childlike wonderment, pausing as if he were at the very brink of the unknown. Then he reached out a tentative hand and stroked the length of her body, bending his head to follow the trail of his fingers with slow kisses. He took her with such shy and gentle cautiousness that they might have been coming together as virgin strangers. Only later did their love wax fierce and hungry. And each culmination brought its own special release, an added affirmation of rightness. Even when they slept, they clung together, until a clap of thunder awoke them.

Forked lightning pierced the room, leaving a dim aftermath, even with the overhead lantern still lit. Matt's body lay slack beside her when she woke. She could feel the static in the air. His hair crackled when she stroked it, making her smile. From now on, she would always cherish thunderstorms.

Matt's eyes opened, and she could see their faint gleam as he looked into her face. His hand reached out, instinctive and loving, closed over her breast, then trailed down over her stomach and circled the swell of her buttocks. Her body began to stir again to his caresses.

"You're mine," he whispered, his tongue darting in her ear. "In every imaginable way. My lover, my wife, the mother of my children. You belong to me. Ali, let's—"

"No," she heard herself say as her body pulled away from him. "No, Matt." She wrenched herself away from the warm haven of his body and left the bed. Thunder roared again as she stood in the middle of the room, and she clapped her hands to her ears to cut out the external distraction. There was enough din, enough confusion inside her head. Surely she wanted this, more than anything. Why had she said no? Who was it who had said no? Where were these unwanted thoughts coming from?

Matt lay stunned on the bed watching her while his words still echoed in the room. *You're mine . . . in every imaginable way. You belong to me.* How could she give him title to something she'd never really owned? How could she belong to him if she couldn't even belong to herself?

He rose and stood beside her, painful bewilderment etching his features. "But I love you, Alex. You can't imagine that what we just shared was— Darling, it isn't just sex I want from you. It's everything. I want you to share a life with me. I want to cherish you always and be with you always."

She shook her head violently, trying to quiet the inner clamor that seemed to crowd out her ability to think straight. "Matt, please, don't. I can't. I can't be what you want."

"For God's sake Ali, don't play games with me now," he begged, frustration cracking his voice. "I'm asking you to be my wife. I love you," he shouted.

"And I love you," she screamed, competing with the thunder outside and the din in her head. "But I will not . . . I can't marry you."

Her fingers, her arms, her shaking legs had lost most of their coordination as she struggled clumsily with her underwear, searching for sanity in the simple act of dressing. Couldn't she even do that without fumbling?

Matt sat heavily on the edge of the bed, his hands

dangling defeatedly between his knees, sensing her critical distress but without comprehension. "I don't understand," he said dully. "I don't understand anything. What just happened here tonight? I thought this changed things for us. We're right together, aren't we? I mean—please, Ali, tell me this wasn't just for kicks?"

When she was dressed, she went to the bed and rested her hands on his slumped shoulders. "No, of course not just for kicks," she said, her voice still sounding strange to her, as if it came from far off. "It was never, never just for kicks. You've got to know that. What I feel for you is beyond sex, Matt."

"Then why?"

There was a terrible, stricken look of misery in his eyes that threatened to annihilate her. She was forced to look away.

"Darling, somewhere in me is the knowledge that I have to claim ownership of this person and learn to live with her. I've spent my whole life belonging—to my father, to a cultural idea, to an imaginary image. I know now that I can't belong to anyone. I can't survive that way."

Dim comprehension altered his face as she spoke, and with it, his body stiffened and his anger flared as he sprang to his feet, his fists tightly curled. *"No!"* he roared. "No, no, no! You're wrong. You've lived your life according to everyone else's ideas, but now it's me, my turn. And for once it's something you can trust. Don't your instincts tell you that? For the first time in your whole damned life you'll be doing the right thing." His control fled as he clutched her, forcing his mouth on hers desperately, as if he could cancel her words and still the enemy voice forever. His hands traveled wildly over her body, as if they were branding irons to claim her.

She battled. A brief tormented conflict, not with him, but with her own desire to yield and be contained within his overpowering love. It was enough, surely it was enough? It would have been more than enough only yesterday. It wasn't fair. There was something new in her, some stranger ripping her up on the inside. That something new gave her the strength to pull away. A few steps beyond the reach of his arms, she stopped. She was on the edge of a dangerous precipice, the rope of her desire still tugging at her.

Matt didn't move. Only his arms reached out mutely to her.

"No, darling," she whispered, shaking her head. "I love you, I'll always love you. But *no*." She opened the door and ran into the high night winds as if she were running for her life.

Boulders loomed up like chunky, misshapen trolls as forked lightning slashed through the darkness around her, blinding, disorienting. Thunder, gale winds and streaks of white light annihilated her senses, but there was no rain, only the relentless wind, crackling dry and hot. It raged out from the desert like the devil's breath. No longer a soft, warming breeze, it was menacing now, tearing up the sagebrush in her path, whipping up spirals of sand and twigs that slapped against her face and arms.

Her eyes stinging from dust, she could barely see where she was going. But she could not return to Matt. She couldn't trust herself not to yield, not to break down and lose that precious step of progress she'd just taken, that small part of herself that felt uniquely her own.

She kept going, guessing wildly at direction, hoping the next flaring in the sky would light up something she remembered that would lead her back to the ranch.

Then the rain began, huge drops of cool water on her hair and shoulders. She turned her face up to the light shower in relief. But in seconds, the rain became a driving torrent as if floodgates had been opened. The earth shook beneath her feet as the thunder crashed overhead. Trying to blink away the blinding rain, she made her way through the narrow ravine that she hoped was the path to the ranch. She was drenched to the skin, and already the parched dirt had turned to thin mud. Although her teeth chattered, the noise was drowned out by the deafening sibilance of the rain.

She hurried as the narrow path through the ravine began to fill with water, forcing herself forward against the whipping slant of the downpour. Watery mud began to slide from the slopes, swirling at her feet until it became a thick rushing stream, licking at her ankles, rising rapidly. The gully was not recognizable, and as soon as she began to question that she was on the right path an aching exhaustion seeped into her flesh. She scrambled up onto a ledge of slippery rocks seeking a safe place to rest and found a scrap of shelter between two enormous boulders.

Minutes later, the rain found her again as the veering wind changed its needling slant. She began to inch further under the overhanging boulder. Then, as the palm of her hand pressed down on something sharp, she moved awkwardly and her wrist twisted under her weight. She slid a few inches and rolled, stopping only when her head and shoulder collided with the massive boulder. The impact jarred her, but it was drier in the new-found shelter.

She drew up her legs and hugged them, resting her head on her knees.

As she waited for the rain to stop, she got the strange, nauseating sensation that even her brain had turned to swirling mud.

Bright daylight penetrated her closed eyelids and she could hear voices . . . words. "*. . . a drowned rabbit . . . lucky you didn't get pneumonia.*"

Alexandra winced as she turned her head to the sound and opened her eyes on Toni Dodd. Sharp concern wrinkled her brow. Vases of flowers were dotted about the room.

As consciousness flooded back, she became aware of the throb in her left wrist, a dull ache in head and shoulder. Then suddenly she was filled with the pleasure of being warm in a clean, dry bed.

"Hello there," Toni was saying. "That was some long sleep. Feeling better?"

Alexandra nodded, then winced as lead weights shifted under her skull.

Toni's mouth grimaced in empathy. "We kept you awake for hours and hours. The doctor thought you might just have a concussion. Scott said you were conscious but not making much sense when he found you. Remember all that?"

"Mmmm." Vaguely she remembered Scott saying something about a rampaging river of mud sweeping by her just a few feet below the rock where she huddled. Anyway, she was safe and sound and blessedly dry, rescued once again by a strong man's arms, she thought disparagingly. Her head began to spin as she thought of Matt. She had rejected him because . . . oh yes, to be her own person, but— The room seemed to shift. . . . She couldn't cope with all that soul-searching now. She would concentrate on the simple facts of existence—a sore head, a throbbing wrist, a comfortable bed.

She sat up gingerly as Toni handed her a steaming cup of tea, aware of her dry mouth and the muddy taste on her tongue. The tea tasted clean and brisk. She could think about that.

"Matt's blaming himself for this," Toni said. "Every time someone leaves your room he pounces on them, demands to know how you're doing, if you've said anything, if you need anything. He's making himself a wreck. Jeez, he's making us all wrecks."

"Can't he come in and see for himself?" she asked, trying to keep her thoughts on the beauty of hot tea.

"No," Toni said slowly, "it seems like he can't."

"Why not?"

Toni shrugged and fixed Alexandra with a wide blue stare. "You tell me, kid."

"I suppose he's proud," Alexandra muttered. "He knows that it's hopeless between us."

Toni snorted. "That's the craziest thing I ever heard. You two are so obviously in love it's—absurd."

The room began to tilt and slide again and Alexandra clutched at the warm teacup. It was impossible to deal with Matt right now. She just couldn't.

When the bed steadied itself once more beneath her, recent memories began to reassemble in her head. A party. She had stepped in as hostess for some reason. Ah, yes. "Toni, you never did tell me why you outbid Matt for that horse. Want to explain that one?"

Toni flushed. "I guess I owe you one after drawing

you into all that unpleasantness with Matt." She moved away to the window and looked out before she continued. "I always had all this money at my disposal and nothing to do with it but have a ball." She looked back at the bed with a self-disparaging smile.

"Doesn't sound a bad way to go, does it? But I couldn't stand my face in the mirror—a taker, a coaster, easing through life on someone else's achievements. I wanted to do something I could point to as my very own thing. I had this yen to be proud of myself."

She came back to the bedside chair, hugging her elbows defensively. "I found some acreage not far from here that was ideal and I bought it and started planning my own horse farm. Matt didn't know for the longest time. He thought Sunstreak was some kind of pet and I was stabling her here till I built this home with a little paddock out back. Sunstreak wasn't any famous broodmare, she was my learning curve. I wanted to learn the business from scratch."

"Did Scott know?" Alexandra asked her.

"He found out. Even encouraged me. After a while, he was helping me, working with me all the way. *With* me," Toni repeated. "He didn't take over, like Matt would have. Scott's different. He respected me for what I could do. It became a partnership where I meant something. I guess that's how I fell in love with him."

"With Scott?" Alexandra felt weak with astonishment. She'd always thought of Scott as suffering from an unrequited passion for Toni.

"Look," Toni said quickly, "Matt and I had a thing once and—well—the guy's got a lot of sex appeal. I didn't notice what was happening, didn't

167

even guess my real feelings for Scott until I had to decide on that bid. Then it came up and slapped me in the face. I wanted that horse because I wanted my stable to be a fantastic success. I desperately wanted Scott to be proud of me and take me seriously. Oh, a lot of men are dazzled by a curvy body and with me being an heiress and all, but I wanted Scott to think more of me than that."

Alexandra smiled. "I don't think it would ever occur to Scott to go after your money."

"I know that. And that was the kicker. Don't you see? I couldn't offer him anything except my own self. Not a sex symbol and not an heiress—but a real person."

"So," Alexandra said, wriggling about to find a more comfortable position against the pillows. She was beginning to feel better. "Now you have the horse. Do you have Scott too?"

"Yes and no." Toni fell down onto the chair again, and when she continued, her voice sounded tearful. "One of the things I love most about Scott is that he's loving and loyal and forgiving." She frowned. "It's also what puts the wrench in the works right now. He won't leave Matt. He says Matt's in a bad way. He has this crazy 'I'm my brother's keeper' notion. He swears that if he walks out on him now, Matt might do himself in with drink or fast cars or fast women. He insists Matt needs someone to stand by him and see him past this phase he's going through."

Alexandra blinked. "Matt's his best friend, I realize that. But you're the biggest thing in his life, Toni. I don't get it. Why can't he have both?"

"Because Matt despises me for what I did and Scott doesn't want to rock his boat right now."

"Despises you? No, Toni. That doesn't make any sense. He's very fond of you. He'll get over—"

"You're wrong. He won't have me in his house. The only reason I'm here right now is—" Toni stood up abruptly, panic and misery in her eyes.

Alexandra breathed in some of that nameless fear. "Why are you here, then. What is it?"

"They thought I should be the one to tell you— another woman. Men are such cowards. And I said I would," Toni murmured gently, and Alexandra, sensing the tone of an unwilling bearer of bad news, felt sore muscles tighten under her skin.

"You need to leave and go home as soon as you can. The doctor said tomorrow would be all right, under the circumstances."

Toni was crying freely now, although Alexandra could see she was trying to be strong, trying to prepare her for something she didn't quite have the nerve to say. She reached for Toni's hand and held it firmly. "What circumstances? Just say it, Toni."

"It's your father, Alexandra. He had a fatal heart attack. He died last night." She bent down and threw her arms around Alexandra.

Alexandra found herself staring past Toni's shoulder at white roses, crisp rust chrysanthemums . . . she could think only of funeral wreaths.

"I'm going to travel with you," Toni whispered. "Make sure you're okay."

She found she could only nod in gratitude. She was deathly tired. Numb.

Later that afternoon, Toni returned with the prescription the doctor had written. "It's for the pain. So you can sleep. You got a lot of bruises and a wrenched muscle and a sprained wrist. Nothing major, but you need your strength back quickly."

Alexandra shook her head at the pills but took the water. "I don't want to block out my feelings with pain-killers, Toni. I'm alive and it hurts, but I need to feel it." The strange feelings in her head had sunk lower, settling over her heart with a dull heaviness. "Where's Matt now?" she asked suddenly.

Toni scraped her sandal toe along the carpet in an evasive movement. "Well, he's . . . uh . . ."

"For heaven's sake!" she snapped, feeling her nerves strained thin. "What is this? I fell down. Twisted a wrist and bumped my head. I didn't lose my wits, for God's sake. My father's death is a shock . . . an aching loss. And I feel rotten, okay? But I'm handling it. I don't need anyone to run interference for me. If there's going to be a scene with Matt, if he's fuming or feeling sorry for himself, I can take care of that, too." She broke off as a cold finger of fear touched the back of her neck. "Toni, he didn't try to—he didn't do anything wild? He is all right, isn't he?"

"He's downstairs in his office," Toni said. "Physically he's fine."

The cold finger lifted. "I'm sorry I snapped at you," she said, reaching out her hand. Toni gave it a quick squeeze.

Alexandra struggled to her feet and slipped into her robe, looking around for some slippers. "I'm going down."

"Jason's with him," Toni added quietly.

"Jason? Then why hasn't he—" But she really didn't need to ask why he hadn't come to see her. She knew that Fortune's Lad was more on his mind than she was.

A sharp tremor of resentment ran through her. Then she smiled to herself. She had no right to object. It really didn't matter anymore. She could never marry Jason. His engagement ring was still on her finger. Another piece of unfinished business— but not at this moment, not in front of Matt. The stiff, awkward scene fizzed through her head . . . her blurting it out, giving him back the ring. Not that she cared about the awkwardness. For her it would be a welcome relief. But for Jason's sake, she would spare him the scene until they were back in Kentucky. It would be easier for him to accept on his own turf.

It was just another burden she would have to carry a day or two longer. As she went downstairs, she was careful to hold herself straight, in spite of the wrenching feeling that with every step she was erasing another little piece of her life.

Jason was standing beside a trophy case and Matt was at the bar. They each held a highball glass, and they both stared at her as she entered the room like a frozen tableau.

"Good afternoon, gentlemen," she said, closing the door behind her. "Can I assume you've finished transacting business, Jason? Or am I intruding?" She swept her eyes over Matt, then looked away. She couldn't look at him without remembering what it was like to be in his arms again.

"I'm glad you're all right, Ali," Matt said quietly. He set down his glass and moved toward her. "I was worried about you."

"Thanks. I think I'll live." The way he was looking at her touched her heart.

"Alexandra, you shouldn't be down here. You should be resting." Jason grasped her upper arms gingerly, as if she might break, and laid his lips lightly on her forehead. "Foolish to take a walk at that time of night."

"Don't overexert yourself, Jason," she said, not responding to the kiss. "There's no need to play the concerned suitor. You knew where you could find me. If you were worried, you could have bounded up those stairs without a moment's hesitation. Before your horse business."

Jason's color rose, lobster pink.

She turned to Matt and saw his face was set in that stonewall expression he had brought to a fine art. "Toni's told me," she said. "It's odd how it took a comparative stranger to break the bad news. Jason was too busy with Fortune's Lad and you, Matt . . . Are you going to make it a trademark of yours? Running out on unpleasantness?"

She noticed a shadow of confusion in the expressions of both men now. She couldn't blame them. She herself couldn't account for why she was acting this way. Was the real Alexandra a pure shrew? Well, it was vicious, but it was the truth. And she was concentrating on holding herself together right now. She felt as if circumstances were testing her bid for independence from both of them.

"I'm very sorry about your father," Matt said.

"Thank you."

"Whatever I can do, Alexandra, you know I'm here." Jason stepped closer to her, recovering his gallantry. "Don't worry about a thing."

"Thank you, Jason." She glanced at Matt. "I guess there's no need for Toni to make that dreary trip home with me now. Jason will be flying back, and I am ambulatory, as you can see. I don't want to bother Toni now I have a traveling companion to satisfy the good doctor."

Jason colored violently again and said nothing. She waited, assuming he'd insist on flying back with her under the circumstances. Aside from the fact that she had flown to California with him, that he still considered them engaged, above all things, he was a Randolph. The Randolphs and O'Neills went back three generations. There was no question but that he would attend her father's funeral.

"Uh, Alex . . ." Jason cleared his throat. "I can't actually go back with you. It's not possible for me to leave tomorrow. I'm so sorry."

"I see." She gave him a curt nod.

"No, please, Alex. I really can't go. There're some crucial business matters that absolutely can't wait." He looked quickly at Matt, a glint of dark anger in his gray eyes.

"It's perfectly all right. It's just that I thought you were my father's friend."

"Fortune's Lad!" Jason blurted out in defense, as if that name could excuse everything.

"Well, of course," she said coolly. "That explains everything." She glanced at Matt.

Matt shrugged. "The decision is Jason's entirely," he put in.

"Alex, be reasonable," Jason blustered. "This is supremely important to me. To us. To our future."

"I can see how important it is, Jason. There's no need to elaborate." She could hardly wait to get out of the room, but at the door she paused.

"You must have had a very successful trip to Chicago, Jason." She saw him take a long swallow of bourbon before she closed the door.

She locked her door that night, and although Jason came and pleaded with her she would not let him in.

"Please Alex," he begged, "let me explain. I must talk to you. I can't let you go on thinking for another minute—"

"Go away, Jason," she ordered through the closed door. "There's nothing to explain."

She crept back into the bed, pulling the covers over her head while he stood at the door, knocking interminably, calling out. But there was such rancor lurking in her throat, she did not trust herself to speak another word. "We're through, Jason. Once and for all, we're through," she whispered to herself under the sheets. But she couldn't summon the strength to face the endless arguments that would follow if she said those words aloud.

At last he gave up, leaving her to a restless, dream-ridden sleep that lasted until a few minutes before dawn.

A quiet strength crept into her as she sat by the window and watched the sunrise cast a soft apricot glow over the hills. All the arrangements for her flight had been made yesterday evening. She had been booked out of Los Angeles so that she wouldn't have to leave the ranch until one in the afternoon and could rest up in the morning.

She stared at the first sunbeam to pierce the window and splash the gray carpet. Arrangements . . . Her life was still arranged so neatly for her, she thought. She stood up, gave one parting glance at the dewy newness of the morning and smiled sadly. It was time she started arranging her own life.

Scott's face looked remarkably chipper and alive as he drove her into San Diego. It was only nine o'clock when they arrived at the airport, ample time for United's nine-forty-five flight.

The last-minute rerouting meant she would have

to switch planes in Chicago and kill two hours, but Alexandra's way had its own advantages. She wanted to see Scott before she left, and the twenty-minute drive into San Diego would not eat into his day the way taking her into Los Angeles would have done. Even better, with no evasive tactics she was able to leave the rancho early enough to avoid seeing Jason and Matt. They would both assume she had taken her medication and would sleep at least until nine, fragile flower that she was. Most important of all, the change in schedule was her own arrangement, taking no more than ten minutes and a couple of phone calls to complete. From now on, she was taking life into her own hands.

Scott glanced at her, frowning as they waited at the departure gate. "Toni will worry about you. She packed last night, and when she finds you've flown the coop already, she'll wonder why I didn't tell her you'd changed the flight."

"It's high time I flew the coop," she said fervently. "Tell her the truth, Scott. I made you promise not to let her know because I don't need a nursemaid. Tell her I need to start doing things for myself. She'll understand. This is a trip I have to make alone." She extended her hand to Scott, then gave him a hug instead. "I probably owe you my life. What can I say besides thank you?"

Scott scratched his head. "Don't say anything, Alexandra. If it wasn't for my crackbrained scheme to get you two back together, you would never have been caught in that flash flood."

"You still saved my life." She grinned. "You meant well, anyway. . . . Scott, I'm grateful for the way you care so much about Matt."

He nudged her gently toward the open gate as the

departing passengers started to stream out to the jetway. She joined the moving line, then turned for a moment.

"What's going to happen to him, Scott?"

"I don't know." His farewell smile began to fade. "He's still got me, and sooner or later I guess he'll get back on an even keel." His face brightened again as he raised his hand in farewell.

Chapter Seven

John Harvey Soames was wearing a black tie. Under the silver thatch, his fleshy but handsome face wore the look of a pallbearer, but he managed a welcoming smile. "Ah, my dear, dear Alexandra," he said, wagging her hand up and down. "What a loss! I am so sorry. My profound condolences." With a gentle hand on her shoulder, he guided her past the receptionist's desk and into the inner sanctum of his law office.

As they took their respective seats, his great antebellum desk stretching between them, he shook his leonine head dolefully. "Thomas O'Neill was truly a great Kentuckian."

"Thank you," Alexandra said, admiring his polish and realizing suddenly that that's all it was, a hundred and ninety pounds' worth of cultivated Kentucky charm. You could sift through it forever without coming across an ounce of sincerity. Soames's rhetorical style was no more than a knee-jerk reflex left over from six unsuccessful campaigns for a seat in the state assembly. She could never quite understand how he had lost; he was so good at this kind of thing. As a young girl, she had thought of him as Santa Claus without a beard.

"Both Mrs. Soames and I will attend the funeral of course." He folded his hands, laying them piously on the surface of the desk.

"My father was cremated yesterday, Mr. Soames."

"Cremated?" The gray winged brows shot up, then lowered in disapproving surprise.

"My father's housekeeper attended the service. Mrs. Farley served him almost thirty years. She was like family. There were just the two of us."

"Yes, well—I see. But your father was an important Kentucky son. He had many, many friends who would have wanted to make their last farewells to such a—"

"Mr. Soames, please. I had no intention of offending anyone, but I had my reasons. . . ." She saw that he expected to hear them. "Which are personal," she added firmly.

"Yes, of course." The merest suggestion of a pout sculpted his lips for a moment, like a child learning of a party to which he was not invited. "We shall move along then with your future." He turned his attention to a folder before him, removing a document, studying it briefly, then handing it to her.

As she read the Last Will and Testament, Soames kept up a running commentary.

"Of course, Thomas left everything to you."

Alexandra cringed. "Left everything . . . yes."

"You'll be quite set, just as he would have wanted. The stables, the house, all the land holdings, stocks and so forth. It's all yours now, my dear."

Alexandra's heart began to sink. "This is it, then, Mr. Soames? Do I need to sign anything?"

"We'll take care of changing title. You'll need to be in touch with the bank, of course. They'll probably contact you, but you can leave all the rest to me. Mere technicalities; that's what I'm here for, my dear."

"And your fee, Mr. Soames?"

He smiled benevolently. "Don't worry your pretty head about that. There's no rush. I'll have Mirabelle get a statement out to you middle of next month. Usually," he said as he walked her to the door, "settlements become quite a hassle where large estates are concerned—contesting heirs, disappointments—but in your case, it's a comfort to me to know you're well provided for. And of course, you'll have the Randolphs to stand by you in your bereavement. Fine, fine family. A splendid match. It's men like Jason Randolph who have made Kentucky the greatest state in the South."

She left quickly, before the trickle of campaign rhetoric became a deluge.

She turned Thomas O'Neill's dark blue Cadillac toward the downtown business district. There were a dozen errands to run, and before she got back to Laurelwood it was dusk.

Mrs. Farley had gone to live with her daughter, leaving without mentioning that she was owed three months' wages. It was the daughter who'd finally called that morning, faltering, apologetic. Alexandra's embarrassment was much worse. Mrs. Farley had kept house at Laurelwood half her life, and now she had no pension, no bonus, not even her current wages. It would be made good as soon as she could manage it, Alexandra had pledged, wondering how long that would be.

Coming home to an empty house was a new sensation, and she regretted she had not left a light on. It was dark and achingly hollow in the front hall, and for the first time she felt the full force of her loss. Deliberately pressing herself through the technicalities of death, she had managed to postpone its meaning. Suddenly she was stricken with it—never to hear that booming voice issuing commands again, no more hearty laughter and Irish jokes and hugs and kisses. Childhood memories overtook her. When the phone rang, it was a few moments before she realized her father could not answer it, nor Mrs. Farley.

By the time she reached the study desk, the phone had stopped ringing. She turned on the desk lamp to dispel the gloom and stepped on some paper. It was a letter, scuffed from something heavier than her own shoe. Mrs. Farley had found Alexandra's father here in the study, collapsed on the floor beside his desk. With a shock, she realized he had probably been holding this letter when he was struck down.

The last thing he'd touched. She smoothed out the creases tenderly, wishing she could have held him one last time. Something irrational made her press her palm to the sheet, as if she could capture some of the warmth of his hand. Absently, she stared at the typed heading of the letter, then stiffened as the words sank in. *Order of Foreclosure.*

She skimmed through the two pages, then sank down into her father's chair. Poor, proud, extravagant Thomas O'Neill. There was no doubt in her now that this bald message had been the final blow.

Laurelwood was his heritage, his life. And with a single sheet of paper from the bank it was gone.

When the telephone rang again, she picked it up like an automaton.

"Alexandra? It's Scott here."

"Oh, yes." She found it difficult to concentrate with the letter staring up at her.

"I'm relieved I got you at last. We've been worried about you. I've been calling for the past three days. Are you okay?"

She pulled her eyes away from the letter. "I'm fine, Scott. And I'm sorry you were worried. There was a lot to do in a short time. The funeral arrangements and so forth. I—I should have let you know I arrived safely but I've been so busy."

Scott paused at the other end of the line. "Oh. The funeral's over then? Toni and I would have sent flowers."

He made no mention of Matt. It was the first time she'd thought of him for several days, and now, as she did, she found the pain intolerable. Her head dipped down reflexively and a drop of liquid splashed onto the sheet in front of her before she realized she was weeping. "How's Matt?" she asked, because somehow she had to say his name.

"I've left him," Scott said. "Toni and I are starting a stud farm. We're getting married."

"Oh Scott, I'm so happy for you," she said, and meant it. It was like a ray of light in the relentless gloom, just to be reminded that some things had a way of working out happily for two people. "Hang on to that girl, Scott. Your loyalty to Matt was admirable, but sooner or later I knew you'd see that you can't mortgage personal happiness for the sake of friendship."

"Well, it was tough, but I made the break. No

more running my life according to the gospel of Saint Matthew," Scott said quickly.

The room was getting blurred and she had to stop for a moment and dash the tears away with the heel of her hand. "Who's taking your place, Scott?"

There was a long silence before Scott said, "No one. There's been quite an upheaval here. Matt's selling Vista—he's put it all in a broker's hands. In the interim, the head groom's taking care of the ponies. Matt's gone."

"Gone where?"

Scott sighed. "There are quite a few of us wondering about that. He's dropped out of sight. I think he's left the state, maybe the country, for all I know."

He was running again. Alexandra felt a spunky little nerve streak along her backbone. "He'll be all right, Scott. Hang on to Toni and don't worry about him. Matt always lands on his feet somehow. It's the people around him who get hurt."

"Yeah, sure. I wasn't planning to lose any more sleep over it." His voice sounded unconvinced.

"Give my love to Toni, and—uh, if you should hear from Matt, keep me posted?"

"Sure. I would have done that anyway, but I'm glad you asked. Real glad."

He was a perfectly nice, ordinary man, Alexandra told herself, wondering if something was happening to her perception of life in general. The gentle, genial Soames of her childhood—what had happened to her yesterday that he should suddenly seem like the caricature of some political cartoonist?

And now it was happening to her again with Birkhoven. The banker had been polite to her, cordial. But all she could think was that he had just stepped out of the pages of a dress-for-success manual. Dark pinstriped suit, white shirt and a muted silk tie with the barest hint of red to add life to an otherwise colorless presence.

Lloyd Birkhoven's flat gray eyes ran back and forth over the tabulations typed on the sheet his secretary had just handed to him. "This has been going on a long time, Miss O'Neill. Your father simply chose to ignore the other preliminary reports about his holdings, perhaps due to his failing health." He shrugged. "It's unfortunate."

"My father ignored nothing, Mr. Birkhoven," Alexandra flared. Thomas O'Neill was only fifty-eight. It was intolerable, this cold-blooded, insulting implication that her father was a decrepit incompetent in his dotage. "He was perfectly aware of the state of his finances." *He died of the knowledge,* she thought.

"He gave me little indication of how he intended to make good the default." The gray eyes were staring blandly at her, unapologetic.

Alexandra made an effort to drop her hostility. It wouldn't get her anywhere. She tried to smile as she asked, "Exactly how much time could I have to make good?"

Birkhoven flipped over the pages he was holding. The last page looked like a carbon copy of the foreclosure notice she had read. "Three weeks from yesterday—it's all here. You did read the notice?"

"Of course." Alexandra sat finishing-school straight, her feet crossed at the ankles, and glanced slowly and deliberately at the portraits of the bank's founder and its first board of directors hanging prominently on the pale ivory wall to her left.

"Perhaps you're not aware, but the O'Neills have been depositors and patrons of this bank since it opened its doors. I am sure a little extra consideration is warranted in a case like this. Surely a reasonable extension could be negotiated?"

Birkhoven followed her glance, then threw the sheaf of papers down on his glass-topped desk. "I appreciate the influence your family has had in the growth of this town. In fact I've used it successfully with the board in the past. The fact is, I've carried those extensions to the limit already. But the bottom line remains. With all the good will in the world, we're not in the banking business to lose money."

Alexandra's hope rose and sank as he spoke. After a moment, she nodded and rose to leave, too depressed to say a word.

"Miss O'Neill!" Birkhoven sprang up from his desk. "I hope you'll forgive me, but it is common knowledge in the banking community, especially since the Randolph family is very much a part of it . . . Perhaps, if the estate is of paramount importance to you . . . well, it would be the obvious place for you to seek a solution."

"The Randolphs have nothing to do with this situation," Alexandra said flatly.

There was a touch of patronizing chauvinism in his smile. "Come now, Miss O'Neill. Your independence is very commendable, but let's face hard facts. You are about to become a Randolph, and that puts a very different complexion on things. It's the main reason your father was able to persuade us to go along with him as far as we have. There was the assumption that when you two tie the knot—"

"No one has the right to assume anything about my personal future," she snapped furiously.

"No, of course not. But considering your name,

the integrity of your family—I naturally believed you would uphold your moral obligations in this matter."

Ice crept into her voice. "I don't believe this institution carries a trust deed on my soul, Mr. Birkhoven."

"There's no need for sarcasm, Miss O'Neill," he said reproachfully. "It was not an unreasonable assumption under the circumstances. Your father—"

"My father is no longer here to honor his commitments. My moral obligations, Mr. Birkhoven, are strictly my own business."

The banker's patience was exhausted. "It's the money or the property. On the fifteenth of next month, and not one day more. I am responsible to my board and I cannot afford to have the mark of such a lengthy default against my name. In view of the offer we have, we've been more than generous in our extensions."

He turned and took an eight-by-ten photograph from his out-tray. "Here," he said, offering it to her.

It was a reduction of an artist's rendering showing a boxlike housing development. Alexandra glanced at it momentarily but did not take it from his hand.

"Sunrise Development is ready to take Laurelwood off our hands the day we foreclose. We've already worked out the preliminaries on the construction loan for the first phase. The board of supervisors is looking very favorably on the subdivision plan. As soon as it's rezoned, they plan to have three hundred home-size lots as the rendering suggests. The bank is even considering a joint venture with Sunrise. In view of all this, you should be more than grateful for that last extension. If the offer had been brought to us a day or two earlier you wouldn't have the next three weeks. I explained all this to your father."

"The day he died, Mr. Birkhoven? By any chance was the subdivision the last topic you discussed with him?"

Birkhoven thought for a moment. "Perhaps it was. I can't quite recall." He looked uncomfortable, and she was glad.

"Well, recall this—for the next three weeks, I have title to Laurelwood. During that period it is my home, and I have no intention of selling to any developer. That's one thing you can be sure that I have agreed upon with my father. It's one moral obligation I intend to honor."

It was a long shot, and that was an understatement, she thought as she loaded the sheet of plywood into the trunk of the car, laying it carefully on top of the art supplies. But there was something about banker Birkhoven that brought out the fighting Irish in her, full force. That ghastly Sunrise rendering was the final red flag that made her grit her teeth and stubbornly refuse to think about the odds against her. *Three weeks and thirty-five thousand dollars and I'll be able to thumb my nose at those ticky-tack boxes.*

After she drove onto the grounds, she closed the gate and placed a padlock on it. Even before she hauled her supplies into the house, she went to the study and took the phone off the hook.

Mrs. Farley had left the house reasonably neat, but she hadn't been able to bring herself to touch the study. Alexandra looked around at the chaos. There was no time to indulge in a thorough cleaning. She merely cleared off the desk, stacking all the folders and knickknacks on the floor by the wall of bookshelves.

Within thirty minutes, the study was a functional

simulation of an artist's studio. The desk had acquired a drawing board at the forty-five-degree angle she preferred. Three standing lamps lit the work area. Old jeans and a work shirt had replaced the linen pantsuit she'd worn to the bank, and a full pot of coffee stood keeping warm on the kitchen stove.

Alexandra unwrapped the package containing a dozen large sketch pads and opened the box of charcoal. Strong men seemed to sap her energies, undermine her sense of direction. For five months she had stewed and wrung her hands and let her mind stagnate, she thought disgustedly. It was time to get back to work. There were no more distractions, and she could begin to feel the creative juices rising. She had five months of idleness to make up for, but perhaps they weren't a total loss. She took up the first stick of charcoal with the half-formed lines pouring out from somewhere behind her eyes. Subconsciously she'd been stashing away ideas for months.

The real Alexandra O'Neill is about to start earning her keep, she thought, as she made the first bold line on the white sheet.

Alexandra returned from the post office ready to collapse. She had worked straight through for forty-eight hours, stopping only to make fresh pots of coffee. Resting for a moment in an easy chair, one dark blue-jeaned leg slung over the armrest, she realized she hadn't even stopped to shower and change before rushing the fruits of her labors into the mail. "How's that for speed, not to mention excellence, Signor Conti, you old Simon Legree?" she whispered to herself, flexing her aching neck and shoulders. An entire season's work in forty-eight hours! She grinned; it was altogether amazing what a fragile Kentucky magnolia blossom could do once the men stopped falling over each other to help and protect her.

They were *good* designs, every one of them—she could feel it in her bones. She dragged herself up and switched off the lamps. She was tired. Perhaps they weren't *that* good. Perhaps she was too punchy from caffeine and exhaustion to have any critical judgment whatsoever. Well, she'd know soon enough, she told herself, reaching for the phone. The postal clerk had guaranteed that Express Mail would reach Los Angeles the following day, and Rome the day after that.

"Alessandra, carissima." Fabio's voice sounded hurt. "You disappoint me. I thought maybe you change your mind? Come back to us in Rome?"

She switched to Italian, knowing that Fabio was crisper, more businesslike in his native language.

"I will look," he said cautiously. "Of course, for a good designer I always have time to look. It costs me nothing. So you'll call me back, *si? Va bene."*

Va bene. She would give him his money's worth. He knew it.

Carla was much more encouraging. "Right on, babe! If it's anything near as good as the wardrobe you had in St. Moritz a couple of years back . . . yeah! The American market would go for the European influence in ski wear. I'll call you as soon as I've looked them over. I'll get 'em tomorrow, you said?"

A blue haze was settling on the grass. As she peered from her open bedroom window, even the trees seemed to have taken on that blue cast in the twilight. There was a haunting beauty about Laurelwood, even in its sad state of neglect. She should try to sleep, but it was hopeless; she was too hyped up from the hours of exertion and pints of strong coffee.

As she leaned against the window, the smell of late fall bathed her, and shadows shifted under the changing light, playing tricks with her tired eyes. For a moment, she could see Matt moving slowly away from the magnolia tree at the far end of the overgrown lawns. The apparition appeared again, fading in and out of the rising mist. There was a befuddled moment when the illusion was caught in stillness, as if it were quietly staring up at the house.

But Matt was gone, just as permanently as her father was gone. She shook her head to clear it. No more self-pity; time heals all. Just a cliché, but it was true all the same. She rubbed her eyes. *You're in a bad way, girl—overstimulated, undernourished and delirious from lack of sleep.* She headed down the stairs to make a sandwich and clean up the litter of the last two days. That was one way to work out all the caffeine. Then she'd take a long hot shower and have a very long sleep.

Sixteen hours later, after fixing and eating a hearty breakfast, Alexandra was back at the drawing board. A pile of discarded sheets lay on the carpet, and a growing stack of finished sketches of swimwear and cover-ups lay on the filing cabinet, when she broke off reluctantly to answer the insistent pounding at the front door.

She had deliberately padlocked the gate to avoid intrusions, and she was furious when Jason entered the hall. He looked around with a slightly harried air, the collar of his blue shirt askew, his knit tie crooked and a rip on one shoulder of his jacket.

"I would have come to the funeral, Alex, but I hear there wasn't one. It's made us all look very

189

shabby. I suppose you were too upset to think clearly and do the right thing."

Her mind was still on her design—a particular curve like a swallow's wing. If she could make it work for the one-piece swimsuit and echo the curve in the cover-up, it would be the eye-popper for the whole line. But it wasn't quite coming together. The halter line didn't do it, and she couldn't see it as strapless—that was too limited a market. Damn Jason!

"I did what I thought was best at the time," she said offhandedly, with a distracted pounce at the lock of hair that had fallen over her eyes. "I'm sorry if it didn't suit you. I was somewhat in shock. It's not as if my father was an old man. I couldn't have anticipated anything like this happening."

"I realize you're still upset with me, Alex." Jason touched her arm in a conciliatory movement.

Alexandra turned away and started back for the study. "Let's not discuss it now—I don't have time."

"For heaven's sake, we've got to. What do you mean, you don't have time?" His voice followed her back to the study.

"What's this?" he said, as she stooped down for an armful of trash and stuffed it into the wastebasket.

He was riffling through the stack of finished tempera designs that lay on the filing cabinet. He stopped, turned to the drawing board and began to shake his head.

"Alex, Alex! You're as out of touch with real life as your father was. You've shut out the world and lost yourself in this—this fantasy life. For Thomas it was horses, for you it's these doll clothes. And all around you . . ." His arm gestured at the room, suggesting the house and grounds beyond it. "It's a nightmare! D'you realize I had to climb over the gate to get in here? And your phone's already been—" He broke off, reached for the receiver and slammed it down into the cradle. "You paint pretty pictures while Rome burns?"

"Those pretty pictures, as you call them, are intended to put out the fire, Jason." She tried to be patient. Creative ideas flew out of the window when she got angry; she'd learned that long ago. "I haven't shut out the world by any means. As a matter of fact, I have plans for making Laurelwood the center of a whole new world."

He laughed gently. "Okay, I get it. This is your career. You're very depressed and you're throwing yourself into your work to cope with it. That's all very well, but these papers mean that you're going to be out on your pretty little rump in a couple of weeks." He withdrew a folded sheaf of bank documents from his jacket pocket and waved them in front of her, demanding attention.

Alexandra slammed her fist on the desk. "Birkhoven gave you that? He had no right whatsoever to discuss my financial affairs with you." She glanced down at the drawing board, the elusive solution to the design almost formed before her eyes. She must get him out of here before it vanished.

"He had every right. You know very well I'd never allow a hint of scandal—"

"Jason, *please*, not now. I don't want to talk now." She clapped her hands over her ears.

"I will not have a slur on my wife's family name," he said, pulling her hands away from her ears. "And you will listen to me, young lady."

"Then you needn't be concerned," she shouted. "I am not going to marry you."

He faltered, but only for a moment before he gave

a placating smile. "All right, Alex. I'm sorry about putting down your work. I'm sorry. There! There's no cause to go off the deep end just because I insist on doing what's right. My God, anyone would think— Now let's forget your tantrum. I realize you're half Irish, and I'm prepared to live with your artistic temperament, but we really have to resolve this here and now."

"I don't love you Jason."

His expression changed, his body seemed to collapse into a defeated droop and his face paled. She was no longer angry, but simply wretched. She'd wanted to postpone this inevitable scene until she could handle it in a civilized way. She hated the blunt brutality of what she'd just done, the betrayed expression distorting the muscles of his face as he tried to cope with it.

Jason slipped his hands into his pants pockets and turned to stare out of the window behind the desk. "It's because of Farraday, isn't it?" he said quietly.

"No, it's because of me, Jason. Me." A wave of sharp regret swept over her. Suddenly she felt utterly lacking in grace. Why had she postponed telling him for days, and why did she have to botch it so badly?

"I know you've never felt the way I feel, Alex. I've always known that. But it was only because you'd never let go of him."

She touched him lightly on the shoulder. "I thought that too, Jason, for a long time. But I've let go now. I'm free of all the strings. This is me finally, making up my own mind. I'm telling you what's true for me, not for you or for my father or Matt or Birkhoven. For me. This is my work, Jason. And this is my home."

"You're going to lose it," he said in a flat voice.

"I'm going to save it if I can," she whispered.

He turned from the window, squaring his shoulders and hardening his face with derision. "Thirty-five thousand dollars? You think you can produce cold cash in two weeks with these? You're a fool!"

She walked to the door and held it open, an unmistakable gesture that she wanted him gone. "I don't need this. Just go. Please."

"Marry me." He came to her, blocking the doorway. "It's the only way out of this mess. Don't you see that? Your father died for this place and you're going to throw it away, all for the sake of some stupid, prideful notion about making your own living. Don't you know that Laurelwood meant more to him than anything in the world? Isn't it worth facing up to the truth in order to save it?"

He caught her in his arms and kissed her roughly. "Marry me next week Alex, and I swear to you I'll have those debts made in twenty-four hours. You'll be able to spend all you want, fixing this place up the way he would have wanted it to be."

The push to wrench herself free of him was fierce, but her voice stayed gentle. "I'm sorry, Jason. I can't do that. *Won't* do that."

A dull red color returned to his face and he stiffened with an ominous, quiet fury. "If you don't, I promise that I'll have every magnolia, every blade of grass, every flower bed on this land razed to the ground by bulldozers and hundreds of little houses dotting every square inch. I'll see to it personally. The Randolphs own sixty-five percent of Sunrise Development."

As all her body's warmth deserted her, she leaned against the doorjamb and watched Jason's expression soften to regret, then shame.

"Oh God, Alex, I'm sorry. I just want you so.

I'm planning on it. Don't make me say these things. . . ."

"Would you do more than say them? Would you really do that to Laurelwood, just to get your own way?"

Staring at her defiantly, he didn't answer.

"Why not?" she answered for him. "Just as you went to great lengths to get Fortune's Lad. You did get it, I suppose?"

He nodded.

"Then you must have dug up something marvelously vicious to twist Matt's arm. Congratulations."

Vaguely she expected him to launch into a prize attack on Matt's character, but he only slid the bank papers back into his breast pocket and sighed. The mention of Fortune's Lad seemed to restore his composure. "You're just tired and overwrought, darling. It's understandable, but it'll pass. I don't expect you to think clearly right now, but have a good night's sleep and you'll see things in a different light in the morning. I'll be home all day tomorrow. Come over when you've gotten your head together."

Alexandra's mind flew back to her work the minute Jason was gone. Instead of casting her down, his threats seemed to add fuel to her creative energy. Three more rough sketches and she finally had the graceful arc she'd been searching for. She switched pads and began to draw the finished sketch, her mind coasting now the idea was complete. She remembered suddenly that her phone had been off the hook ever since she'd started working until a few minutes ago. Perhaps Carla had been trying to call. Surely she'd received her mail by now.

It was nearly four P.M. in California. "Did you get them?" she asked, when Carla came to the phone.

The pause was too long, much too long. She could feel her confidence ebbing away and a devastating fatigue sapping her bones. "Carla? Are you still there?"

"I don't know how to put this without sounding . . . Ah, what the hell, Alex. They're inspired."

Elation began to surge through her, and she was aware of her thudding heartbeat as the receiver almost slipped from her clammy hand. She clamped it to her shoulder for a moment while she wiped the perspiration from her palm. "Carla, this isn't too cool, but I need some cash. Fast."

"I can give you ten thousand dollars up front against ten percent of sales once we go into production."

"How soon can I get the advance?"

"Like—when the bank opens tomorrow."

Chapter Eight

Hope, revitalizing and nourishing as a high-protein meal, refreshed every muscle and lifted her spirits. It carried her though a dozen more completed sketches; it colored her dreams golden that night and sent her sketching contentedly through another fiercely productive day.

Carla had wired the money that morning and Alexandra's bank account fattened. Ten thousand dollars wouldn't bail her out, but it was a start—a sure sign that she could reasonably expect to dig herself out of her hole. And she had yet to hear from Fabio.

She caught a brief snatch of sleep, then she called him. It was five A.M. in Kentucky, but late morning in Rome. Fabio would be working on his second cup of espresso as he finished up dealing with the morning's mail. He'd be a harder sell than Carla; he was a knuckle-buster when it came to making a lira. But she was good. Inspired, Carla had said.

Yes, he liked them. But he was no soft touch. A firm commitment was something else. She kept him on the line, pressing him, wearing him down.

"You know I cannot decide to launch a new line myself, *cara.*"

Like hell you can't, she thought, but heard the indecision in his voice that meant she was wearing him down and waited, her hand tightening on the receiver.

"I must show them to Guido. And as for money, *bella mia*—you know those things are left to the accountant. . . ."

It was coming, she felt it.

"But since the season is only a few weeks off now, and you say you must have a firm answer, perhaps we can arrange a little commitment of our good faith."

It had taken her thirty minutes. Her mind was spinning from the gyrations of Italian wheeling and dealing by the time she hung up. She was only five thousand dollars richer—an option, but with more money to come if they agreed to take the whole line. For that, she would have to agree to a lower percentage.

But at least that five thousand would be in the bank by tomorrow; Fabio had agreed to wire it. Perhaps she could borrow against future income or buy a few more precious weeks from the bank with half the cash in hand.

Birkhoven personally watched her endorse the drafts when the bank opened the following day. But he was adamant. She couldn't borrow against promises, and fifteen thousand dollars was not thirty.

"This doesn't alter the terms of foreclosure, Miss O'Neill. Payment must be made in full."

As she drove away from the bank, the hope that had buoyed her for two days began to leak away, leaving a dull headache in its wake. At least, she thought as she pulled up to the post office, she would take care of some of the lesser debts. After mailing a check to Mrs. Farley, she headed for Prentice Mortuary.

"Here's payment in full for my father's burial expenses," she said, handing a check to the book-keeper.

The heavy woman in the tent dress frowned as she put on her glasses. "I don't find it in the receivables, Miss O'Neill. I seem to recall you paid it already." She bent down to a file drawer in her desk.

"No," Alexandra said. "I can assure you it's still outstanding—"

"Yes, here it is. Paid in full." She drew out a ledger and placed it open on the desk, her forefinger trailing down a line of neatly penned columns. "Yes, I remember now. Mr. Prentice handed it to me himself. It was a cash payment and I entered it yesterday. Look."

Slightly bewildered, Alexandra headed for the phone company. She couldn't afford to have the phone cut off.

"You're up to date," the clerk at the window assured her testily, while she insisted he go through the files and verify it.

"My records show that my account was two statements behind," Alexandra insisted. "Check again, please."

"Who paid it?" she demanded at last, after the clerk finished a protracted phone call.

The man shrugged. "I assume you did."

"But I didn't!"

"It all goes through our central office in Lexington. If you didn't, someone did."

It was the same at the gas company, the power and light company—all her utility bills were current. Her slate was clean. A distinct uneasiness grew in her until it was a full blown fuming conviction. She nosed the Cadillac down the highway and headed for Windermere.

"What audacity!" she screamed at Jason. "How dare you interfere in my life!"

"I don't know what you're talking about," Jason said coldly.

"I don't want your money. I don't want the strings attached to it. You've just settled all my bills. Tell me how much this instant. I will not have myself indebted to you."

"I'm not that much of a fool," Jason said, his face darkening with anger. "If you insist on drowning—go ahead. I'm not going to stop it, and I promise you I haven't paid a nickel of your piddling utility bills or the funeral expenses."

Alexandra remembered the engagement ring nestling in its velvet-lined box in her purse. She drew it out and placed it on the hall table. "That belongs to you," she said softly. "I'm sorry, I should have returned it earlier."

Jason blinked and picked up the ring box. "I'm still a Randolph," he said gently. "You're still an O'Neill. Neighbors. You don't have to stand out in the hall just because we're no longer engaged."

He took her into the library and offered her sherry, his manner so polished that he made her feel almost boorish. She could not bring herself to refuse his civilized gesture.

"Jason," she said, staring into the amber liquid, "I

believe you if you say you haven't paid my bills. But somebody has. It's important to me to find out. Do you have a clue who it could be?"

Jason drained his glass and a look of impotent rage suddenly tightened his mouth. "Who do you think? He's come back, damn him to hell!"

Matt! Only Matt could wreak such swift havoc in his face, cause that startling contortion of the refined, intelligent features. Jason rose from his armchair without a word, taking the ring box from his shirt pocket and tossing it on the wine table. At the mahogany desk in the bay window he lifted the telephone and dialed.

"Randolph here. Has my horse been brought in yet? Yes, yes. I haven't forgotten the conditions. Tomorrow. I'll be there."

After he slammed down the phone, he stared morosely through the window, then turned and glanced absently at the bookshelves as if he were sifting through choices. When he looked at Alexandra again, his face had calmed. "Excuse me for a moment, Alex. I have something to show you."

He returned with a miniature antique chest in his hands and sat on the sofa beside her with the receptacle on his knees. Inside the chest, a costly collar of diamonds glinted softly on black velvet.

"They're worth a fortune, Alexandra. They've been in the family for over a hundred years. They could do more than rescue Laurelwood from foreclosure, they could restore it to its former glory." He picked up the small case on the wine table and held up the solitaire diamond of her engagement ring. "They go together Alex. If you'll wear this, it's all yours. You can do whatever you want with it— Laurelwood—start a fashion business— I won't stop you."

He took the elaborate diamond collar and dropped it in her lap. The weight of it was monstrously heavy on her thighs; for a panicky moment, she thought of leg irons on a slave.

"Maybe I've been unreasonable," Jason was saying, the words spilling out with a desperate, final-hour urgency. "It's been a bad year for you, I know. I won't insist you marry me next week—or even in December as we planned. We'll wait, Alex. Put this awful time behind us. I won't even insist we set a date right now. Just—just slip that ring on your finger again and I'll know," he added, twisting the knife, "that your father can rest easy in his grave."

She flinched as if he'd struck a nerve. All that she owed her father; that debt, that guilt, would weigh her down for the rest of her days if she couldn't save Laurelwood.

There was a tremor in her hands as she replaced the diamonds in their nest of velvet. "I meant what I said, Jason. I don't love you, I won't marry you and I can't tell you how sorry I am that I ever misled you. It wasn't deliberate."

His shoulders jerked in a tiny spasm and his hands curled into tight fists. A strange stiff expression froze his face, but he neither moved nor spoke as she said good-bye. She left him in the cool of the early evening, wondering at the sheen of sweat that coated his forehead. He wanted her as much as it was possible for a man to want, she thought. As much as he wanted Fortune's Lad. Poor Jason, how he hated to lose at anything.

As she drove away, she saw a young man in jeans striding across the paddock. He was lithe and tousled and work-hardened in a way that sent her thoughts flying back to Matt. Matt wanted to possess her too, but there were deep anguished feelings involved in that wanting, the kinds of feelings a mere piece of horseflesh could never inspire. A fierce streak of longing, physical and spiritual, raked her with an almost literal pain. The price of independence, she thought. She'd never dreamed it was so high.

The thought of Matt tracking down her debts and paying them filled her with a blend of heartache and rebellion. He was trying to control her life just as Jason had tried. She'd committed herself to independence. It was why she'd wrenched herself out of his arms that last time, against all the yearning of her heart. She wasn't going to let all that painful effort go to waste. She would not tolerate this meddling, but to cope with it would be hard. She wouldn't be strengthened by the single-mindedness that upheld her when she coped with Jason.

Matt was somewhere in the vicinity, obviously. She would simply have to track him down, reimburse him, and make it quite clear she was unwilling to accept his help in the future. It shouldn't take long to find him, she thought, heading for town. There were only three decent hotels.

There was no Farraday listed at any hotel. No guest by that name had registered within the past week. Alexandra returned to the car after she'd drawn the third blank and tapped her fingers nervously on the steering wheel. Perhaps he'd stayed in Lexington? No, it was too long a drive. It was infinitely more logical for him to— Suddenly she sat up straight.

A new thought occurred to her and a picture of his old home passed before her eyes. Could he be making some sentimental journey? She knew the tremendous hold his childhood home had on him. She thought of the similar tumbledown shack in

California. That miserable arrangement of rotting beams and floorboards had been enough to make him buy the vast expanse of Vista del Lago. Yes, she thought, as she drove back along the eight miles of highway that led to Windermere, there was some powerful symbolic attachment there for Matt.

It was still there, forlorn and forgotten in its overgrown weedpatch of land, even smaller than she remembered. But it was empty, no sign of any recent visitors. The door was gone, and through the warped, sagging doorframe she glimpsed the crumbling interior, decayed from time and neglect, abused by vandals. The screen door lay out front on what was left of the porch, so twisted and corroded that not even the meanest scavenger was tempted.

Moonlight filtered through the broken windows where cobwebs filled up the gaping spaces. An overturned table with only one leg lay discarded in one corner, and there was a rocking chair set on its side; she felt the need to right it. Once on its rockers, she saw it was beautifully made of hand-rubbed wood. Two rungs were missing from the backrest, but otherwise it was spared from the vandals.

She ran a finger along one arm and saw the soft gleam of the wood as her finger made a path in the dust. Matt had once told her about making a rocker for his mother. Suddenly, she wanted it, wanted to take it back to Laurelwood and clean it up carefully, repair the damage to the back. It was senseless, whimsical, but she found herself carrying it to the trunk of the car and balancing it precariously. It was a treasured possession once, she thought. She wanted to treasure it too.

The absurdity struck her when a lone car went by on the nearby lane, its headlights catching her red-handed as she tried to settle the chair more securely in the trunk. But the car went by without stopping, the driver apparently not seeing the act of burglary in progress, or not caring.

Once she was home with her booty, she cleaned it off with a rag from the garage and carried it up to her bedroom. There were nicks in the wood. She would sandpaper them smooth again the next day, she decided, caressing the dark red stain, sensing the care that had been poured into the hand-rubbed finish.

She showered, changed into jeans and went downstairs to fix a meal. As she sat at the kitchen table eating an omelet, she took a quick inventory of the situation. Laurelwood was still threatened, Matt had still not been dealt with. But meanwhile she'd earned some money, there were still a few more days to think of some way of salvaging the estate, and her utilities, like it or not, were paid. Her frantic attempts at free-lancing her way to solvency might even pay off, if there were only more time.

She began to feel small, helpless and close to tears as she cleaned and dried the dishes. She'd planned on more sketching during the evening, but suddenly she was overtired, her mind a blank.

In her bedroom, the rocking chair beckoned. Rocking herself in it, she felt comforted, almost held, as if there were still traces of love and affection in the fine oak grain.

It was crazy, but she didn't care. Impulsively, she left the house and, armed with a flashlight, poked through the tool room off the stables, searching for sandpaper, rope, nails. Suddenly, the simple repairs couldn't wait until the morning. She ransacked the garage, the tool room, even the cupboard in the storm porch off the kitchen door. Half an hour later, she ran back up the stairs to her room, carrying a carton full of tools, rope, lemon oil and sheets of fine sandpaper; she'd even found a small bottle of wood stain.

She heard the front door chimes as she reached her room, set down the carton and ran back down-stairs, irritated at an interruption so late in the evening. Another realtor? Surely not this time in the evening without calling first? *Please,* she said to herself, *don't let it be Jason.*

Jason stood on the porch closing his dripping umbrella. He smelled of wet Harris tweed, she noticed, and she had to fend off an unspeakable weariness at the sight of him.

"I wouldn't have disturbed you at this time of night, Alex," he said, coming into the hall and closing the front door, "but it's important. Strictly business."

Her mind jumped to his involvement in the land company, the threats he'd made to chop up Laurel-wood. "I don't want to hear a word about Sunrise Develop—"

"No, no." He caught her arm, and she saw the intense pallor in his face under the bright hall light. "I didn't mean a word of it, Alex. Honestly, I was just desperate."

"Are you all right, Jason?" Reluctantly, she began to lead him to the study. He followed her, then sank into a chair as if his knees were buckling.

"There should be some brandy in here," she said, opening her father's liquor cabinet. "Yes—can I get you some?"

When he nodded, she found a balloon glass and poured him a measure. He sat silently clutching the stem, swirling the golden liquid, not drinking it.

Leaning against the edge of the desk, she waited

for him to speak, sensing his strange mixture of urgency and terrible reluctance. "Business, you said?" It was an effort to hide her impatience under a gentle voice.

"This would be easier to say, Alex, if only—" A nerve twitched at the outer corner of his eye, a tiny insistent pulse.

"What does Matt Farraday mean to you?" he asked, setting the glass down untouched and averting his face.

His hand was shaky. On the table beside his chair, the brandy continued to swirl in the crystal snifter. She watched the liquid swing from side to side in the bowl of the glass. What business was it of Jason's to ask her that? Their engagement was over. There was nothing between them. She glanced up at him. His eye still pulsed and he clutched the chair arms with stiff fingers.

A wave of pity made her bite her lip to stop the critical answer behind it. He had been generous—offering family jewels to bail her out. She should never have agreed to marry him. As a result of her blindness, her immaturity, she had hurt him unnecessarily. However tepid it seemed in retrospect, they had once been partners in a relationship. She owed him her honesty and generosity.

"He means a great deal to me, but if it's any consolation, Jason, Matt asked me to marry him before I left California and I told him no."

"But now that you've broken our engagement?" he urged.

"The answer would still be no."

Jason rose and went toward her. "Alex, I don't pretend to understand what's changed you, but I was a fool to let you go to the Coast with me. Everything was fine until then. Can't we forget the past few days ever happened?"

She shook her head. "If they hadn't happened, if I'd gone through with our marriage, it would have been a disaster. For both of us."

"Not for me, Alex," he said, gripping her arms fiercely. "Not for me."

"Jason, you said you had business to—" She heard chimes again and a sick tightness in her stomach relaxed. "It's the door, Jason," she said, and after a moment he dropped his hands, freeing her to answer it. He looked sickly pale. "Why don't you sit down and have your brandy?"

Before she crossed the study, the door chimes sounded again, impatiently. Whoever it was this time, she was grateful for the interruption. She hurried from the dim back hall, around the stairwell toward the front entrance where a bright light still burned.

"The front door was unlocked," Matt said. "I see his car. Where is he? Has he told you?"

Water streamed from his hair and face and his dark raincoat was sodden. Suddenly he seemed aware of it, blinked and passed the heel of his hand over his dripping eyelashes, then smoothed back his hair. "Has he told you?" he repeated.

She was staring at him, wondering how she could feel happy and heartsick at the same time. "Told me what?"

His hands clenched. "Alex, take me to him."

She felt something chilly on her arm. It was his soaked sleeve as he came closer and cupped her elbow. But his hand was warm. Gloves, she thought. Or he had his hand in his pocket.

"Alex, where is he?"

The crack in his voice made her collect her wits and she motioned with her head to the rear of the house. As he guided her along the hallway, she said nothing. When he saw the lit room beyond the open door, he left her and hurried forward into the study. "Randolph has a debt to pay," he said.

She followed him into the study like someone trapped in a senseless dream. She had lit only the table lamp by Jason's chair. The chair was empty. They both stood in the shadowy center of the room, but somehow they were not the two men she had known most of her life. A distancing veil had dropped over them. She closed her eyes as if something had distorted her vision, then opened them again.

"She's got to know all of it, Randolph. Now!" Matt's voice was like the wrath of God.

Suddenly she needed to sit down. She sank into the easy chair, her eyes not leaving the confrontation. She was watching them from some unimaginable distance.

They stood squaring off like opponents in some life and death struggle, both suddenly terrifying. Matt towering like an avenging archangel, Jason locked in some inferno of hate that sent bolts of energy spiraling through his body. Was she dreaming some Dantesque nightmare? she wondered as she huddled in her chair.

Gradually her fevered imaginings cleared. As she watched, the two men seemed to shrink back to normal human size. Jason was speaking.

"You thought I never knew about your affair with him. I did. I knew you were making love." His voice was as dry as paper as he leaned against her father's desk. It made her think of an interrogation victim at breaking point, finally talking without hope and without guilt. He stared at the photograph of a champion horse on the wall with a sightless, catatonic gaze, while his lips moved mechanically.

"It used to goad me, drive me crazy, wanting you the way I did and knowing he was with you, touching you, his filthy hands all over you. If only you knew what that was like, Alex—that rage inside me and that awful sense of impotence. There wasn't a thing I could do to stop you going to him." A brief smile stretched his lips. "Until his father got sick."

An awareness of her physical presence seemed to touch Jason for a moment; he paused and glanced at her. It would have been almost a commonplace movement, but his eyes were still glazed.

Poised rigidly three steps away from him, Matt suddenly leaned forward at the pause, ready to force Jason on if he failed to continue.

"Old Farraday was in the critical ward, Mrs. Farraday at her wit's end. It was a massive stroke, and the doctor's gave him little chance of survival. There was no money for the hospital bills." Jason stroked his jaw for a moment, his opaque eyes widening slightly.

He inclined his head toward Matt. "When he asked me for a loan, we made a deal. I'd take care of all the medical expenses and fly a specialist in from Houston, but only if he'd leave you alone, if he'd leave town and never come back. And never tell you why he left. That was the deal. I did it for you, Alex. But you can only make a gentlemen's agreement between two gentlemen," he added bitterly, as if a wand had been waved and human feeling had suddenly been restored to him.

Alexandra looked at Matt, his faced suffused with

dark, angry passions that he seemed to keep locked tightly under the skin. And she thought of the lonely years they had spent in hate and love and nursed grievances. Jason's deception had succeeded so well for so long. She could only ask, "What makes you tell me this now?"

Jason's face hardened with a defiant, almost triumphant grimace. "We have a new deal now. Fortune's Lad—for the truth."

Alexandra stared up at Matt. "Why did you never explain? Why did you let me go on thinking . . . ?"

Matt gave her a sealed look, only his jaw and his fists moving slightly, and the truth sliced through her, razor-sharp.

No one man she had ever known but Matt would have submitted himself so remorselessly to this tyranny of honor. His monstrous, egotistical, anachronistic sense of honor. A gentlemen's agreement, Jason had said. How unerringly he had found Matt's Achilles' heel. How mindless, she thought, how unutterably stupid. Matt had the morals of an uncompromising Japanese warlord. He was capable of making a suicide pact with his personal honor. She felt a ripple of hysterical laughter bubbling up.

Jason was calm now. There was a hint of the family arrogance once more in the way his shoulders squared. "I don't regret it. I regret only that you had to know in the end. I would do it again, except that I'd make sure I won. I should have won this time." He headed for the door, then stopped to turn on Matt.

"A lot has changed in five years, Farraday, but one thing's still the same. You were a bastard then, and you still are. You'll always be a bastard. No amount of money can ever change that." She sensed a silent exchange between the two men that she couldn't interpret. Jason left without another word.

Matt started forward as the front door slammed shut. "You're all right?" he said, careful not to touch her.

"Yes. I'm—all right."

He nodded and moved toward the door. "I did write, you know. After you left. I'm sure they never forwarded my letter." He shrugged. "It wouldn't have made much difference by then. It didn't say much. Only where you could reach me."

She had the fleeting feeling that she was performing the last act of a play, that the curtain would fall and nothing she could do would alter what the playwright had written. He was leaving her alone on the stage. It was simply the way the play ended. But it wasn't right; she must do something to change it. "Matt?"

"Yes?" He stood in the shadow, filling the doorway.

"I . . . I wanted to thank you. It makes a difference to me, knowing why you left. I've always—I—don't think Jason would ever have brought himself to tell me if you hadn't just happened—"

"I didn't just happen through your door, if that's what you're trying to say," he broke in gruffly. "Jason and I had our own private confrontation earlier this evening. He was here because I sent him to spill his guts to you. It was part of the price for Fortune's Lad. I came just to make sure he didn't welch on the deal. It was an afterthought." A grim smile crept over his features. "I guess I'm only just beginning to get you Kentucky aristocrats pegged right."

She began to guess at a small and devastating

truth about him. The adamantine quality of his behavior toward her, his fanatic code of honor. He carried through life a profound sense of unworthiness.

"Matt." She rose and stood just an arm's length from him. "I never ever slept with Jason. I've never made love to any man except you," she blurted out. "If I ever made you think otherwise . . ." *It was my devastated pride, my wounds. . . . I wanted you to hurt, too. That was my privilege. I didn't understand.*

She tried to penetrate his expression but it was shadowed. "Not to worry," he said lightly. "You're making a lot of changes in your lifestyle. I'm sure you'll change that too. The liberated woman is entitled to liberated sex."

"Don't. There's nothing wrong with taking charge of my own life. You were the one who told me to!"

She heard a light sigh. "There's a kind of independence that everyone should have. But it doesn't seem to be the kind you're developing."

When he left, she realized she'd been asking him to love her once more. She had longed to express her gratitude, to erase the bitter years of misunderstanding with kisses, to comfort him in her arms. She had told him how she loved him the night of the storm. He had sworn he felt the same. Had he been too proud to remember? Or was her love for him not enough without possession—total, chattellike ownership?

For an hour she sat brooding in the study, bitterly envious of the hard male strength in Matt that made him able to leave her so easily, his sovereignty intact, while she ripped herself inside out, clawing tooth and nail for every step toward selfhood simply because she was a woman.

Bastard, Jason had called him. How she wished

that bastard had stayed, stoic or angry or tender or consumingly possessive. The evening had left her pitiful attempt at dignity in shreds; she would have yielded to Matt on any terms he chose if only he had stayed to hold her through the long night.

And how she despised herself for wishing it.

Chapter Nine

By morning, Alexandra had whipped herself back into a kind of functioning machine, firing on all cylinders with no respite for thoughts except those of survival. With a scratch pad on her knee, she sat in the study, surrounded by stacks of bills and officious looking forms and notices, and laid out the complete situation for herself. It was a gloomy picture.

The livestock were taken care of, the two mares repossessed by an agent of their former Virginia owner, the broken-down stallion pensioned off to serve as a tame hack at the Ardley Riding Academy. But the list of liabilities and debts was endless, and sorting through her father's papers she came across new ones: a roofing contractor, the feed store and tack shop, state disability owed on the former stable employees, property tax installments. . . . Her life was ringed with creditors. She still owed Matt for the bills he'd settled without her knowledge, vital payments that kept the precarious roof over her head operable. She owed Matt for life-support, she thought grimly.

She was reminded of that particular debt by a realtor, who had tricked her way into Laurelwood to get an exclusive listing on the house. Lola Carpenter was brash, but Alexandra couldn't resent a woman who was merely trying her best to make a living. For almost an hour, she had acted the gracious hostess, guiding the woman on a detailed tour of the house and stables. Why not? she thought. If Ms. Carpenter found a buyer who wanted to live at Laurelwood, it was infinitely better than seeing the estate chopped into hundreds of pieces. She'd even offered the woman a cup of coffee, relishing the presence of another human being filling the endless lonely vastness of the house for a few more minutes.

Over coffee she learned that Matt had just closed escrow on one of the finer county homes and was making offers on all the adjacent parcels of land he could get his hands on. After the realtor left, Alexandra didn't dwell on Matt's proximity; she was too busy putting out fires in her besieged existence. Matt was just one more creditor who would have to wait until there was a semblance of order in her life, she told herself. First things first.

The first thing was Laurelwood. In a last-ditch effort to close the gap between what she'd paid on the foreclosure note and what was still owed, she consulted with a corporate attorney. After two long sessions, she had incorporated herself—O'Neill Enterprises, Inc., with a trade name of Alessandra. She spent two days running up a long-distance phone bill, coaxing promises from everyone she'd ever met in the fashion industry. Would they care to buy stock in her brand-new corporation? Were their partners, associates and bosses interested in a very modest investment?

Three days later, the responses started to trickle back, small nibbles of three thousand dollars, two as large as five thousand. Some verbal commitments, she knew, might never come through. But by six days to Birkhoven's zero hour, she had exactly $9,000 of investor money in her hand. At a small independent bank in Lexington, she opened a corporate account and deposited the full amount. She wasn't exactly AT&T, but if all the verbal commitments came through it would cover the note, if she could persuade her miscellaneous creditors to wait and not attach her bank account.

It was an awful lot of "ifs," she thought, but she couldn't afford gloom and doom. She had another six days before Birkhoven could evict her, and she relished the thought of seeing his astonishment if she pulled it off right at the final hour. She turned her efforts to cooling the creditors' heels, offering them payment schedules and a small first installment, talking them out of litigation.

Face to face, most creditors were cooperative, and she began to realize how loved her father was in the community, in spite of his reckless ways with money. The enormous sense of pressure began to ease, she noticed, after her second day of facing the creditors. Perhaps she was just learning to live with uncertainty, but she was beginning to feel less like a computer and more like a woman again. She realized it the afternoon she let her mind stray back to Matt. It was hard not to.

In a small town, a wealthy out-of-towner was good news to the economy. A few old-timers remembered his beginnings and marveled at the amounts he was spending. He had hired a rather expensive interior decorator, had been seen dining with a woman at La Cuisine, the best restaurant in town.

Alexandra was back at the drawing board, staring disgustedly at the rough charcoal lines of a sundress, a design that didn't quite work, when the phone rang.

It was her new attorney, Mel Zeigler. "Those papers have arrived for you to sign," he said, sounding relieved. "You're legal now. You were shaving it rather close, you know, accepting money before the papers came through. Can you come right in and sign them now?"

"Mel, I'm busy," she said distractedly. "How about if I come in Monday?"

"Look, I'm your lawyer, and I won't rest easy until your signature is on this, fair and square." Mel paused, then said, "You still have to eat. How about a dinner at La Cuisine and I'll bring the papers with me? A little wine, a little business, and you have the rest of the day to clean up your desk."

How often did Matt dine there? she wondered. She tried to picture the scene if Matt *were* there, she seated at a table with Mel. Mel was attractive in his own way, a rising, clever young man with an extravagantly chic wife who was on her way back from a buying spree in Europe. Mel's manner was relaxed but strictly professional, she thought, remembering exactly how he looked—vital, intense, intelligent. He was always very attentive when she spoke, very, very attentive. Yes, she hoped Matt would be there to see them.

"Thank you, Mel," she said after a moment. "It's the best offer I've had all day. I need just a couple more hours at the drawing board."

Shame set in as she replaced the receiver. What was she trying to do? Make Matt jealous? What was the point? She had no clarity of purpose. But then, she thought swiftly, he probably wouldn't be there anyway.

Half an hour later, she gave up on the sketching, got out her calculator and reached for a large envelope. On the outside she had penned OWED TO MATT. The total came to one thousand eight hundred forty-seven dollars and ninety-six cents. Lola Carpenter knew the address of the Brierson house. She called her and asked for it. She would write a check for the full amount and mail it to him. Somehow she couldn't face the possibility of seeing him that night, knowing she was still in his debt. On her way to meet Mel, she dropped the letter in a mailbox. Matt wouldn't know for a couple of days, but at least she would have the satisfaction of knowing she was free and clear of strings.

He was at the restaurant! With a tiny thrill of pleasure, she took Mel's arm and swept by Matt's table in the candlelit dining room of La Cuisine. She gave him a slight nod of recognition and took in the woman dining with him. She felt her tension relax. The woman was fiftyish. She was holding out a swatch of paneling. An open bulging briefcase at her feet was stuffed with glossy magazines or catalogues —Alexandra couldn't quite tell which—but she knew the woman was the decorator.

Alexandra rejoiced that she had dressed with care—a green wool suit that matched her eyes, a high-necked cream blouse with Victorian ruffles that were blatantly feminine. Her hair was up, softly draped away from her face in a faintly Victorian style that complemented the ruffles.

Why did it still matter so much to her? She had refused Matt. *Let go, let go,* she told herself. What if he'd been on a date, not a business dinner? Didn't he have a right to his life? Yet she kept expecting his eyes to stray her way, as her eyes seemed pulled to him.

During the meal, Mel kept up a recital of facts on tax laws, corporate bylaws, loopholes and shell structures. She tried to listen, but her mind kept wandering to the table beyond Mel's left shoulder.

There'd been drinks at Matt's table when she and Mel walked in, and by the time Alexandra's veal escalope arrived, she knew Matt's meal was no further along than hers with Mel. She lingered over coffee, with the growing apprehension that they might meet awkwardly on the way out.

Their checks arrived very close together. "Thanks for coming, Alexandra," Mel said. "Now I'll sleep easy." He rose, tapping his briefcase containing the sheaf of papers now signed and in order. "I'm picking Sandy up at the airport tomorrow in Lexington. I have to be up at the crack of dawn."

Matt and the decorator were rising too. There was nothing she could do now but brazen it out. *You asked for it,* she told herself as they headed for the door.

"How are you, Matt?" she asked brightly.

"Fine, Alexandra." He gave a polite smile but his eyes were cold.

"I've heard you've bought the Brierson house."

"Yes. Fran, this is Alexandra O'Neill and—"

"I'm sorry—Mel Zeigler," she said quickly.

"Fran Johnson," Matt said. "She's transforming the old place for me. I'm afraid I've been overworking her."

"I'm sure it will be beautiful," Alexandra said, feeling Mel's hand gently steering her out the door. "It was nice seeing you."

Mel stole an amused look at her face as he walked her to her car. "An old flame? You suddenly got very red in the face. Sorry to pull you away like that, but I have a long drive."

"Nonsense, Mel. You imagined it."

"Oh," he said quietly, and stood watching her drive away.

Jumbled thoughts ran through her febrile mind like hobgoblins as she tried to sleep. Her life seemed tied to the calendar—just four more days for Laurel-wood, unless more checks arrived. Should she start packing? Should she cast around for fresh ways of raising funds? Dollar signs danced before her eyes. Perhaps tomorrow's mail would solve it. After all, she needed just ten thousand now, no, twelve! What a fool she was to deplete her account by almost two thousand dollars in order to write that check to Matt. It wasn't as if he were needy or dunning her for the money. *Matt.* Would she never get him out of her system?

She gave up the attempt at a decent night's sleep and slipped downstairs to her makeshift art studio. More Alessandra designs, she demanded. But her mind was blocked.

She forced her hands into action and saw a mediocre nothing of a dress materializing on the white sheet.

In disgust, she ripped it up, tossed it furiously into the wastebasket and tackled a new sheet, doodling in short, choppy strokes. "No, no and no," she growled behind gritted teeth, as Matt's grin emerged from the charcoal doodle. "Leave me alone!"

"No more cat and mouse games, okay?" She stared at the face. "I'm on my own two feet now, more or less. And if I have normal sex urges once in a while—that doesn't mean there's only one man who can satisfy them. The world's full of men, Matt. There's no such thing as a one-man woman. I'm going to be responding to new men. I'm going to open myself up to life and throw away the key!"

It was two A.M. when she climbed back to bed. It was over now, she'd purged herself by saying it all out loud. Only it didn't seem to help. Crying softly into the darkness, she knew all the games she could play with her mind, all the little head trips, didn't alter facts. Adult or childish, rich or poor, clinging or fiercely independent, her feelings for Matt remained.

A second check arrived from Conti the next day, and her problem shrank by another five thousand dollars. Again, she began to feel that it could just happen, even if there were only three days left.

When Birkhoven's phone call summoned her imperiously to the bank at eleven o'clock, she made out a deposit slip, endorsed Fabio's check and took it with her. Birkhoven insisted on being mysterious, refusing to mention over the phone why she should come.

She made her deposit at the teller's window and was turning for Birkhoven's private office in the rear, when Matt emerged from it, Birkhoven unctuously walking him across the threshold. There was a leather pouch and two envelopes in Matt's hands, and the banker was grinning ear to ear.

Although her grip reflexively tightened on her purse, it seemed to jump out of her hands as Matt walked toward her, the deposit envelope fluttering down after it. He bent quickly to pick them up.

"Thank you," she said. "I—I—dropped them." Her tongue was suddenly as inept as her fingers.

"Yes," Matt said with a deadpan look. "I thought that's what might have happened."

As she took her things back from him, she could feel herself blushing like a shy teenager. "So! How's the house coming?" she asked, trying to sound casual.

"Fine."

She heard herself mouthing idiot small talk as he glanced over her shoulder toward the door.

"And your new venture? I hear you're free-lancing now." His interest was perfunctory.

"Fine, fine," she nodded as he muttered something minimally polite and headed for the street.

Birkhoven grinned at her like a magician who'd just performed the most magnificent sleight of hand. "I appreciate your coming so promptly. This is an extraordinary windfall, Miss O'Neill, from your point of view. Last night we received an offer on your property. Someone with a large family who actually wants to live in the house and keep the estate intact. The buyer is willing to open escrow and clear the default before Friday."

Not now, she thought, *not when I'm so close to keeping it.* Her eyes glanced down at the document he thrust into her hands. It was a bona fide offer, but, "I'm not prepared to sell my property," she said, handing him back the offer.

Birkhoven's reaction was startling. For some reason, he wanted her to accept this offer desperately, greedily. "Don't be foolish like your father!" he snapped, then broke off remembering his manners. "There really is little alternative," he coaxed. "I should have thought this was far more attractive than foreclosure and Sunrise Development." He paused, as if he were casting about for persuasive arguments. "I'm sure it's what your father would have wished."

"My father would have wished to keep Laurelwood in the family," Alexandra said quietly.

Birkhoven attempted a sympathetic smile. "Of course, but let's be realistic, Miss O'Neill. With half the note still to be raised and only three days to do so . . ."

Alexandra bridled at the patronizing tone. "I am not obliged to reveal all my resources to you at this time, Mr. Birkhoven. But you're not the only bank in the county. I'm just not ready to consider the offer at this time."

He shrugged. "Have it your way. But the buyer does have other choices. I doubt if he'll wait on you."

A deep sigh heaved up from her ribs, and she picked up the document once more. "All right, I'll give it some consideration. May I take it with me?"

"Of course, of course, my dear," he said, escorting her out of his office with such a jubilant spring in his step that she began to wonder what kind of kickback he might be getting on this particular transaction.

If Laurelwood does have to go, she told herself as she drove home, *a private buyer is the lesser of two evils. I already decided that when I spoke to Lola Carpenter.* But all thoughts of her finances fled as she recognized the car parked in the driveway.

Matt was just coming down the steps from the front door as she pulled up. "I was just going to give up," he said, opening the car door for her.

223

"I had some errands to run," she said, unlocking the front door. "Come on in." Her hand shook as she placed her purse and papers on the hall table. For one awful moment she thought she might drop them again. She was extra careful, determined to redeem herself from her moronic performance at the bank. "It's kind of messy and run-down," she said as he walked past her down the hall. "But I've been so busy, I've had no time to get anyone in to clean."

"I've never been in this room," he said, when she steered him into the spacious living room. "It's lovely."

As Matt studied the family portraits on the wall, she suddenly regretted bringing him in here. Somehow, from the chandelier to the dusty antique clock on the elaborate marble mantelpiece, it reeked of faded glory.

Matt moved from one portrait to the next as he said, "I understand you're looking for investors for your corporation."

"You seem to know an awful lot about my private affairs," she said tartly.

Matt turned to face her, suppressing a smile. "It's a small town. And since you're obliged to publish a DBA in the newspaper before you can get a business license, I'd hardly call it a private affair."

She began to feel foolish, thinking of the legal announcement that had already appeared three times in the *Press-Telegram*.

"I'm raising some funds, yes," she said evenly, making it sound like a question of choice, not desperation.

"Then I'd like to add my name to your list of investors."

He sounded businesslike enough, but this was one

source of money she couldn't afford to accept. "I'm afraid that's not possible." Her voice came out cold and clipped.

"Why not?"

"I'm—limiting my investors to those people directly involved in the garment industry."

He pretended to think about it for a moment. "That's a bit unusual. Isn't it a rather severe restriction?"

"It's my decision."

"Fine." His expression was either amusement or contempt; she wasn't sure which. "Fine," he repeated, "but idiotic under the circumstances."

"Under the circumstances?" She bristled. "I don't know what you mean by that."

Matt tossed his head with impatience. "Oh, come off it, Alex. It's no secret that this place is in foreclosure. I know you've made a gallant effort, but it's too late now. Why don't you let me help you out?"

She felt her jaw tighten. "You know why, Matt. I won't fall into that trap again—letting myself be manipulated by what some man can offer to do for me in return for favors."

Matt's eyes flashed with anger. "The only thing that's manipulating you is this ridiculous false pride. You've swung from one extreme to the other. From Miss Magnolia Blossom to—to—"

"I'm doing what I think is right," she broke in.

"Then you'd better give more careful consideration to what's right, while you're at it," he muttered, buttoning his jacket and heading for the door, "or you may wind up with nothing but your pride left intact. Believe me, Alex, pride never kept anyone warm in bed."

* * *

"It's the right thing to do," she told herself dolefully as she drove home from the bank through sheets of gray rain the following day. "You'd better take good care of the place," she said to the future owner of Laurelwood, "whoever you are."

She had stuck it out another whole day, but who was she kidding? The checks had stopped coming. Why prolong the agony? Her only choice was between a private buyer and Sunrise Development. At least she'd avoided the latter by accepting the offer. Birkhoven had been very brisk when she walked in with the offer in her hand. "You're doing a wise thing, Miss O'Neill. The old place will be in good hands."

She must return tomorrow and sign the final documents, she remembered dully. It wouldn't be official until then. When she got out of the car, she trudged through the grounds in spite of the rain, saying a last farewell to the paddock, the lawns, the stables and the unkempt rose garden.

If it rained much longer, she thought, she might never get to see Laurelwood in sunlight again. In the hall, she hung up her wet raincoat, then picked up the papers she'd brought back yesterday and laid on the hall table.

A white envelope lay there from Fabio's second check. She had brought back the deposit slip and forgotten to file it, she remembered, because she'd arrived home to find Matt on her doorstep. She picked it up, laid it on top of the house documents and took them to the study. She would tackle the filing later. Usually it bothered her to leave banking papers lying around, but this day was different from all other days. Right now she needed to do something very strenuous.

For hours, she raged through the house, sorting

out the few family possessions she would keep, packing her own things in trunks, throwing books and mementos into cartons she found on the storm porch, making piles when she ran out of cartons. When the antique furnishings went under the auctioneer's gavel, that would take care of most of the creditors, she assured herself. But the idea brought little consolation.

In the makeshift art studio she'd created in the study, she began packing her supplies away. She would have to begin apartment hunting immediately, she thought. She'd spend the day in Lexington. Maybe she'd find some place with a north window where she could set up her studio until she could afford a business address. Yes, Lexington was the place to look; it was far enough away not to be reminded constantly of her failure. No, she told herself fiercely, not total failure. This was no time to stop and get maudlin. If she thought about how her life was diminished in the past few weeks, she would come unglued. It was the pluses she must dwell on.

She was *not* diminished, a rebellious small voice insisted; on the contrary, she'd done more growing in the past month than in twenty-two years. *You've started a business, which is beginning to pay off.* It might not be enough to save Laurelwood, but she'd proved she had worth. Her talent was salable, even to a skinflint like Fabio.

She searched for the last deposit slip she'd made for Fabio's check. It was time to file her bank papers. She reached for it, then found herself staring blankly instead at a business envelope with a typed address. To Mark Chandler, Jr. It was odd. This wasn't her deposit slip. Where was her deposit envelope, and how had she acquired Mark Chandler's mail?

She turned the envelope over thoughtfully, re-membering something. The other day at the bank, she'd dropped everything at Matt's feet and he had retrieved it for her. He'd been carrying papers too—something got switched. Although why Matt should be carrying someone else's mail she couldn't fathom. It was irrelevant, she decided. The deposit slip wasn't critical, it merely offended her mild obsession with filing.

But something made her stare at the envelope in her hand. That name, Chandler, rang a bell some-where. Then suddenly, letting out a yelp, she thought she knew and tore a legal-size sheet from a manila envelope. The offer to purchase Laurelwood.

Her hand shook as she read the name of the buyer at the top of the offer. . . . Mark Chandler, Jr. The typed address was care of Lloyd Birkhoven at First Merchant's Bank of Kentucky. But the address on the mysterious business letter was Grange Meadows, Waverley Lane. She had written that address herself just days ago, the old Brierson house. So that was why Matt was carrying Mark Chandler's mail. That presumptuous megalomaniac wouldn't quit. Under some phony name, he was trying to bail her out by buying Laurelwood, still trying to own her by own-ing her home.

Tears of indignation began to well up at the thought. With a stroke of the pen, he could make a travesty of all her blood, sweat and tears, her superhuman efforts of the last few days. *An extraor-dinary windfall*, Birkhoven had said.

"Windfall, my foot!" she muttered, slipping the offer back into the legal-size envelope. She was going to settle his hash once and for all. She was not Miss Magnolia Blossom and he wasn't Rhett Butler.

Or Mark Chandler. Phony names to save a Southern lady's honor, indeed!

A thought struck her just as she was leaving the house. In the front hall, she fished out the white envelope from her purse and read the letter to Mark Chandler. It was notification of a board meeting, signed by the corporate secretary of Kenicrest Mills.

Matt frowned at the intrusion and rose from the sofa where he was cozily seated with Fran Johnson. "As you can see, I'm in the middle of a meeting."

"I don't care what you're doing," Alexandra fumed. She had demanded from the manservant who had answered her furious knocking, that she see Mr. Farraday. When he had hesitated, she had simply brushed past him into the house, flinging open doors until she found him. Nothing could stop her impetus now.

"You and I are about to have a private discussion," she announced loud and clear.

"Would you excuse us a moment, Fran?" Matt said apologetically, then turned back to glare at Alexandra.

She glared back. "It's going to be more than a moment. You have some explaining to do."

Matt looked undecided, as if he might just throw her out of his house. Then he walked back into the room, leaving Alexandra standing adamantly by the door. "I'm awfully sorry, but perhaps we can pick this up tomorrow? Something's come up."

The woman looked slightly bewildered, took the coat he handed her and left obediently.

"Exactly who are you?" Alexandra demanded when Matt had closed the door to his study. "And what do you think you're doing invading my private life?"

"What's that supposed to mean? I'd say you got that reversed." He turned his back and reached for a glass at the bar. "You look slightly bedraggled. Maybe you're working too hard—you're obviously confused. Do you want a drink?"

"No." She came up behind him and folded her arms stiffly. "I want answers. Who is Mark Chandler, Jr., for instance?"

Matt made a great show of pouring a Scotch and soda, as if he were stalling for time.

"I'm not accepting your money for Laurelwood. How dare you try to pull that? Jason said you were up to all kinds of crooked deals—I didn't believe him. Now it's all quite clear—"

"The only thing that's quite clear is that you don't know what you're talking about," Matt said softly, then took a deep gulp of Scotch.

"Oh no?" Alexandra slammed two envelopes on the bar, a white one addressed to Mark Chandler, and a large manila one containing Mark Chandler's offer to buy Laurelwood. "You handed me this by mistake when I dropped something in the bank. But this"—her hand slammed down on the manila surface—"is no damn accident!"

"Sit down," he ordered roughly, spinning around to face her and pointing to an armchair. "And don't open your mouth until I've finished. You want an explanation? By God, you're going to get one! And by the time I'm done, you'll know as much about Mark Chandler as I do."

Matt threw himself down on a leather sofa. "Two years ago," he began, "I received a letter from a Boston law firm."

* * *

Chandler money was quiet money, old Boston money. Even into the Second World War, the caste system of aristocrats still ruled in the Chandler world.

Martin Chandler was the only son of a man who wore his business empire in place of a crown. The scion of a vast and glittering dynasty, Martin was also the victim of its tyrannous protocol. At the age of seventeen, when he found his manhood in the arms of an Irish maid, the breach of protocol was not to be tolerated.

Trifling with the help, his parents explained patiently, was not altogether unknown in the dim reaches of the Chandler family tree. But an illegitimate child with that kind of mother was unthinkable. Pretty little Katherine Mary Purdy, only six months off the boat from Ireland, was unmistakably pregnant.

In spite of Martin's protests, his romantic adventure was abruptly terminated. Katherine Mary was sternly handed an envelope and a fine letter of recommendation. It was clearly understood she would never show herself again.

Romantic adventure was not Martin's term; he ached and grieved in a most un-Chandler-like fashion, which his parents attributed to the foolishness of youth. He would recover. He pined and fumed and argued and searched in vain. The girl had vanished without a trace, taking his unborn child with her.

Seven years later, the grief a fading memory, he married one of Boston's most desirable daughters. To Monica Debenham Chandler, he confessed his youthful error, and began to devote a steady stream of money to the cause of tracing Katherine Mary with the intention of supporting her child. Monica shrewdly threw her efforts into giving him other, more acceptable heirs, but theirs remained a childless marriage.

At the age of fifty he renewed his efforts, knowing his days were numbered. Martin Chandler was dying of cancer. Through an orphanage, then a foster home, through a dozen private agencies, after twenty years of wondering, one Matthew Purdy was found, son of Katherine Mary Purdy (deceased) and the foster son of one Jake Farraday and his wife, Gertrude.

A resourceful investigator from Detroit had found his way into the wilds of Kentucky. On a shaky wood porch, Jake Farraday had supplied the long-sought answer with his last intelligible speech on the day of his crippling stroke.

The subject was known as Matthew Farraday, the investigator reported to his wealthy client. His whereabouts were presently unknown. But it was established that he was alive, his parentage verified and a copy of his birth certificate in the mail on its way to Boston. It was surely only a matter of days before he was tracked down.

Unfortunately, the subject had left the state abruptly without a forwarding address, but there was at least the name he went by, and a photograph less than three years old.

It was enough for Martin Chandler. Just weeks from his death, he was able to make the gesture he had struggled to make throughout his life. Through due process of law, he granted his entire interest in all Chandler holdings to Matthew Farraday, last known address in Fayette County, Kentucky, with the proviso that Matt's involvement in Chandler Enterprises be conducted only under the name that was rightfully his to use, as the oldest grandson of the empire's founding father, Mark Stanford Chandler. Only Butterworth, Gemmings—Martin's principal law firm—was aware of the real identity of Mark Chandler, Jr.

Matt stretched and went to refill his glass. "Now you know as much about me as I do," he said hoarsely.

"So that's how you got all that money." Alexandra's voice was soft with wonder at the revelation.

"Not exactly. The way I live, everything I spend, I've earned myself. Through my own sweat—call it guile if you prefer, but it's legal guile." He flexed his shoulders in a stiff shrug. "I suppose I inherited something long before all this caught up with me: the Chandler genes for making money. But the Chandler income is frozen. It goes into a trust for—for my own offspring, should I have any."

"You mean you've never been able to touch a penny of it?"

"No. I mean I don't care to," Matt said fiercely. "I'm the one who froze it."

Alexandra was a little subdued by the long, poignant story, but it didn't alter the real reason she had come to see him, she remembered, stiffening in her chair.

"Whoever you are—captain of industry, crown prince or whatever—it still doesn't give you the right to try to buy Laurelwood by deception. You knew how important it was to me to handle my own life without interference."

Matt stared at her intently. "What's the matter with you, Alex? I'm not trying to control you. I only wanted to help. When you love someone, you don't want to see them hurting; you do anything to stop the hurt. Anything, even if it means crossing some wild notion they cherish of what independence means."

She shook her head sadly. "Don't you see what you're doing to me by undermining me like this?"

Matt bent and lifted her gently from the chair. "I only see that I love you."

She pulled away. "But that love expresses itself in domination. Ownership."

His shoulders sagged. "All right," he said defeatedly. "I can't change your mind."

The cool stony indifference she had seen so many times settled into his expression, but this time there was something final about it. "I won't try again. I get the message loud and clear. My offer on Laurelwood is unacceptable." He reached for the manila envelope and tore the offer in two.

"My God, what's the matter with me?" she whispered as she drove home. "Haven't I done exactly what I set out to do?" But despair seemed to thicken the very air she breathed. *It's because Laurelwood is about to disintegrate*, she supposed. Matt had been the only way of stopping it, and the only way she couldn't consider. It wasn't because she despised him. She loved him, loved him so much that she was in danger of losing herself in that love and becoming a mere extension of Matt.

Did women like Carla pay such a price for selfhood? she wondered. Had her life been so complacent until this moment that she'd missed some glaring truth?

She could hear the telephone as she fumbled with the front door key and she grabbed for the receiver in the entryway.

It was Carla. "Well? Don't you have anything to

say for all my efforts? Don't tell me the post office blew it again. I sent it Express, for crying out loud."

"What?" Alexandra tried to gather her wits. "What did you send, Carla?"

"Jeez! Didn't you get any mail today?"

"I—uh—yes—I don't know. I haven't looked in the mailbox yet."

"*Yet?* Seven—ten," Carla muttered obscurely, as three thousand miles of cable began to crackle with static. "It's ten o'clock at night out there in the meadows. Talk about lazy rustic ways! Get on the stick, kid. Read your mail and call me back."

Alexandra stared at those exquisite pieces of paper, two pale green, one pale blue. Cashier's checks to O'Neill Enterprises. She counted again, as if she could not trust her grasp of simple arithmetic. Ten and five and three made eighteen. Eighteen thousand dollars. She desperately wanted to blink, but didn't dare. She was afraid the mirage would disappear. Her eyes remained glued to them as she reached for the phone.

An hour later, the checks began to take on meaning. Slowly she began to retrace her steps in every room in the house, unpacking, uncrating, erasing the work of the day, stopping every half hour to run back to the study and gaze upon the precious checks again. Never had money seemed so beautiful.

By midnight, the house was restored to the way it had looked that morning, shabby, neglected, but hers now. Hers tonight, the next day, and next week and next year. She sat in the rocking chair in her bedroom, the checks on her lap, like some preposterous miser in silent communion with his gold.

She had enough; she'd done it. In the morning, she would take infinite delight in giving Birkhoven the shock of his life. She would despoit the checks in her new account along with a personal check. Then she'd drive over to First Merchants and, with a glorious flourish, she would write that check for thirty thousand dollars. That would enable her to tear up the foreclosure note under Birkhoven's nose.

Mel Zeigler wouldn't approve of commingling funds, but her investors were in good hands, she knew. She'd work up a storm to see that O'Neill Enterprises turned a profit for them. If she could do what she'd done during the past three weeks, she could do anything.

At last she returned the checks to her bank folder. No, it wasn't the money that was beautiful, she decided, climbing into bed. It was the power, the deep, satisfying sense of autonomy. Alexandra O'Neill was at last at the helm of her own life.

Chapter Ten

$\mathscr{I}$t had all been accomplished amazingly fast, she thought, frowning at the mediocre sketch and ripping it off the pad. Just a few strokes of the pen while Birkhoven managed to look both astonished and glum at the same time, and it was done. She had earned the right to keep title to Laurelwood.

The whole operation had been far less dramatic—and less gratifying—than she'd imagined last night. By midmorning, she was back in the study and once more working at the drawing board. Or trying to work.

She had just experienced the most fulfilling moment of her life, so why was she so unproductive? Where had the night's elation gone to? The work was grueling. It was always grueling when nothing came out, nothing but awkward lines, derivative ideas, purposeless strokes of the charcoal. Nothing was meshing on the board. In less than an hour, the study floor was littered with wrinkled discards.

Anticlimax, she decided; everything considered, she really deserved a day off. It was an occasion to celebrate. The rain had stopped finally, and the sky looked crisp and clear. She put on a leather jacket and went out for a walk.

Dead sycamore leaves crackled under her step as she took the path skirting the paddock, heading for the pasture that separated Laurelwood from Windermere. How did one celebrate alone? she wondered.

Celebrations I Have Known.

She could see the words in fat wobbly cursive writing, like the title of a fifth grader's English composition. Her mind teemed with pictures. Memories of Rome. Hugs and kisses and laughter and tears and toasts and spilled champagne and dancing and handclapping . . . Italian celebrations. She kicked at a bright scarlet toadstool, snapping the stem.

The clouds shifted, unveiling the sun as she strolled toward the elm grove where a tiny stream formed the northeast boundary of Laurelwood. Italian, American . . . all celebrations were basically the same. They all seemed to require at least two participants.

The sun felt gentle as she lifted her face and closed her eyes. "It's okay," she whispered. "Sure it's lonely, but there will be other men. Less domineering men who'll give me the space to be myself. Give it time."

When she returned to the house, it got no better. The mellow old mansion, so warm and redolent with generations of love and laughter, felt just like a morgue. She hung up her jacket and wandered disconsolately through the upstairs rooms, lingering by the four-poster bed her father had slept in all his adult life.

You'd have been proud of me this morning, father. I wish you were here to celebrate the occasion with me. The Irish, you once told me, were good at celebrations. You'd be dancing a jig on the kitchen table. . . .

I blamed you for a while for stifling me, protecting me too much. I thought you'd sapped my strength. Forgive me. It was just your expression of love, what you thought would make me happy. Possessive, yes—fiercely possessive. But it was love all the same. And love can never really hurt anyone. Your love nourished me, protected me, cherished me—but it never suffocated me. I did that to myself. It's taken me twenty-two years to see that. But who's counting?

Her face was hot and wet. She splashed cold water on it, then raised her head to the mirror above the washbasin to look at this new and undisputed owner of Laurelwood. A stubborn redheaded Kentucky Irishwoman, just as willful, just as reckless as her father.

What was it Matt had said? When you love someone, you can't bear to see them hurting? You'll do anything to stop it? Well, she'd stopped that hurt all by herself. At least part of it. She'd discovered who she was, proved that inside her was something inviolable that no one's strength or love or possessiveness could touch. She'd had her victory.

But oh, dear God, what use was it without Matt?

Matt had needed to give, just as her father had needed to give. It was the expression of his love. And she had been so frightened of being swallowed

239

up in it, so unsure of her own selfhood, that she had spat on it.

He had made a love offering. As stunningly simple as that. Not to take her over, as she had accused him of doing, not to own or control. He had done it simply because love must express itself, must offer what it can. She could feel that need to give now. It was hunger in the center of her body.

A few nights ago she had plumbed the depths of Matt, his sense of unworthiness. She had told him she loved him but couldn't marry him. How would she have felt if their positions had been reversed? Anguish rocked her at the thought of the pain she had inflicted. Her mind raced with improbable remedies. Matt needed to prove he was worthy of her. He had needed that vital chance to help her. To rescue her.

If only she'd had a shred more confidence in herself, she could have had the grace to accept, to yield just a tiny bit. But she'd been hard as iron. By the skin of her teeth, she'd rescued herself.

A mad thought struck her. Only Birkhoven knew she didn't need rescuing. She winced. Only Birkhoven and about eight hundred employees at the bank, the title company and who knew how many other interrelated agencies. Matt didn't know yet, probably, but he'd doubtless find out; he seemed to be able to find out anything he chose to.

Suddenly she remembered the chilling indifference in his eyes when they had parted last night. He had washed his hands of her once and for all. No, Matt wouldn't know she was out of the woods as of this morning, simply because he was no longer interested.

As she started the car, she offered a small prayer that he would never know. It was just past noon.

There was plenty of time to stop payment on that check.

It was a wild chance she was taking, it was crazy, but . . . if she could genuinely persuade Matt she needed him, perhaps she could undo the damage she'd done. It was at least worth a try.

She gunned the engine and crossed her fingers for luck as she sped down the driveway.

"What now?" Matt opened the door himself. His eyes looked tired, disinterested.

She couldn't smile, she couldn't leap into his arms. She was desperate, about to lose Laurelwood, she reminded herself. But it was all she could do not to fling her arms around him. "Matt, I've been an ungracious, stubborn idiot. I'm so embarrassed. May I talk to you for a minute?"

He hesitated, wary and defensive.

She almost sighed with relief. *He didn't know yet. He would have offered some scathing congratulations. He wouldn't have been able to resist it.*

"I don't mean to be rude, Alexandra, but I don't feel like socializing right now."

"Oh." Her heart somersaulted. "Matt, I need your help—desperately."

His dark brows furrowed slightly as if she weren't making sense, then he turned away. "Come on in," he said, his voice giving no indication she was welcome.

There was fresh Regency striped wallpaper in the entryway and soft colors in the living room accented by cut flowers and green plants.

"Drink?" He went to a carved antique sideboard.

"Scotch, please."

He brought it in an exquisite Venetian glass. As their fingers brushed lightly, she felt her arm shake with the desire to touch him and she wondered achingly if he still felt anything for her. It didn't seem so as he walked to the fireplace.

"Won't you sit down?" he said stiffly. The thin shell of civility was awful. She almost expected him to glance covertly at his watch. Then he actually did.

She sank down on the sofa, wondering if there was any point in her playacting, trying to remember the phrases she had rehearsed on the way over. *Nothing you'll ever do is as important as this. Try, just try. Keep going.*

But it was no longer in her to say anything but what was in her heart. "Matt, I know now that I'm losing the only thing I ever wanted. I've waited too long and now it's too late. I've been such a fool. Arrogant, proud. And it was a false pride. You were right. I was going to tell you I needed you, Matt. But I'm afraid it's too late."

She looked at the artfully casual arrangement of fine furniture, the splendid dieffenbachia that rose gracefully from its elegant planter. A man who was lost and unhappy didn't hire a decorator and surround himself with such joyful beauty. He was fine now. He had lived through the hurt and was continuing with his life without her. "I'm sorry I bothered you," she said miserably.

Her muscles ached with regret and the burden of heavy silence as she rose from the sofa to go. "You've got better ways to spend your time. I can see that."

"You don't have to lose everything," he said in a tentative voice. "Laurelwood's yours if you want it. You only have to ask."

Her eyes closed in utter confusion as she headed for the door. "Laurelwood? Is that what you thought I meant?"

"Isn't it Laurelwood? What else would make you put yourself under the slightest obligation to me?"

She heard herself lying in a voice she barely recognized. "Matt, I scraped some money together. But it's not quite enough. I don't care about obligations anymore. I was crazy to turn you down. Is the offer still good?"

"Which offer?" he said stiffly.

She felt dizzy. "All of them. The offer to marry me, share your life with me and help me financially. Will you—are you—do you—?"

"I'm happy to do it," he said strangely, heading for the door. He was half out of the room. "First I'm calling Birkhoven," he said over his shoulder.

She waited for him trembling, not sure she had made sense. Oh Lord, he was acting so strangely. Did he truly understand? Could he ever feel exactly the same about her?

When he came back into the room he kissed her chastely. Then he turned and held out his hand. "Discretion," he said, smiling gently. "I don't want to lose my new housekeeper."

She followed him up the curved staircase to his bedroom. "Birkhoven's at a luncheon," he said, touching the top button of her blouse. "Did you eat lunch?"

"No. Yes. I'm not hungry."

His finger traced her mouth, then slid over her chin. He cupped her breasts lightly. "His secretary made an appointment for us. After closing time. Three-fifteen." He had undone the two blouse buttons, then closed them again. His voice shook. "Two hours. All right if we wait in here?"

She felt like melting ice cream, and as he stroked his fingers through her hair, she found herself fumbling to open his shirt.

"What a fool I've been, Matt," she muttered over and over as she drew him closer to her. She was covering his warm skin with kisses, touching him with her tongue, her fingertips, her eyelashes, driven by the hunger to give. Suddenly she was no longer trying to speak, dumb with the knowledge that merely to touch this beautiful beloved man, to supply his basest needs and feel his response, could bring such a leaping joy.

She heard her voice again as she moved against the deep silken thrusts inside her. "Matt, oh Matt. I want to belong to you."

"Ali, Ali, sweetheart," she thought he said. But his voice was hoarse with passion.

In no time at all, she heard his words distinctly. He was saying it was time to leave.

She glanced at his bedside clock. Could an hour and a half have really passed so quickly? "But it's only two-thirty." She wrapped him in her arms and legs, wanting him again. "We've still got half an hour," she whispered. She was besotted with desire, unable to move.

He extricated himself and sat up. His voice was firm. "The owner of Laurelwood is not about to walk into First Merchants' Bank looking like that."

She slid her cheek along the smooth narrow part of his back. "'Course not, love. I'll put my clothes on," she said, smiling and kissing the ridge of spine she saw as he bent forward.

"You'll do more than that. You'll go home and change into fresh clothes." He headed toward the bathroom. "I'll meet you at the bank."

Reluctantly, she began to dress and saw he was right. She had disrobed in such unseemly haste, three buttons had ripped from her blouse. *Hussy,* she told herself, grinning like a Cheshire cat as she drove home. *Lucky for you it's fall and you were wearing a raincoat. He still loves you. He still loves you. He still loves you!*

She had learned something in the last hour. The physical dimensions of sex, of giving and taking pleasure in total surrender to the heart's dictates, transcended carnal passion to a degree she had never imagined. It was like some spiritual act of faith, trailing glory and exaltation. There were no more ambiguities.

She felt strangely newborn as she hurried into Laurelwood to bathe and change. Less than twenty minutes—just time for a quick shower. As she hastily put on some makeup, she noticed that lovemaking had performed wonders on her face. The pressure of the past weeks had made her hair limp, her eyes dull with suppressed desperation, her face drawn and pale. After being with Matt, she glowed. Her hair was shining, and her eyes were a clear bright green. She dressed in a suit designed by Guido Conti, a formfitting jacket in soft amber wool with free-swinging kick pleats in the skirt.

On the short drive to the bank, she remembered a phrase. *I'd be happy to help you.* It bothered her that Matt had said nothing about marriage. Was he too proud to ask her again after rejection? Or was that offer simply no longer valid. She didn't care. She'd take him on any terms. She knew she made him happy.

One thing was sure, she realized as she pulled into the parking lot of First Merchants', there were no reservations in her feeling for Matt. Her career, her pride, her independence were all secondary to that feeling. She'd had her identity crisis and come out on the other side. Her love for Matt had endured as strong as ever.

Birkhoven's demeanor was subservient in front of Matt, but she could sense the thinly disguised confusion. He displayed the odd glance first to Matt, then to her, as if they had both taken leave of their senses.

"I believe that everything is taken care of now," he said, handing her the last document to be signed and taking the cashier's check Matt handed him with a tiny bow of the head.

Twelfth Night, she thought whimsically, aware that she was gazing dreamily at Matt through a constellation of stars. Tricks, disguises, misunderstandings, all for love, and love always wins out. I feel like the heroine of a romantic comedy.

"That takes care of the property," Matt said, shaking her out of her daydream as they walked to the parking lot. "Now we have other debts to clear up, don't we Alex?"

"Matt, there's no need—"

"Hush," he said. "Go home and I'll follow you." He turned away decisively and walked to his car.

Love, she was discovering, did strange things to her personality. It made her smile at odd intervals when there was nothing particular to smile at. It sent warm currents up her spine when Matt so much as caught her eye, and it plunged her into a wild roller coaster ride of physical longing when his voice suddenly lowered to a purr.

Love was also hard on her muscle coordination. She was forever dropping things, she observed in the study, as she bent to retrieve the scattered contents of her folder marked "Unpaid Bills."

"Oh, don't bother with that now, Alex," he said,

taking her shoulders and straightening her up. "Why don't you just leave it all here, and I'll send my secretary over tomorrow with a check. How much will clear it up?"

"Huh?"

"Ali," he said gently, "may I see your bank book and figure it out? I don't think figures are your strong point."

"Bank book?" she echoed. He'd see around forty thousand dollars on deposit. He'd know about her stupid trick. She wasn't ready to explain that yet. She wasn't sure enough of him. Suddenly she was terrified of losing him.

"The bank book, Alexandra?" His voice was mildly patient, as if he were speaking to a small child with a minimal concentration span.

In the awful silence that followed, she saw a tiny smile pulling up the corner of his mouth as he waited for her to speak. "Alex, I know," he said softly. "Birkhoven told me about the check you stopped while we were waiting for you to arrive."

She buried her face in her hands. "Matt, please don't think I was trying to make a fool of you—"

His laughter burst through the room in a prolonged uproar. "You idiot, you beautiful, insane, idiot." He pulled her out of the chair, his shoulders still shaking with laughter. "I sure hope you're better at business than you are at petty deceit. You did it because you *love* me, Ali. Of all the hokey, pea-brained schemes. And I spent five years schooling myself to be sophisticated enough for you."

He perched on the edge of the desk, his laughter subsiding but the amused grin still stretching his mouth wide. "Alex, did you honestly think you could pull off a stunt like that?"

"It was the only thing I could think of. I want to be

your wife, Matt. I want to make babies with you. The whole stupid romantic works, as you put it. I made such a hash of things in California. I guess being insanely in love makes you hokey."

"Hokey or not, you've got yourself a deal, lady," he said, smiling broadly. "All the offers are still good." His fingers reached out, flicked aside her unbuttoned jacket and began to trace the curve of her breast beneath the silk blouse. "An hour and a half was definitely not enough." He grinned and withdrew his hand as her nipples responded to his touch.

"Let's go upstairs," she said breathlessly.

"We're going to my place." His voice was crisp as he took her left hand and pressed her fourth finger. "We're going to put something official right here. It may be too late to make an honest woman of you tonight, but the next time you take off your clothes, you'll at least be wearing an engagement ring."

"You bought me a ring?" She wondered when on earth he'd managed that.

"I've bought several over the past few years. First an emerald to match your eyes. Then a second, much larger emerald when I could afford it. But I thought you might find it too pretentious, so I kept the first one just in case. Then it occurred to me you might prefer something more traditional, so I got a square-cut diamond. Two weeks ago I got a sapphire because I discovered Jason gave you a diamond. I am not Jason." He pulled her face around until it was an inch from his. "I trust you gave it back."

She nodded, stupefied.

"Don't look so surprised," he said as they pulled out of the driveway. "I told you I knew all about head trips, didn't I?"

* * *

"Oh, Matt. How could I ever have imagined I could be happy without you?" she said as they held each other that night. She felt she might float away if he weren't holding her so close to him.

"I'm sure you could if you were determined to. That's why I finally decided to give up on you. If you hadn't come today, Ali, I would have closed up this house and never tried again."

It was too dark to see his expression, but there was a somber tone to the words. She shivered as if a cold wind had touched her. "I don't even want to think about it," she said.

His lips tightened over her nipple briefly, then he burrowed his face between her breasts. "I know a way to drive it out of your mind," he growled, nuzzling into flesh. . . .

Later, he lay beside her very still, his chin resting on her shoulder. "Any objection to becoming my wife in the morning?" he mumbled, half asleep.

"Just try and stop me." Her palm, resting over his navel, began to slide downward slowly.

He groaned softly. "I hope I can handle the wedding night. Trying to make up for five years in one day is somewhat ambitious. And you can stop that . . . it will get you nowhere."

"Sorry." She took her hand away.

Matt took it in his and squeezed. "Don't be. It's just I'm not used to quite so much ardor in one night."

"Should hope not," she breathed, as sleep crept into the corners of her mind. "Me neither."

The morning sun filtered pale and hazy through the windowpanes, and Alexandra's eyes drifted lazily around the room. It was a beautiful house, the old Brierson place. She'd be more than happy to call it home.

Home, she thought, stroking Matt's hair as he slept in her arms. A house could be bought or sold or mortgaged, but not home. She knew that now. Home was not Laurelwood, nor this house in particular. Home was the feeling she had at this moment, as she felt the rise and fall of his light breathing. You couldn't define it with property lines, and no money in the world could save it from foreclosure.

Only the heart could do that.

If you enjoyed this book...

...you will enjoy a Special Edition Book Club membership even more.

It will bring you each new title, as soon as it is published every month, delivered right to your door.

15-Day Free Trial Offer

We will send you 6 new Silhouette Special Editions to keep for 15 days absolutely free! If you decide not to keep them, send them back to us, you pay nothing. But if you enjoy them as much as we think you will, keep them and pay the invoice enclosed with your trial shipment. You will then automatically become a member of the Special Edition Book Club and receive 6 more romances every month. There is no minimum number of books to buy and you can cancel at any time.

MORE ROMANCE FOR
A SPECIAL WAY TO RELAX

$1.95 each

2 ☐ Hastings	21 ☐ Hastings	41 ☐ Halston	60 ☐ Thorne
3 ☐ Dixon	22 ☐ Howard	42 ☐ Drummond	61 ☐ Beckman
4 ☐ Vitek	23 ☐ Charles	43 ☐ Shaw	62 ☐ Bright
5 ☐ Converse	24 ☐ Dixon	44 ☐ Eden	63 ☐ Wallace
6 ☐ Douglass	25 ☐ Hardy	45 ☐ Charles	64 ☐ Converse
7 ☐ Stanford	26 ☐ Scott	46 ☐ Howard	65 ☐ Cates
8 ☐ Halston	27 ☐ Wisdom	47 ☐ Stephens	66 ☐ Mikels
9 ☐ Baxter	28 ☐ Ripy	48 ☐ Ferrell	67 ☐ Shaw
10 ☐ Thiels	29 ☐ Bergen	49 ☐ Hastings	68 ☐ Sinclair
11 ☐ Thornton	30 ☐ Stephens	50 ☐ Browning	69 ☐ Dalton
12 ☐ Sinclair	31 ☐ Baxter	51 ☐ Trent	70 ☐ Clare
13 ☐ Beckman	32 ☐ Douglass	52 ☐ Sinclair	71 ☐ Skillern
14 ☐ Keene	33 ☐ Palmer	53 ☐ Thomas	72 ☐ Belmont
15 ☐ James	35 ☐ James	54 ☐ Hohl	73 ☐ Taylor
16 ☐ Carr	36 ☐ Dailey	55 ☐ Stanford	74 ☐ Wisdom
17 ☐ John	37 ☐ Stanford	56 ☐ Wallace	75 ☐ John
18 ☐ Hamilton	38 ☐ John	57 ☐ Thornton	76 ☐ Ripy
19 ☐ Shaw	39 ☐ Milan	58 ☐ Douglass	77 ☐ Bergen
20 ☐ Musgrave	40 ☐ Converse	59 ☐ Roberts	78 ☐ Gladstone

Silhouette Intimate Moments

Coming Soon

Dreams Of Evening by Kristin James

Tonio Cruz was a part of Erica Logan's past and she hated him for betraying her. Then he walked back into her life and Erica's fear of loving him again was nothing compared to her fear that he would discover the one secret link that still bound them together.

Once More With Feeling by Nora Roberts

Raven and Brand—charismatic, temperamental, talented. Their songs had once electrified the world. Now, after a separation of five years, they were to be reunited to create their special music again. The old magic was still there, but would it be enough to mend two broken hearts?

Emeralds In The Dark by Beverly Bird

Courtney Winston's sight was fading, but she didn't need her eyes to know that Joshua Knight was well worth loving. If only her stubborn pride would let her compromise, but she refused to tie any man to her when she knew that someday he would have to be her eyes.

Sweetheart Contract by Pat Wallace

Wynn Carson, trucking company executive, and Duke Bellini, union president, were on opposite sides of the bargaining table. But once they got together in private, they were very much on the same side.

Silhouette Special Edition

Coming Next Month

Love's Gentle Chains by Sondra Stanford

Lynn had fled from Drew believing she didn't belong in his world. Then she discovered she was bound to him by her love and the child he had unknowingly fathered.

All's Fair by Lucy Hamilton

Automotive engineer Kitty Gordon had been in love with race driver Steve Duncan when she was sixteen. But this time, she would find the inside track to his heart.

Love Feud by Anne Lacey

Carole returned to the hills of North Carolina and rediscovered Jon. His family was still an anathema to hers, but he drew her to him with a sensuous spell she was unable to resist.

Cry Mercy, Cry Love by Monica Barrie

Heather Strand, although blind since birth, saw more clearly than Reid Hunter until love sharpened his vision and he realized that Heather was the only woman for him—forever.

A Matter Of Trust by Emily Doyle

After being used by one man, Victoria Van Straaten wanted to keep Andreas at arm's length. However, on a cruise to Crete she found Andreas determined to close the distance.

Dreams Lost, Dreams Found by Pamela Wallace

It was as though Brynne was reliving a Scottish legend with Ross Fleming—descendant of the Lord of the Isles. Only this time the legend would have a happy ending.